She was trapped by the incoming tide

Morwenna shivered violently, light-headed with cold and fear. She was going to drown, to be taken by the high tide at midnight. The same tide that had claimed the life of her namesake, Morwenna Trevennon, centuries before.

But the other Morwenna had died in the arms of her lover, Morwenna thought remotely, *and Dominic isn't here with me. Dominic....*

Closing her eyes, she envisioned Dominic's face. The waves, which enfolded her, felt as strong and comforting as Dominic's arms. The call of the sea resembled his voice, urging her to stop struggling. And, weakening, Morwenna gave herself up to her fate.

Other titles by
SARA CRAVEN
IN HARLEQUIN PRESENTS

STRANGE ADVENTURE 191
A GIFT FOR A LION 195
WILD MELODY 199
TEMPLE OF THE MOON 215
A PLACE OF STORMS 235
PAST ALL FORGETTING 243
THE DEVIL AT ARCHANGEL 251
DRAGON'S LAIR 255

Other titles by
SARA CRAVEN
IN HARLEQUIN ROMANCES

GARDEN OF DREAMS 1943

Many of these titles, and other titles in the Harlequin Romance series, are available at your local bookseller or through the Harlequin Reader Service. For a free catalogue listing all available Harlequin Presents and Harlequin Romances, send your name and address to:

HARLEQUIN READER SERVICE,
M.P.O. Box 707,
Niagara Falls, N.Y. 14302
Canadian address:
Stratford, Ontario, Canada N5A 6W2
or use coupon at back of book.

SARA CRAVEN

high tide at midnight

Harlequin Books

TORONTO · LONDON · NEW YORK · AMSTERDAM
SYDNEY · HAMBURG · PARIS

Harlequin Presents edition published June 1979
ISBN 0-373-70791-6

Original hardcover edition published in 1978
by Mills & Boon Limited

Copyright © 1978 by Sara Craven. All rights reserved.
Philippine copyright 1979. Australian copyright 1979.
Except for use in any review, the reproduction or utilization of
this work in whole or in part in any form by any electronic,
mechanical or other means, now known or hereafter invented,
including xerography, photocopying and recording, or in any
information storage or retrieval system, is forbidden
without the permission of the publisher.

All the characters in this book have no existence outside the
imagination of the author and have no relation whatsoever to
anyone bearing the same name or names. They are not even
distantly inspired by any individual known or unknown to the
author, and all the incidents are pure invention.

The Harlequin trademark, consisting of the word HARLEQUIN
and the portrayal of a Harlequin, is registered in the United States
Patent Office and in the Canada Trade Marks Office.

Printed in U.S.A.

CHAPTER ONE

'WELL, I wish to make one thing perfectly clear at the outset. She cannot remain here.'

The new Lady Kerslake's voice, almost strident in its vehemence, resounded plainly through the closed drawing room door, freezing Morwenna where she stood, her hand already raised to knock. A number of thoughts chased wildly through her head as she assimilated Cousin Patricia's words—among them that it would be far more honourable to turn and walk away, pretending to herself that she had heard nothing, and that eavesdroppers never heard anything good of themselves anyway, but at the same time she knew that wild horses could not make her budge an inch. And it might be a relief to find out what her cousin really thought, as opposed to the saccharine sweetness she had been treated with up to now.

'Oh, Mother!' It was Vanessa speaking now, her voice slightly impatient. 'You can hardly turn her out on to the streets. She has no training and no qualifications. You know as well as I do that she simply wasted her time at school. What on earth's she going to do?'

'That is hardly our responsibility,' Lady Kerslake returned coldly. 'She chose to neglect her opportunities. She can hardly complain now if they no longer exist. And it was up to her father to make suitable financial provision while he was alive. He knew quite well what the entail involved.'

'Perhaps, but he could hardly foresee that he and Martin would both be killed in the same accident. Martin was the heir, after all, and he would have looked after Morwenna.'

Standing motionless in the hall, Morwenna felt a fresh stab of pain inside her at the casual words. But Vanessa was right in a way. No one could have foreseen on that bright autumn day, only a few weeks before, that before night came she would have been quite alone in the world, her father and brother both dead, victims of a freak collision with a lorry whose brakes had failed on the steep hill outside the village.

She had always known that the entail existed, of course. Had even laughed ruefully with Martin over the male chauvinism in this era of Women's Lib of the insistence that the baronetcy and the estate should still descend through the male heirs only. The future hadn't filled her with a great deal of concern. She was barely eighteen, after all, and more interested in having a good time than considering her future prospects. And her father had encouraged her in this. Always he and Martin had been there like bulwarks, and she had basked secure in the certainty of their affection and spoiling. Until that day—when the chill wind of reality had shown her how fragile her shelter had been.

The solicitors had been very kind, and had explained everything in great detail, including the fact that there was not a great deal of money for Cousin Geoffrey to inherit. Her father, she learned for the first time, had been speculating on the stock market and suffered some considerable losses. Given time, Mr Frenchard had said, he would have recouped these losses—his business acumen was considerable. Only he had not been given time.

During the weeks since the funeral Morwenna had felt that she was existing in a kind of curious limbo, and this impression had been emphasised with the advent of Cousin Geoffrey, whom she hardly knew, and his rather domineering wife, whom she did.

Cousin Patricia, she knew, had expected to find herself a wealthy woman and had been less than entranced with the true state of affairs, although becoming Lady Kerslake and occupying the house, a gem from the reign of Queen Anne, must, Morwenna surmised drily, have been some consolation at least.

At first she had been inclined to gush over Morwenna, but as the days passed, her manner had become more distant. Not that they had ever been close, Morwenna thought. And she had never been on friendly terms with Vanessa either, even though her father had insisted they attend the same school and had paid both lots of fees to achieve this. She had wondered since whether Vanessa had resented this, or whether her main source of grievance had been simply that her younger cousin had the ability to skate lightly over the academic waters where she had frankly floundered. Whatever the cause, Vanessa's hostility had at times been almost tangible, and there had been little softening of her attitude since her arrival at Carew Priory. On the contrary, Morwenna felt at times that Vanessa was frankly gloating over the reversal in their fortunes. She'd had to be very careful over everything she did and said, making certain that Mrs Abbershaw the housekeeper went to Cousin Patricia for her instructions, even remembering to knock before she entered rooms where the family had gathered. Suddenly she was the outsider in her own home. Yet no longer her own home, as Lady Kerslake was reiterating with some force.

'And I can't imagine why you should be so concerned, Vanessa,' she added with asperity. 'You've never cared for her particularly.'

'I don't care for her now,' Vanessa retorted waspishly, 'but we have to consider what people will say, and her father and Martin were extremely well liked locally. We don't want to start off on the wrong foot.'

'Indeed not.' Lady Kerslake gave a deep sigh. 'What a problem it all is! I had no idea the wretched child was simply going to hang around here aimlessly. Wasn't there some talk of a painting school?'

'There's always talk of something where Morwenna's concerned. But you're right, she was supposed to be joining Lennox Christie's class at Carcassonne this month. Whether he'll be so keen to have her now that the fees are not forthcoming is a different matter. It's a well-known fact that he fills up his class with rich dilettantes in order to pay for the pupils he really wants.'

Morwenna's fingers, clenched deep in the pocket of the loose knitted jacket she was wearing, closed shakingly round the envelope she had thrust there not half an hour before. She had seen the postman coming up the drive from her bedroom window and some premonition had told her what he was bringing, and she had run down to intercept him. All the letters were taken as a matter of course to Cousin Patricia now before they were distributed to the appropriate recipients, and Morwenna knew that a letter with a French stamp would have attracted just the sort of attention that she least wanted.

And her sense of foreboding had been fulfilled. Vanessa might almost be a thought-reader, she told herself despairingly. Lennox Christie's letter had been courteous but adamant. The work she had shown him at her initial interview in London, he wrote, did not justify him offering her a non-fee-paying place in his class as she had requested. However, he would be back in London in the spring, and she could always contact him then with any new work she had produced, so that he could review his decision. It was the final humiliation. The offer of a review in the spring was, she knew, put in as a salve to her damaged pride.

She had never had a lot of faith in her ability as an artist. She had inherited some of her dead mother's talent, and had been the prize pupil at school, but she had had few illusions about how she would fare in the fiercely competitive art world if ever her livelihood depended on it. It hadn't before, of course, and only a sense of utter desperation had prompted her appeal to Lennox Christie. She had sensed during their brief interview earlier that year that he had been unimpressed with the range of landscapes and still life she had shown him, but she knew at the same time that she was capable of better things, if not the touch of genius which had been stamped on so much of Laura Kerslake's work. She had not mentioned her mother's name to Lennox Christie. There seemed little point. Laura Kerslake had been dead for over ten years and she had painted little after her children were born. Besides, her work was no longer fashionable.

Cousin Patricia had said as much soon after she had arrived at Carew Priory. Morwenna had little doubt that those of her mother's paintings which were hanging in the house would soon be relegated to an attic, and replacements sought for them in the trendy gallery in London which Lady Kerslake patronised. She had hoped very much that she would be long gone from the Priory before that happened.

She had never intended to stay there in any case. This was what made it so doubly hurtful to hear herself being discussed as if she was some parasite. She had always known that she would have to get a job of some kind. This was why she had been on her way to speak to Cousin Patricia, to ask, cap in hand, if there was any prospect of a job, however menial, at the trendy gallery. At least she had been spared that particular shame, she thought fiercely.

But that was all she was to be spared. Vanessa was speaking again. 'And are you sure that she is just hanging around aimlessly? After all, she was seeing quite a lot of Guy a few months ago before all this happened. Perhaps she's hoping to revive all that again and use him as a meal ticket for life.'

Guy's mother gave an unfeeling laugh. 'I can't believe she's that naïve,' she exclaimed. 'Guy may have paid her attention while Robert and Martin were alive, but the circumstances are different now, very different. Guy isn't a fool by any means. She's quite an attractive girl, I'll grant you that, but if she's hoping for anything more from him than just a casual affair, I'm afraid she's going to be severely disappointed. Guy can do better for himself than a penniless cousin.'

Vanessa's 'Mother!' was half laughing, half scandalised, but Morwenna waited to hear no more. She turned precipitately and fled back across the wide hall with its rich Turkey carpet and dark panelled walls, and up the gently curving stairs.

In the past few weeks, one room in particular had become her refuge—her mother's small sitting room in the West Wing. This was one of the few places where Cousin Patricia and her 'little changes' had so far not penetrated. Morwenna slammed the door behind her, then flung herself down on the shabby brocaded sofa and gave way to a storm of tears. In a way, it was a catharsis she had been needing. She had hardly shed a tear at the funeral or afterwards, and had meekly accepted the tranquillisers that the doctor, worried by her pale face and shuttered eyes, had prescribed.

Now grief, humiliation and rage all had their way with her, as she lay, her face buried in the silken cushions. It was dreadful to contemplate how near, how very near she had come to falling in love with Guy. As children, they had been largely indifferent to each other on the few occasions they had met. Then, in the early summer, she had met him again at a party after a gap of several years. In fact they had hardly recognised each other, but the attraction had been, as she thought, instant and mutual. Now she had to face the fact that she had been the one who was attracted, and that Guy had only had an eye to the main chance. She pressed her knuckles against her teeth until they ached.

So many things began to make sense now, particularly the fact that she had seen so little of Guy since the funeral. True, he had been working, and only came down to the Priory at weekends, but even then he had held aloof. She had been grateful then, telling herself that it was respect for her grief that held him in check, but now she knew differently. It was simply that Guy had nothing to gain now in prolonging their relationship. She could only be thankful that she had never yielded to the frank temptation to turn to his arms for comfort.

She had sometimes wondered in the past why it had always been Guy who had drawn back in their lovemaking. There had been several times when she had longed for his kisses and caresses to sweep her away on a tide of passion past the point of no return. Now she wondered if it had been self-control which restrained him, or simply a disinclination to get too closely involved with her. Whatever his motive, it had been enough to keep her eating out of his hand all through the summer, she thought unhappily. In fact, she had come close to quarrelling with Martin on the subject. Martin had been unimpressed with Guy's blond good looks, and had disliked his sense of humour which tended to poke sly fun at everyone outside the charmed circle in which he moved.

Guy was one of the few subjects they had disagreed on, and now she had to acknowledge that Martin had not simply been playing the heavy brother. He had been wiser than she knew, and she understood his motives now in encouraging her to apply for a place on the painting course. Apart from wanting to get her out of Guy's way, he had been concerned about her lack of purpose in life, her lighthearted assumption that there would always be someone around to look after her. She was quite aware, without conceit, of her own attractions and knew there were few men who would not be drawn by her pale silky hair, twisted up into a loose knot on top of her head, and her large grey eyes with their long fringe of dark lashes. She supposed now that this was why she had been so easily taken in by Guy. She was accustomed to men's attentions and admiration, and it had never even occurred to her that her good-looking cousin could have an ulterior motive.

'What a fool!' she whispered aloud, pressing her knuckles childishly against her streaming eyes. 'What an utter fool!'

At last she lay quietly, her eyes closed, capable only of an occasional aching sob. She felt physically and emotionally drained, and she was scared as well. One certain thing had emerged from the unpalatable comments she had heard downstairs—she was going to have to leave the Priory, and fast. But where was she to go? Even the potential refuge of the painting school had been taken from her, and the remnants of her pride forbade her to ask for any kind of help from Cousin Patricia.

She sat up unwillingly, pushing her tumbled hair back from her face, while her brooding gaze travelled round the room, resting with a kind of painful affection on the few pieces of antique furniture that she knew her mother had chosen for this room when she had first come to the Priory as a bride. The fact that the chair covers were faded and the curtains and carpet had also seen better days only added to their charm. Above the white marble fireplace hung Laura Kerslake's only attempt at a self-portrait, painted only a few years before her death. Morwenna's eyes lingered on it with peculiar intensity, as if that serene face with the humorous eyes and the wryly twisted mouth, suggesting that the artist knew only too well that portraiture was not her *forte*, could provide her with some clue what to do for the future. She gave a small weary sigh at her own fancifulness, and her eyes wandered on past the portrait to the small group of landscapes on the adjoining wall.

Here, Laura Kerslake had been thoroughly at home. These were what Morwenna had always thought of as the Trevennon group. They were scenes done from memory of the place where Laura had spent her girlhood. Although she had been born and lived in London during her early years, the outbreak of the Second World War had caused her parents to seek a safer home for her, and so Laura, on the brink of her teens, had made a long, solitary journey to Cornwall to stay with some distant relatives. She had never returned to London. When the news had come that her mother and father had been the victims of a direct hit on their house during the Blitz, she had simply remained at Trevennon.

Trevennon. Morwenna climbed off the sofa and walked across the room to study the pictures more closely. Of all her mother's work, these seemed more deeply imbued with the almost mystical, fey element which characterised it than any others. When she was small, Morwenna had gazed at the big, dark house on the cliff top with its twin turrets and tall, twisted chimneys and set her young imaginings of Camelot, of Tristan and Iseult among those sombre stones. Laura had laughed indulgently at such fancies, although at the same time she had pointed out that Trevennon owed more to the tin-miners than it did to any fabled knights and ladies.

Morwenna knew that the rugged coast nearby was littered with the remains of the mine-workings, and the ruined buildings and chimneys stood now only as the landmarks of a vanished prosperity. Trevennon, her mother had said, had been founded on that prosperity, but Laura had never given any hint as to what it owed its present subsistence.

In fact, when she looked back, Morwenna realised that her mother had said very little about her life in Cornwall. But she had been happy there, or that was the impression Morwenna had always received. Besides, her own name was a Cornish one, and her mother would hardly have chosen it if it had revived any unhappy memories, although at the same time she was aware that her father had not approved the choice. 'Pure romanticism', he had called it, but with an edge to his voice rather than the indulgent note with which he usually greeted his wife's whims. And he had used the same phrase, Morwenna remembered, when he had looked at the Trevennon group—the house on the cliff-top, the deserted Wheal Vaisey mine, the tiny harbour village of Port Vennor, and the cramped beach of Spanish Cove with the dark rocks standing up like granite sentinels against the swell of the tide.

'Why do you say that?' As if it were yesterday, Morwenna recalled the lift of her mother's chin. 'I wasn't just painting a place. I was painting my youth, and all I knew then was peace, security and love.' She had risen from the sofa and walked over to her husband, sliding her arm through his and resting her cheek against his sleeve. 'I don't doubt that you're right, but leave me my illusions.'

'Peace, security and love.' As the words came back to her, Morwenna felt herself shiver. They were like an epitaph for her own hopes, she thought unhappily. Then she stiffened. A purposeful step was coming along the passage outside, and she turned to face the door as it opened. Lady Kerslake came in.

'Oh, there you are, Morwenna. I've been looking all over the house for you,' she said rather pettishly. 'I was wondering whether you intended being in for lunch.' She hesitated, then went on, 'You see, Guy has just phoned to say that he's coming down and bringing a friend with him and we thought....' She let the words drift into silence and gave Morwenna a significant look.

Morwenna bit her lip. So Guy was bringing his latest fancy down to lunch, and his mother was checking to see that their inconvenient house-guest would accept the situation without showing that she cared, or making any kind of scene. Her temper rose slowly.

'How nice,' she said with assumed indifference. 'But if my presence is going to cause any embarrassment I can easily pick up a snack at the Red Lion.'

'Oh, my dear!' Lady Kerslake's lips parted in a smile of total insincerity. 'As if we would expect you to do any such thing! What a silly girl you are, sometimes. Not, of course, that we would wish to interfere if you *had* made any plans. After all, you're a grown woman now, and you have a life of your own to lead. It's perfectly natural that you should want to be independent, and we don't want to interfere, or feel that we're holding you back in any way.' She paused again, invitingly, as if waiting for Morwenna to confide in her. Her tone had been all interest and motherly concern, but Morwenna knew she would not have been deceived for an instant, even if she had not overheard that brief conversation in the drawing room. Cousin Patricia's whole tone and attitude was hinting broadly that she had outstayed her welcome, and that they were waiting to hear what plans she had made to shift herself.

The humiliation of having to admit that she had no plans, and that even her embryo career as an artist had died an undistinguished death, was suddenly too much to bear. A germ of inspiration lodged in her brain, and before she could reason with herself or question the wisdom of what she was about to do, she spoke.

'You really don't have to bother about me any more, Cousin Patricia. I'd intended to tell you over lunch that I'm going away. I—I've been invited to stay at Trevennon— with my mother's people—until I go to Carcassonne in the spring. The letter came this morning. It's a wonderful opportunity for me. Cornwall's a marvellous place for painters. My mother used to say that she got all the inspiration for her best work from her time at Trevennon,' she ended, rushing her words nervously, as the thought occurred to her that Cousin Patricia might demand to see this mysterious invitation.

Lady Kerslake's eyes rested wonderingly on the group of paintings over Morwenna's shoulder, then came back to search her face rather frowningly. 'Your mother had relatives in Cornwall? I wasn't aware....'

'Very distant relatives,' Morwenna broke in. 'Cousins heaven only knows how many times removed.' Wildly she searched her memory for names that would add weight to her story. 'It—it was Uncle Dominic who wrote to me.' That was the name her mother had mentioned most of all. Dominic Trevennon who had taught the city-born girl to climb barefoot over the rocks, to row a boat, to fish, to lift the lobster pots and relieve them of their snapping contents. It had been Dominic too who had told her the legends that Morwenna remembered as bedtime stories. Tales of the 'knackers', the small malevolent spirits who inhabited the tin mines, whose tapping hammers presaged disasters, such as flooding or earthfalls. Tales of the galleon which had foundered off Spanish Cove during the storms that pursued the ill-fated Armada, and the gold it had carried, still to be found, Laura had said, among the sand of the cove by anyone reckless enough to climb down the cliff to search there and risk being cut off by the racing tide. And Morwenna had lain there round-eyed among the comfort of the blankets, hearing the screech of gulls and feeling the sand gritty under her bare toes as she delved among the shifting grains for the doubloons.

'It all seems very sudden,' Lady Kerslake was saying, her lips drawn into a thin line. 'But I suppose you know what you're doing. Have you met any of these—er—cousins before?'

'No, but I feel I know them. My mother told me so much about them.' Morwenna, guiltily conscious just how far this was from the truth, surreptitiously crossed her fingers in her jacket pockets.

'Well, it's very kind of them to offer you a home, under the circumstances,' Lady Kerslake said sourly. 'I do hope you won't take advantage of their generosity, Morwenna. You can't expect to be a burden on other people all your life, you know. But if it's only until the spring, I don't suppose it will matter too much.' She gave a brisk nod. 'Now, what about lunch?'

'Oh, don't bother about me.' Morwenna's nails dug deep into the palms of her hands. 'I think I'll go and see about my packing.' Another meal in this house, she thought, would choke me.

'As you wish,' Lady Kerslake concurred, not troubling to hide her relief at the way the situation seemed to be resolving itself. She turned towards the door, then hesitated as if a thought had occurred to her. 'If there are any of your mother's paintings, Morwenna, that you would care to take with you, I hope you won't hesitate to do so. Geoffrey and I were talking last night, and we agreed it would only be fair that you should have some keepsake of her, although there is no actual legal entitlement. I'm not suggesting, of course, that you should take any of the better-known canvases hanging downstairs, but if you want any of the pictures in this room you may have them. I don't think they can be regarded as her best work by any means, but naturally they will be of sentimental value to you.'

If she had expected a show of delight, she was disappointed. Morwenna's face was impassive and her few words of thanks merely polite. Lady Kerslake went away to arrange her lunch party reflecting that the girl was probably put out because she had not been allowed to take her pick of the more valuable paintings.

As soon as she could be sure that she had departed, Morwenna sank back again on the sofa, her legs shaking. She stared across the room at the painting of the lonely house on the bleak headland and her stomach contracted nervously. She thought wildly, 'Oh, God, what have I done?'

She had always tended to be impulsive. It was a family trait, but it had never carried her to these lengths before. It had been impulsiveness that had led her to apply to the painting school. Many of the friends she had been at school with were rather desultorily pursuing careers as personal assistants or secretaries, but they seemed to be little more than glorified dogsbodies as far as Morwenna could see. Or they were helping to run boutiques, or serving in West End department stores. Somehow she had wanted more than that. And it hadn't particularly pleased her when people said tolerantly, 'Oh—Morwenna? Well, she'll get married, of course,' their eyes lingering appreciatively over her slender figure with the gently rounded hips and small, firm breasts.

She tried to control her whirling thoughts. After all, she wasn't committed to going to Cornwall. Trevennon had been a let-out—the inspiration of the moment—something to save her face with Cousin Patricia. She didn't have to actually do anything about it. Anyway, a wave of colour flooded her face, she couldn't just wish herself on a group of strangers, in spite of her brave words to Lady Kerslake. She had no means of knowing whether the Dominic of whom her mother had spoken with such affection was still alive. He would be in his sixties at the very least, and the years that Laura Kerslake had spent at Trevennon would only be a distant memory.

She had sometimes wondered why her mother had not maintained contact with Trevennon over the years, but at the time it had never occurred to her to ask. She had been too young to consider the complexities of the situation, she thought, and after her mother's death, too much probing into the past had never seemed quite appropriate. Besides, she had always had the feeling that her father had not shared her mother's nostalgia for Cornwall. Nothing had ever been said, but the impression had been a strong one. Perhaps it had been nothing more than ordinary, and only too human jealousy of a time when she had lived and been happy without him, Morwenna thought wryly. Sir Robert's love for his wife had been all-encompassing. But somehow she had felt the past was an area where she should not trespass with her questions, and now they could never be answered—unless of course she went to Trevennon herself.

She shook her head slowly, clenching her fingers together in her lap. She must stop thinking along those lines. The fact of the matter was that she was homeless, but that wasn't the disaster it seemed. Friends were always flouncing away from the shelter of the parental roof after some devastating row or other, and they managed to survive. There were a number of names in her address book which she could call on in an emergency. People were always swopping flats, or marrying and moving out. There would be someone somewhere wanting another girl to make up the numbers. And there were jobs too. Not the sort of creative work she had planned on. For those she would need training—qualifications. But she would find something to do which would pay her share of the rent and food bills, and there were always evening classes she could go to.

She suppressed a grimace. It was a far cry from the spring in the South of France that she had envisaged, but she had only herself to blame. She was capable of far better work than that she had shown Lennox Christie. But she had known the money was there to buy her a place in his class, and she had simply not tried too hard. If she were trying now, it would be very different.

She took the crumpled letter out of her pocket and read it again slowly. While it held out no definite hope, it did offer her a second chance. But she would need to work very hard over the next few months to convince him that she had sincerity and application as well as talent, and wasn't just another wealthy playgirl looking for an undemanding few months in the sun.

She got up restlessly and walked over to the window, staring out at the prospect of smooth lawns and leafless trees which unfolded itself before her. What she needed was a few months' grace to do some serious painting, when what confronted her was the urgent necessity for job and flat-hunting. She tried to do some swift mental calculations, but the results were depressing. The pitifully small amount of money she had in her bank account would not be enough to feed and house her while she pursued this tenuous dream. It was time she recognised her hopes of a career — even on the fringes of the art world as the fantasy they were, and got down to realities.

She sighed and cast a regretful look back over her shoulder at the group of paintings on the wall. Their appeal had never seemed more potent. If she took any of her mother's work away with her when she went, it would be those, and the self-portrait above the mantelpiece. But if she did take them, heaven only knew what she would do with them. She could not imagine them as a welcome addition to the decor in any of her friends' flats. She supposed drearily they would have to be stored somewhere until she could find a proper home for them. Whenever that might be.

She was halfway to the door when the thought came to her. She stopped dead in her tracks and swung round again to survey the pictures. She might not be able to claim a temporary home at Trevennon, but surely, for her mother's sake, they might be willing to store the paintings for her. If she took them down to Trevennon and explained the situation.... As long as she made it clear it was only a temporary measure. They would be far better there than locked away in some warehouse. And it might give the Trevennon family some pleasure too to know that Laura Kerslake had never forgotten....

There was some relief to be gained in knowing she had solved at least one of her problems, minor though it was. It was doubtful whether she would find such ready solutions for those that remained, nevertheless as she went to her room to begin to sort through her clothes and belongings, a tiny ray of hope began to burn deep inside her.

The next few days were not comfortable ones. Morwenna was thankful that she had announced that she was leaving in advance, otherwise she felt the atmosphere in the house would have been well-nigh unendurable. As it was, she could remind herself that the little barbs and snide remarks which came her way were only for a little while longer.

She had been totally ruthless with her packing. Most of her extensive wardrobe was now at the Vicarage awaiting the next jumble sale, and she had retained only the most basic elements. But this did not grieve her as much as parting with the childhood books and possessions that still occupied her bedroom. She had thought sentimentally that one day all these things could be passed on to her own children, but she knew she had to travel lightly, and the cherished articles were disposed of to the charity shop in the nearby town. She had soon reduced her possessions down to the contents of one large suitcase, while her painting gear was consigned to the depths of an old rucksack which she found in one of the attics. The Trevennon pictures and her mother's self-portrait were carefully taken from their frames under Lady Kerslake's eagle eye and made into a neat parcel.

Life did not become any easier with the arrival of Guy with his latest girl-friend in tow. She had dark, elaborately frizzed hair and a giggle that made Morwenna want to heave, but judging by Guy's air of smug satisfaction, he saw nothing amiss.

Morwenna also had to cope with the added humiliation that Guy had obviously told this Georgina all about her, possibly with embellishments, and that Georgina's reaction to the situation was to treat her with a kind of pitying contempt, mixed with triumph that Morwenna's loss had been her gain.

Morwenna suffered this in a kind of teeth-grinding impotence, but she knew there would be no point in trying to convince Georgina that her relationship with Guy had been very much in the embryo stage, and that she was not stoically trying to conceal an irrevocably broken heart. It would have given her immense satisfaction to tell Georgina that she was welcome to Guy, and that her only regret was that she had not had the wit to see the truth behind his advances in the first place, but she knew that the other girl would not believe her.

However, it was Vanessa's attitude that Morwenna found the most surprising. As the time approached for her departure, her cousin became almost cordial, even to the point of insisting on driving her up to London to catch the Penzance train. Morwenna accepted the offer, but she did not deceive herself that it was promoted by any new-found liking for herself. She suspected that Vanessa was taking her to the train merely in order to make sure that she was in fact going to Cornwall, and was seeking her company during her remaining hours at the Priory simply to enable her to avoid Georgina to whom she had taken an instant and embarrassingly open dislike.

Life at the Priory, Morwenna decided on reflection, seemed likely to become hell for man and beast quite shortly, especially if Guy decided to marry Georgina and her father's money of which she spoke so often and with such candour, and in a way this helped to alleviate the pain of parting from her home. Nevertheless she cried herself to sleep each night, her tears prompted not merely by grief for the losses she had suffered but fear as well. It was all very well to tell herself robustly that no one need starve in these days of the Welfare State, but there was no escaping the fact that she had led a reasonably sheltered existence up to a few short weeks ago, and that what faced her was likely to be both difficult and unpleasant. Nor was it any consolation to remind herself of the thousands of girls of her age who were far worse off than she was herself. She felt totally and bewilderingly alone. From being the pivot on which the family's love turned, she was now an outcast, and she felt all the acute vulnerability of her position.

But when the day of her departure actually arrived, she was relieved. She said a stilted goodbye to Sir Geoffrey in the study which had once been her father's and was acutely embarrassed when he handed her with a few mumbled words a slip of paper which turned out to be a sizeable cheque. Blushing furiously, she managed a word of thanks and as soon as she was outside the door, she tore the cheque into tiny fragments and stuffed them into a jardiniere, conveniently situated on its pedestal further along the corridor.

Lady Kerslake returned to her former saccharine amiability, giving the impression that it was only Morwenna's own intractability that was taking her away from the Priory. Morwenna, putting her own cheek dutifully against the scented one turned to her, wondered with a wry twist of her lips what Cousin Patricia's reaction would be if she suddenly took her at her word and announced that she was going to stay.

Vanessa was waiting in the hall tapping her foot impatiently. She made no attempt to help Morwenna with her case or rucksack but walked briskly ahead of her to the car and sat revving the engine while her cousin stowed her luggage in the boot. Morwenna climbed into the passenger seat and looked steadily ahead of her. There was no point in looking back. The Priory was closed to her now and lingering backward glances as the car started down the drive would only distress her.

Vanessa gave her a sideways glance as they waited to emerge from the drive on to the road.

'You're a cool customer, I must say, Wenna,' she remarked. 'One moment you're drooping about the place like Patience on a monument or something, and the next you're off—and to Cornwall of all places! You must be completely mad. I mean, it may be all very well in the summer, except for the crowds, of course. But in winter time—my God!'

She paused but Morwenna made no response, so she continued, 'I thought Guy might have made the effort to come down and say goodbye—especially under the circumstances.' She waited again, but there was still no reply, and her voice was slightly pettish as she went on, 'I suppose he thought if he made a fuss it might upset the frightful Georgina.'

Morwenna said calmly, 'There was absolutely no reason for him to make any kind of fuss.'

'Oh, come off it, Wenna.' Vanessa put her foot on the accelerator and overtook a van on a slight bend to the alarm and indignation of its driver. 'You know quite well that you and Guy had a thing going. It can't be pleasant for you to see him with someone else. I don't blame you at all for going off to lick your wounds somewhere—I think I'd do the same in your position. But if it's any consolation to you, Mother was furious over Georgina. It's been almost amusing watching her try to be civil to her. I think in some ways she would have preferred it if Guy had insisted on sticking to you.'

'Thank you,' Morwenna said drily.

Vanessa hunched a shoulder. 'Oh, you know what I mean. After all, you were pretty involved with him. He's lucky to have got away as lightly as he has.'

'Without having to make an honest woman of me, do you mean?' Morwenna was controlling her temper with some difficulty. 'Is that what you all think?'

Vanessa shot her an uneasy glance. 'Well—not precisely. But Guy is sleeping with Georgina—and being utterly blatant about it, so....'

'So naturally you all assumed that I'd fallen into bed with him with equal ease.' Morwenna forced a smile. 'I can't pretend I'm flattered, or does Guy usually restrict his attentions to pushovers?'

'Well, let's say he doesn't usually waste a great deal of his time on frightened virgins,' Vanessa returned derisively.

Morwenna caught her bottom lip savagely in her teeth. 'I see.' She was silent for a moment. It was difficult to know which was worse—the assumption that she had been Guy's pliant mistress or the alternative inference that she had not been sufficiently attractive to him for him to have attempted seduction. She would have preferred not to be ranged in either category.

She managed a light laugh. 'Actually our relationship was based more on mutual convenience than anything else,' she said, digging her hands into the pockets of her sheepskin coat to conceal the fact that they were trembling. 'We—we both needed someone to be seen around with. And I don't blame Guy at all for confining himself to ladies with money. Now that our positions are reversed, I'm doing more or less the same thing.'

'You are?' Vanessa gave her a slightly flabbergasted look. 'I don't follow you.'

Morwenna allowed her smile to widen. 'Well, I'm not going down to Cornwall for my health's sake, let's say.'

'No?' Vanessa was openly intrigued. 'Is there a man?'

Morwenna achieved a giggle quite as smug as anything Georgina had produced.

'Of course there's a man,' she said without a tremor,

crossing her fingers superstitiously in the shelter of her pockets. 'I'd hardly be travelling to the back of beyond at this time of year otherwise.'

'Well!' Vanessa's tone was frankly congratulatory. 'I always knew you couldn't possibly be as innocent as you looked. Have you known him long?'

Morwenna shrugged. 'Long enough,' she said airily. Since I was a small child, she thought hysterically, in dreams and stories, and please don't let her ask me how old he is or any other details. I don't care if she does think me a gold-digger or worse. Anything's better than being regarded as a charity case. And I'll never see any of them again, so they can think what they like.

Vanessa was speaking again. 'And do your plans include marriage, or is that an indelicate question?'

'Oh, that would depend on a lot of things,' Morwenna said hastily. 'I—I prefer to cross that bridge when I come to it.' She gave a little laugh. 'And if I can persuade him to provide the money to send me to painting school next year, I may never have to cross it at all.'

'I see,' Vanessa said blankly. 'Well, all I can say is that I wish you luck.'

'Thank you,' Morwenna laughed. 'But I don't think I shall need it.' Her tone implied a total confidence in her own power of attraction, and for a moment she despised herself for playing Vanessa's game, but what did it matter after all? They were never likely to meet again. Once she was out of the way, Morwenna guessed that her cousins would breathe a sigh of relief and put her out of their minds. In a way she could see their point of view. While she had remained at the Priory, they could never feel their inheritance was truly theirs. She was a wholly unwelcome reminder of the old days, and relations between the two families had never been on the most intimate terms.

But it was chilling to have to recognise that she was now alone in the world with her own way to make. There had been times, not long ago either, when she had inwardly rebelled against the loving shelter of the Priory, when she had been sorely tempted to thrust away her father's and Martin's concern for her and take off on her own like so many of her contemporaries. In some ways now, she wished she had yielded to the impulse. At least now she would not feel so bereft.

Later, as she stowed her solitary suitcase and her haversack, with the bulky parcel of canvases attached, on the luggage rack and felt the train jerk under her feet as it set off on the long run to the West, a tight knot of tension settled in the pit of her stomach. She watched the platforms and sidings slip past with increasing despondency. In spite of her brave words to Vanessa, each one of which she now bitterly regretted, she knew she might well be embarking on a wild goose chase.

She swallowed past a lump in her throat. The request that the Trevennons should store her mother's pictures until she was able to come for them had seemed quite a reasonable one when she had first formulated it. Yet what right had she, a stranger among strangers, to ask any favours at all? Wouldn't she have done better to have stayed in London and hardened herself to sell the pictures? That would have been the sensible thing to have done instead of tearing off on this quixotic journey to a corner of England she only knew from bedtime stories and a few romantic images on canvas.

She sighed unhappily. For better or worse, she had started on her journey and she wished very much that she could put out of her head the fact that someone had once said it was better to travel hopefully than to arrive.

CHAPTER TWO

HER mood of depression had not lifted by the time she reached Penzance, and matters were not improved by the fact that it was pouring with rain from a leaden sky. Morwenna surveyed her surroundings without enthusiasm. She wished that funds permitted her to summon a taxi and order it to drive her to Trevennon, but she knew that would be a foolhardy thing to do when she had no idea how far the house might be situated from Penzance. For a moment she toyed with the idea of finding somewhere to spend the night in Penzance, but she soon dismissed it. Top priority was getting out to Trevennon and leaving the pictures there.

Her hair was hanging round her face in wet streaks by the time she had found a newsagent and bought a map of the area, and she was thankful to find an open snack bar where she could shelter and study the map in comparative comfort. Trevennon itself was not marked, but she soon found Port Vennor as she drank her coffee and ate a rather tasteless cheese roll. Spanish Cove was marked too, so she knew roughly the direction to aim for.

As she emerged from the snack bar, a gust of wind caught the door, almost wrenching it from her hand, and catching her off balance for a moment. Morwenna groaned inwardly. Her mother had told her all about the south-westerly gales, but she had not bargained for meeting one as soon as she arrived. Walking down to the bus stop, it occurred to her that she wasn't sure exactly what she had bargained for. In fact, the more she thought about it, the more hare-brained and impulsive her actions seemed. She eased the rucksack into a more comfortable position on her shoulder and bent her head against the force of the rising wind.

One thing was certain. She would soon find out if she had been a fool, and she found herself hoping with something very like a prayer in her heart that Dominic Trevennon would be a kindly and understanding old man who would not demand too many stumbling explanations of her arrival, unheralded, on his doorstep.

When she arrived at the bus stop, she found that she was not alone. Another girl was waiting, sheltering from the wind in a nearby doorway. As Morwenna stopped to put down her case, she gave her a frankly speculative look. She had a short, rather dumpy figure which wasn't helped by being enveloped in the voluminous folds of a black cape reaching to her ankles. Her face was round and friendly, and quite pretty, and she smiled as Morwenna put down her case.

'Miserable day.'

'Yes.' Morwenna looked around her. 'And it gets dark so quickly at this time of the year.'

'Have you got far to go?'

'I'm not sure really. I'm trying to get to a house called Trevennon.'

'Trevennon?' The other looked startled for a moment. 'It's quite a long way. You want to ask to be set down at a place called Trevennon Cross.' She was silent for a moment, then she said, 'Look—I'm not trying to be rude. But are you quite sure that's where you want to go?'

Morwenna was no longer very sure of anything, but she lifted her chin with a confidence she was far from feeling. 'Of course. I'm looking for a Mr Trevennon—Dominic Trevennon. Do you know him?'

'Not personally.' The other girl's mouth twisted wryly. 'He doesn't exactly welcome outsiders on his sacred preserves.'

Morwenna groaned inwardly. So much for the benevolent old gentleman of her hopes, she thought.

'You make him sound a formidable character,' she said, trying to speak lightly.

'He's a bastard,' the other girl said shortly. 'Behaves like one of the Lords of Creation, hanging on to that barn of a house and his piece of crumbling coastline as if he was defending one of the last bastions of Cornwall. He hates tourists and he doesn't go a bomb on casual callers either, but if he's expecting you, it should be all right.'

Morwenna's heart sank even more deeply. The white-haired grandfatherly figment of her imagination was turning into one of the autocrats of all time, so what kind of a reception was she going to get?

'You seem to know a great deal about him,' she commented.

'Not through choice, I assure you. My brother and I have a small studio pottery at St Enna which is pretty near Trevennon. We want to extend it and open a small shop, but we were refused planning permission, and Dominic Trevennon was behind that. He was afraid it might attract tourists near his precious estate. He values his privacy very highly, does Mr Trevennon.'

Thanks for the warning, Morwenna thought bleakly. She glanced at her watch. The bus would be arriving any minute now. It still wasn't too late to change her mind. Could this really be the man her mother had spoken of with such nostalgic affection, or had the passage of time simply changed him out of all recognition?

'I'm Biddy Bradshaw, by the way,' the girl went on. 'I've been doing the rounds of some of the gift shops, trying to get some firm orders for the Easter trade.' She gave a tight little smile. 'If we had our own shop, it would make things much easier. The shops are fairly co-operative round here, but they want commission on what they sell for us, naturally, and there isn't that much profit just at the moment to share around.'

Morwenna nodded, conscious of a slight feeling of awkwardness as she introduced herself.

Biddy's eyes were alight with interest. 'Morwenna? But that's a Cornish name. I didn't realise you were from this part of the world.'

'I'm not. But my mother spent most of her childhood here, and I suppose it seemed a natural choice for her.'

Biddy shrugged slightly. 'I suppose so—if you have a taste for tragic legends. Oh, here's the bus at last.'

She clambered up the steps of the single-decker while Morwenna followed. 'You want the stop after mine,' she directed as Morwenna paid for her ticket. 'Turn left at the Cross and follow the road until it brings you out at the house. You can't miss it,' she added. 'It doesn't lead anywhere else.'

Morwenna would have liked to have questioned Biddy

further about Trevennon, but the bus was fairly crowded and she was aware of all the potential listening ears, so she confined her questions to general ones about the area itself. Biddy was cheerful company, and Morwenna felt oddly desolate when she announced eventually that they were coming to her stop.

'You want the next one, don't forget,' she said as she got to her feet. 'Good luck.' She paused. 'If you—do decide to stay for a while, look us up at the pottery.'

'I'd like that,' Morwenna smiled up at her. As the bus lurched away again she took a deep breath to steady herself and began to retrieve her belongings. In less than five minutes she found herself standing in the darkness, the wind whipping at her hair and tangling across her face. She shivered, huddling her sheepskin jacket round her for warmth and wishing that she was just about anywhere but the chill of this unknown country road.

She began to walk towards the faint glimmer of the signpost at the crossroads, glad of the shelter of the hedge. It was raining still and the drops stung her face. When she licked her lips she could taste salt on them, and in the distance above the howl of the wind, she could hear the sea roaring.

'Good night for wrecks,' she murmured aloud, and grimaced at the thought. At the crossroads she turned left as Biddy had indicated and found herself in a narrow lane, bordered on either side by high hedges. It was really dark now, the faint moonlight almost totally obliterated by the mass of rushing clouds chased by the gale.

She had walked perhaps two hundred yards, practically feeling her way along the hedge, when she stopped and said flatly and aloud, 'This is silly.'

She set down her case and the rucksack and began to unfasten the buckles. Among the oddments she had thrown in at the last moment, she thought, was a torch, although she wasn't sure if it worked or if there were even any batteries in it. Naturally the missing article had slipped right to the bottom of the rucksack and she was obliged to repack it almost completely before she could fasten it again. Grimly she stood up at last and tentatively switched on the torch. The faintness of the glimmer of light that fell on the road in front of her indicated there was not much life left in the batteries, but it was better than nothing, and it was a heavy, comforting object to have in her hand anyway on this evening when the whole world seemed full of movement and menace and unidentifiable sounds. She shone the torch ahead of her, and her heart almost leaped into her mouth when it picked out something large and white in the hedge, something which bent and swayed in the wind. A large notice board, she realised, with hysterical relief, and what an utter fool she was making of herself. She had spent the greater part of her life living in the country, so why was she behaving like a townie, leaping at every shadow, letting her imagination play tricks. It was nonsense to think that this dark, unfamiliar landscape was rejecting her. She was letting Biddy's warnings really get to her.

Or was she? she wondered drily a moment later as she allowed her torch to play over the lettering on the board. 'Private Road to Trevennon Only', it stated unequivocally. No sign of the welcome mat there, she thought philosophically, and walked on.

She had been walking for about ten minutes and wishing that the notice board had given some idea of the distance involved when it happened. The shriek of the wind had been rising steadily, and now in a sudden boiling crescendo of sound there was a loud crack just ahead of her, and with a slithering rumble a tree fell right across the road in her path.

She stood very still for a moment, then put her case down, and began to shake. She wasn't hurt. For God's sake, it hadn't even touched her, but it had been close, and at this rate her nerves were going to be shot to pieces and she was going to arrive on Dominic Trevennon's doorstep a gibbering lunatic.

What was more, although the tree on closer examination did not turn out to be particularly large, nevertheless it had blocked the road. She could climb over it, but that was not the problem. Private road it might be, but presumably people at the house had vehicles and visitors with other vehicles, and the tree had fallen awkwardly between two bends in the lane. A driver wo... be on top of it almost before he realised.

She caught hold of one of th... ...dier branches and tugged, but to no avail. It migh... be large, but it was heavier than it looked. She su... ...sed her most sensible course of action would be to hurry on to the house wherever it was, and warn someone, trusting to luck that no one drove along the lane in the meantime.

Ironically, the wind now seemed to be lessening, as if aware it had done its worst and could now be satisfied. And behind her, in the distance, she could just hear the sound of a car engine, coming fast. Morwenna swung round, her eyes searching the darkness. She was not all that far from the main road, she told herself. There was no reason to think that the traveller would not go straight on. But even as she watched, she saw the glare of a pair of powerful headlights and knew that against all the odds the car had turned off towards Trevennon. And the driver knew the road. He was covering the narrow twisting road without a check, and any moment now he would be here, unaware of the waiting danger.

Morwenna almost hurled her case and rucksack into the shelter of the hedge and ran, stumbling, back to the bend. She stood in the middle of the lane, swinging her torch from side to side in a desperate attempt to attract attention, but wouldn't the pitiful light it afforded be swallowed up in the darkness?

The car lights seemed to slice across the evening sky, and then with a snarl of the engine the car was upon her. She gave the torch one last wave, then dived towards the hedge, but not quite soon enough. Something grazed her—perhaps a wing—and she fell, not hard but sufficiently to wind her. The car stopped with a squeal of brakes, a door slammed and Morwenna found herself being hauled to her feet with considerably more force than she felt was necessary.

He was tall, and his hands were hard and bruising. That was the first, the most immediate impression, and more than enough, Morwenna thought feelingly, as she was dumped unceremoniously back on to her feet. He seemed to be very dark, or was that just the suggestion of the darkness around him, and he was, she realised radiating an anger that was almost tangible.

'You bloody little idiot.' He wasn't shouting; he didn't have to. 'What the hell do you think you're doing? You could have been killed!'

His grip on her upper arms was really hurting, and furiously she pulled herself free. 'You call me an idiot!' she blazed back at him, fright and stress making her voice younger and more breathless than she would have liked. 'And what about you—driving like a maniac on a rotten night like this? If I had been killed, it would have been all your fault!'

Even as she spoke, she knew she was not being totally fair. He had seen her pitiful attempt to cause a diversion and had managed to stop, in spite of the speed he was driving at, almost within the car's length. But this had been the final straw in a pretty abysmal day, and now reaction was taking its toll of her.

'Your logic fascinates me,' he said with a cool contempt that seared its way across her skin. 'May I point out to you that this is in fact a private road, and under those circumstances one expects to be preserved from the antics of lunatic hitch-hikers. And might I also suggest you make your way back to the main road, and ply your trade there.'

'I was not hitch-hiking!' She was furious to find that she was shaking like a leaf. 'What I was doing was trying to save your life, or at least trying to prevent you from being injured. That, of course, was before I met you.'

There was a long electric silence.

'You'd better explain,' he said grimly. 'Oh, not your last remark. I've managed to work the implications of that out for myself.'

'There's a tree down,' she said tonelessly. 'Just round that bend. I was going to warn someone at the house, then I heard you coming, and thought I'd better stay and warn you instead. Only all I had was that damned torch, and the batteries aren't too good—and now they've gone all together.' She began unavailingly to push the switch on the torch backwards and forwards as if her very insistence could make it work again.

There was another silence, then he said abruptly, 'Wait here.'

He walked across to the car, climbed in and started the engine. He drove the few feet to the bend, then stopped. Another pause, then she heard his footsteps returning.

He said without emotion, 'It seems I owe you an apology.'

'Well, don't let it ruin your life.' She tried to sound flip, but the quiver in her voice betrayed her, and she heard him sigh, swiftly and sharply.

'But that still doesn't explain precisely what you were doing on this road in the first place,' he said. 'What happened? Did you miss the main road in the dark? This lane only leads to....'

'To Trevennon,' she finished for him wearily. 'I know. I can read, actually, if the print is big enough. And I haven't missed my way, though God knows it would have been easy enough. I'm going to Trevennon. I have to see Mr Dominic Trevennon.'

She heard his startled intake of breath and wondered resignedly if she was to be the recipient of another Awful Warning about Mr Trevennon's intolerance of casual callers and general irascibility, but when he spoke his voice sounded cool and disinterested.

'Indeed, and has Mr Trevennon the pleasure of expecting you?'

'No,' she admitted. 'And I've already been warned that he's arrogant and awkward and imagines that he's some uncrowned king of Cornwall, but all the same, I'm going to see him.'

'I can't imagine why,' he remarked. 'Judging by the description you've received of him, I would have thought it would have been infinitely preferable to keep your distance.'

'I have to see him, she said abruptly. 'I want to ask him a favour.'

'Do you think he sounds the kind of man likely to provide favours for chance-met strangers?'

'On the face of it, no.' Morwenna shook her head. 'On the other hand, he's obviously a supreme egotist, and he might just be flattered to think someone has travelled half way across England to ask him to do something for them. Besides, I'm not wholly a stranger to him.'

'Well, I wouldn't count on it,' he said bitingly. 'And what do you mean—you're not "wholly a stranger"?'

But Morwenna was already regretting that she had said so much.

'I'm sorry, but I think that's my business,' she said, biting her lip. 'And I don't doubt you're a lifelong friend of his and that you can't wait to get down to Trevennon and tell him what I've said. Well, go ahead. I don't suppose that in the long run it will make much difference anyway.'

'As a matter of fact,' he said slowly, 'at this precise moment, I'm wondering whether I've ever known him at all. As for proceeding with all haste to Trevennon to drop you in it, may I remind you that the road is blocked by a tree. Besides, I'm going to make a detour round to the farm to get Jacky Herrick to bring his tractor down to shift it, so if you hurry you should arrive at Trevennon with your version first.'

'A tractor?' Morwenna let her voice register exaggerated surprise. 'You mean you're not going to pick it up with one hand, and toss it lightly into the hedge?'

She was sorry as soon as she had said it. There was something about him that got under her skin, but that was no excuse for behaving with gratuitous rudeness.

When he spoke, his voice was cold with anger. 'If I was in the mood for tossing anything into a hedge, believe me, young woman, you'd get priority over any tree.'

'I think we've already established that,' she said ruefully, wincing a little as she moved forward.

'Are you hurt? The car hardly touched you....'

'Oh, please don't bother about me.' She felt as if one side of her was one terrific bruise. 'I still might manage to finish fourth.'

'Stand still,' he ordered abruptly. 'You might have broken something.'

She stood, teeth clenched more with anger than with pain as he completed a swift but comprehensive examination of her moving parts.

'Thank you,' she said with awful politeness when he had finished. 'You should have been a vet.'

'I won't complete the analogy,' he returned with equal

courtesy. 'Although several members of the animal kingdom do suggest themselves. Which reminds me—when you get down to Trevennon, watch out for the dogs. They're not trained to encourage strangers.'

'Oh God!' Morwenna, retrieving her case and rucksack from the hedge, swung round to look at him. It was maddening that it was too dark to see his face properly, let alone the expression on it, and she could hardly ask him to stand in the car headlights for a moment so that she could judge whether he was joking. He hadn't done a great deal of joking up to that point, certainly, and there was no reason for him to start now, so the dogs probably existed. She moistened her lips uncertainly. 'Do—do they bite?'

'It has been known,' he said laconically. 'The thing to do is stand your ground. Don't try to outrun them—that's fatal.'

'I can imagine it would be.' Morwenna knew an overwhelming desire to sit down on the wet lane and scream and drum her heels. 'But you don't have to worry. I doubt very much whether I could outrun a tortoise at the moment. Would it help if I knew the dogs' names?'

'It might. They're called Whisky and Max. Do you think you can remember that?'

'Oh, I think so,' she said grimly. 'I imagine I shall have great difficulty in remembering anything else.' Wincing slightly, she settled her rucksack on her shoulder then picked up her case.

'Dear God!' He was still standing in the shadows well out of range of the headlights. 'Not just a casual call, I see. Just how long were you planning to stay at Trevennon?'

It was on the tip of her tongue to confess that she would be satisfied with a roof over her head for the night, but she suppressed it. After all, it was none of his business.

She sent him a smiling glance over her shoulder as she prepared to negotiate the tree. It was one of her best, slightly teasing, deliberately provocative, aimed at leaving him with something to think about.

'We'll just have to see how things work out,' she said lightly. 'Maybe the king of Cornwall will take a fancy to me.'

But if she had counted on having the last word, she was to be disappointed.

'I'm sure he'll take something to you.' His voice was bland. 'Preferably a riding crop. *Au revoir*, my pretty wayfarer.'

She held her head high, and wouldn't allow herself to limp until she was round the next bend and out of the range of those too-revealing headlights.

The force of the wind seemed to have spent itself, and now the air was full of the sound of the sea, a sullen booming roar as the breakers hurled themselves against the granite cliffs. Nor was it rain on her face any longer, but spray.

As she trudged on wearily, Morwenna found herself wondering how easy it would be to miss the house entirely and walk straight over the cliff into the sea. She grinned wanly at the thought, and then stiffened, peering almost incredulously into the gloom. Somewhere just to the left she could see a light, a steady, purposeful light like a lamp set in the windows of an uncurtained room. And at that moment the moon emerged from behind the flying clouds, and Morwenna saw the dark mass of the house, its chimneys and roofs clearly outlined against the sky.

Under the circumstances, it was madness to feel such a sense of relief, of homecoming even, but the familiarity of the building's shape, imprinted on her mind by her mother's painting, caught at her heart, and she felt childish tears prick at the back of her eyelids.

Somewhere close at hand a dog began to bark, deep and full-throated, and then another took it up, and in the house another light went on, as if the occupants were responding to the animals' warning. Of course, she thought, they would be expecting a visitor—the man she had met on the road.

Summoning all her courage, she walked up to the front door. The notice she had seen had been perfectly correct, she thought wryly. The road indeed led to nowhere but Trevennon—straight to its door in fact. And what kind of arrogance had decided to build a house in this very spot anyway—out on a headland, exposed four-square to the elements? 'A barn', Biddy had called it, she thought, and wished that her first view of it had been in daylight.

There was an old-fashioned bell pull at the side of the front door, and Morwenna tugged at it half-heartedly, not really expecting any results. But to her surprise, a bell did start jangling somewhere inside the house, and the dogs began barking again tumultuously. They seemed to be penned up somewhere in the outbuildings which rambled away from the side of the house, and as Morwenna waited, she heard the barking rise almost to a frenzy and the sound of heavy bodies banging against some kind of wooden barricade. It was altogether too close for comfort and Morwenna hoped devoutly that it would hold.

'Whisky!' she called out, trying to sound firm. 'Max! Quiet, good dogs.'

The good dogs were clearly puzzled by this personal appeal from an unfamiliar voice, but they stopped barking. There was a lot of subdued whining, and convulsive sniffing, and paws scrabbling on a hard surface, but that, Morwenna felt, was a far more acceptable alternative.

And someone was actually coming to answer the door. Morwenna felt her stomach flutter with nervousness, and clenched her hands into fists deep in the pockets of her coat as the heavy door swung open with an appropriate creak of hinges.

She was confronted by a small stocky man, almost enveloped in a large and disreputable butcher's apron. His face was wrinkled like a walnut into lines of real malevolence, and bright eyes under grey shaggy eyebrows glared suspiciously up at her.

'Wrong 'ouse,' he snorted, and attempted to close the door.

Morwenna stepped forward quickly to circumvent the move. She smiled beguilingly at him, ignoring the scowl she received in return. Her thoughts were seething. Was this—could this be Dominic Trevennon? He would be about the right age, she reasoned, and he seemed to fit the portrait of unlovable eccentric which she had begun to build in her mind.

'Mr Trevennon?' she asked, trying to speak confidently.

'Not 'ere,' was the discouraging reply. 'So you may's well take yourself off.'

'Do you mean he's away?' Morwenna's heart sank within her. 'Or is he just out?'

'Tedn't none of your business,' the gnome remarked with satisfaction. 'Now go 'long with you. I want to get this door shut.' Somewhere in the house a telephone began to ring, and his face assumed an expression of even deeper malice. ''Ear that?' he snarled. 'I should be answering that, not stood 'ere, argy-bargying with you.'

'Oh, please,' Morwenna said desperately, seeing that he was about to slam the door on her. 'I—I've come a long way today. If Mr Trevennon isn't here at the moment, couldn't I come in and wait?'

'No, you couldn't.' He looked outraged at the thought. 'If Mr Trevennon'd wanted to see you, he'd have left word you were expected. You phone up tomorrow in a decent manner and make an appointment. Now, go on. I'm letting all this old draught in.'

The door was already closing in Morwenna's face when a woman's voice called, 'Hold on there, you, Zack. You're to let her in.'

''Oo says?' Zack swung round aggressively.

The woman approaching jerked a thumb over her shoulder. ''E does. Good enough for you?'

Apparently it was, because Zack held the door open—not wide, it was true, but sufficiently to allow Morwenna to squeeze herself through it into the hall. She put her case down and eased the rucksack from her aching shoulder, ignoring Zack's mutter of, 'Seems mazed t'me.'

'You keep your opinion until you'm asked, Zack Hubbard.' The woman gave Morwenna a searching but not unfriendly look. 'You can wait in the study for the master, miss. There's a nice fire in there.' She paused doubtfully, taking in Morwenna's chilled and generally bedraggled appearance. 'Would you fancy a cup of something hot, while you'm waiting?'

Morwenna accepted gratefully and followed her rescuer across the wide hall. She was too bemused by the suddenness of her access to the house, just when she had almost given up all hope, to take much account of her surroundings, but the paramount impression was one of all-pervading shabbiness.

And this was confirmed by the room in which she found herself. A big shabby desk, littered with papers and crowned by an ancient typewriter, dominated the room. A sagging sofa covered in faded chintz was drawn up in front of the fireplace, and these with the addition of a small table just behind the sofa constituted the entire furniture of the room. The square of dark red carpet was threadbare in places, and the once-patterned wallpaper seemed to have faded to a dull universal beige, with lighter, brighter square patches seeming to indicate depressingly that pictures had once hung there.

Morwenna sank down on to the sofa and held out her hands to the blazing logs. What she had seen so far gave her no encouragement at all. The Trevennons, it seemed, had fallen on hard times since her mother had last visited the house. And it could furnish an explanation as to why Laura Kerslake had never returned there. Perhaps the Trevennons themselves had discouraged any reunions, preferring her to remember things as they had been. To remember people as they had been.

She glanced at the rucksack which she had placed on the sofa beside her and began to fumble with the buckles. She took out the parcel of paintings, and after a moment's hesitation walked across and laid it on the desk. Her own equivalent, she thought wryly, of putting all her cards on the table.

There were some newspapers and magazines piled rather untidily at one end of the sofa and she riffled through them casually when she sat down again. They were an odd mixture, she thought, giving little clue as to the tastes and personality of the subscriber.

There were some local newspapers as well and Morwenna unfolded one of these and began to glance casually through the news items on the front page, but the newsprint had a disturbing way of dancing up and down in front of her eyes, and at length she gave up the effort, acknowledging that she was more tired than even she had guessed.

The door opened and the women came in carrying a tray, which she placed down on the sofa table. Again Morwenna was the recipient of one of those searching looks.

'Is—is something wrong?' she asked.

'You have a look of someone I know. Can't bring to mind who it is, but I daresay it'll come to me.'

Morwenna's heart skipped a beat. Was it her mother that this woman recognised in her? She was quite aware that there was a resemblance, but before she could ask further, a door banged nearby and Zack's voice shouted pettishly, 'Inez!'

The woman tutted and moved towards the door. 'Dear life, doesn't he go on,' she remarked placidly, and went out closing the door behind her.

Morwenna studied the tea tray with slight amusement. It had been laid with a tea towel, and bore in addition to a fat brown earthenware teapot, a cup and saucer, neither of which matched, and a small plate holding two buttered cream crackers. But the tea itself was strong and fragrant, and by some miracle not made with teabags. She sipped it as if it was nectar.

When she had finished, she leaned back against the shabby, comfortable cushions and closed her eyes. She felt warmed through, and oddly at peace in spite of her inner uncertainties. All kinds of curious images began to dance behind her shuttered eyes, and it was pleasant to lie back and contemplate them while the warmth of the fire began to dissolve away some of the ache from her tired limbs.

Trees danced in the wind, and dogs with eyes as big and golden as the headlamps on a car went bounding through the night, baying at the moon. And somehow Biddy was there too, the wind filling her black cape. 'Private road,' she seemed to be saying over and over again. 'Private road. Keep out.'

Morwenna had no idea how long she had been asleep or what had disturbed her, but she was wide awake in an instant and sitting up startled. It was much lighter in the room and she realised that someone had switched on the powerful lamp which stood on the desk.

It was a man, and she knew as soon as she saw him that it was the man she had encountered in the lane. Her instinct, she saw, had not misled her. He was dark, as dark as the stormy night outside the windows, tall and lean. His face was thin and as hard as if it had been hewn from the granite cliffs—a high-bridged nose, a jutting chin, firm lips and dark, hooded eyes that stared down at her mother's paintings spread on the desk in front of him.

Men who looked like that, she thought dazedly, had once sailed ships bringing contraband from Brittany into the coves along this coast under the noses of the Excisemen. And men who looked like that could even have hung lanterns on lonely rocks to lure unsuspecting shipping to a terrible doom.

He must have sensed her eyes on him because he looked up, and Morwenna found herself shrinking from the mixture of angry disbelief mingled with contempt that she saw in his face.

She tried to tell herself that she was still asleep and that her dreams had crossed the frontier into nightmare, but then he spoke and she knew that it was all only too real.

'Who the hell are you?' he said. 'And what are you doing here? You have two minutes to answer me before I have you thrown out.'

CHAPTER THREE

FOR a moment Morwenna was stunned into silence, then impetuously she jumped to her feet, regardless of her hair which had come loose from its topknot and fell about her shoulders in a silken shower.

'And just who are you,' she raged, 'to speak to me like that? And how dare you open that parcel? It was for Mr Dominic Trevennon—a private matter. But you have the unmitigated insolence to walk in here and....'

'I can't imagine who has a better right,' he interrupted with icy hostility. 'You are the intruder here, not I. And your time is running out, so I advise you to answer my questions.'

Her head came up defiantly. 'I need tell you nothing,' she said. 'I wish to speak to Mr Trevennon and no one else.'

There was a long electric silence. Then,

'I suppose,' he drawled, 'that it's just within the bounds of possibility that you aren't playing some devious provocative game of your own to attract my attention and that you really don't know who I am.'

For a minute Morwenna felt numb. Her eyes travelled over him desperately rejecting what her brain told her was the truth.

'No!' she whispered. 'It—it's not true. You can't be....'

'But I assure you I am—what was it you called me?—the uncrowned king of Cornwall. And this'—he showed his teeth in a mirthless smile—'is my castle.'

'No!' Morwenna pressed her hands against her burning cheeks. 'It's you that's playing some game. You can't be Dominic Trevennon. You're not old enough.'

He laughed contemptuously. 'If that's an attempt at flattery....'

'It isn't,' she said flatly. 'By my reckoning the real Dominic Trevennon must be in his sixties at least.'

He showed no surprise at her statement. Instead he nodded slightly as if her words had only confirmed what he himself already knew.

'Now,' he said very quietly, 'tell me who you are and what you want in this house.'

She could have ground her teeth. Instead she held on tight to her self-control. 'I've obviously been under a misapprehension,' she said tonelessly. 'I can only apologise, and leave. May I have my pictures, please—and their wrappings?' She held out her hand, but he ignored the gesture completely.

'Not without an explanation,' he said. 'You had enough to say for yourself when we met earlier. Why this sudden reticence? You wanted to ask me a favour—remember?'

She gave a bleak little smile. 'Not you,' she said. 'Someone else who clearly doesn't exist any more. Your father, perhaps, or....'

'My uncle,' he supplied equally bleakly. 'Who does exist, thank you. He's upstairs in his room at this moment studying chess problems.'

She looked at him, startled. 'Then—may I see him, please?'

'No, you may not. Whatever business you feel you may have in this house, you can settle with me.' He flicked a hand towards the paintings. 'I assume it has something to do with these. If you're hoping to sell them, then I should tell you at once that you're wasting your time.'

'I don't,' she denied swiftly, her glance in spite of herself going to the discoloured marks on the walls.

His eyes followed hers and he smiled thinly. 'You're quite right, of course. There were pictures hanging there once, and of considerably more value than these offerings.'

'I admit they're not her best work,' Morwenna said, biting her lip. 'But they do have a certain value—sentimental value, perhaps. Or that's what I believe, or I would never have come here.'

'Why?' he said. 'Because the subjects bear a certain superficial resemblance to certain buildings and landmarks locally? I think you'll have to do better than that.'

'Of course not,' she flared at him, stung. 'Because she—my mother, Laura Kerslake, the woman who painted those pictures, used to live here. This was her home when she was a girl. The Trevennons were her family—the only family she had until she married my father. Oh, I know that she seemed to have lost contact with you all, but....'

'Did she send you?' he interrupted, his voice glacial.

Morwenna shook her head, conscious that there was a sudden lump in her throat, but reluctant to reveal her distress to this man's cold hostility. 'She—died, several years ago,' she said constrictedly.

He made a slight restless movement. 'I'm sorry.' It was a perfunctory remark, made simply to satisfy the conventions, and oddly that hurt most of all.

She lifted her head and stared at him dazedly. 'I'm glad she can't hear you say that,' she said, almost in a whisper. 'I'm glad she's not here to know how little the people she loved really thought of her.'

'You're very quick with your judgments.' He thrust his hands into his pants pockets. 'You said she seemed to have lost contact with us. Did it never occur to you to ask yourself why? I don't know how much or what she may have told you about her life here, but I'll dare swear she never told you about the misery she left behind her when she went.'

'You're lying!'

'What reason would I have to do that?' he shrugged. 'What I've said may be unpalatable, and light years removed from Laura Kerslake's glossed-over version of her time at Trevennon, but it's the truth for all that.'

It wasn't so much his words, but his tone revealing so clearly that it was immaterial to him whether she believed him or not, that carried conviction. Morwenna stared at him numbly, unable to think of a thing to say.

He broke the silence himself eventually. 'And what about your father—the gallant Sir Robert. Does he know that you've come here?'

'My father's dead too.' She had to dredge the words up from some deep, painful recess of her mind. 'And my brother Martin. They were killed in a road accident only a few weeks ago. The estate went to his cousin. All I have left are these pictures.'

'My God,' he said very quietly. 'So that's it. Your mother's stories must really have got to you, my dear. Thirty-five years ago she found a refuge here, so you thought you'd do the same.' He shook his head disbelievingly. 'Well, I give you full marks for tactics. What a pity you were so totally misled about your likely reception.'

The contempt in his voice seemed to curl down her spine. She wanted to strike at him, to rake her nails down his dark face, and had to clench her hands into fists at her side. His face did not alter, but she knew all the same that he was quite aware of her inward battle with her temper and even faintly amused by it.

'You are also very quick with your judgments.' She stared defiantly across the room at him. 'I admit I did come here to ask for a home—but only for these pictures. I thought you might store them for me until I got a place of my own. I thought that if you wouldn't do it for my sake then you would do it for my mother's. I know now that I was wrong.'

He gave a short, unamused laugh. 'Disastrously wrong. So that was the favour you wanted to ask. I'm afraid I can't accede to it. There are still people in this house for whom such an overt reminder of your mother would be undeservedly painful. My uncle is one of them, and he's been a sick man for some years, so I would prefer him not to be upset in this way.'

She could hardly credit what her ears were telling her. What had happened here all those years before to leave this aftermath of bitterness? Whatever it had been she could not believe that her mother had ever been aware of it. Nothing had ever shadowed Laura Kerslake's affectionate memories of Dominic Trevennon. She felt herself shiver, and moved her hands in a slight negative gesture.

'I can't pretend I know what's going on here,' she said, steadying her voice by a tremendous effort. 'But under the circumstances all I can do is leave at once, and apologise for my intrusion.'

She picked up her rucksack from the sofa and walked towards the door, but he stepped away from the desk and into her path.

'Just a minute,' he said peremptorily. 'It isn't quite as simple as you seem to think. Just what did you hope to gain by coming here like this?'

'Very little,' she said wearily, her head bent. Her hands were clenched tightly round the straps of her rucksack, the knuckles showing white. 'Just a few feet of storage space, that's all. I see now of course that it was too much to ask of strangers. It was just that I've never—thought of the people in this house as strangers.'

'How very appealing,' he commented cynically. 'What a pity you didn't take the trouble to write or telephone in advance of your arrival. You might have been spared a difficult journey. And for the record, I'm not convinced by this cock and bull story of yours. It's just unfortunate for you that giving refuge to waifs is no longer among our family failings. And you have your mother to thank for that.'

Morwenna lifted one shoulder in a shrug of resignation. 'Believe what you want,' she said shortly. 'But what I told you happens to be the truth.'

'Come now, Miss Kerslake.' The cynicism in his voice deepened. 'Are you trying to tell me that it never once crossed your mind that there might be a home for you here?'

It would have been wonderful to lift her head and damn his eyes and fling his insinuations back in his mocking face, but she couldn't lie, not even to save her own face. Half-truths had got her into this mess, after all.

'No,' she said at last very quietly. 'I can't deny that it did cross my mind—briefly, once.'

As she spoke, she glanced up and saw an odd look cross his face, as if her admission had surprised him. But why should it have done? It was after all only what he had been waiting to hear, she thought. She gathered all her resolution and moved forward again towards the door. He made no attempt to get out of her way and she had to walk round him to reach it. As she reached for the knob, the door suddenly swung inwards and she stepped back, unable to repress a little cry of alarm.

'Hell's bells, I'm sorry.' The young man standing on the threshold gave her a swift look of concern which swiftly and overtly changed to one of admiration. 'Did I knock you? I just had no idea that you'd be standing there. I thought Dom was alone, you see, and. . . .'

'The young lady is just leaving,' Dominic Trevennon said in a voice as bleak as a winter's gale.

'Really?' The newcomer made no attempt to hide his

disappointment. 'That's too bad. Are you staying in the neighbourhood?'

'Only as a temporary measure. I have to get back to London.' Morwenna did not look at Dominic Trevennon to judge the effect of this deceptively defiant little speech. She was frankly shattered at the thought of having to go out again into this stormy night to find somewhere to stay. If she was honest with herself, she had counted on being offered a night's shelter at Trevennon. She had not wanted to eat any further into her small savings. She reflected despondently that this trip to Cornwall was likely to prove one of the costliest impulses of her entire life, not merely in financial terms either. Her confidence and self-respect had also taken an unexpected battering. All she wanted to do now was to get away from this big dark house and the harsh insensitive man who dominated it and lick her wounds in peace. She needed desperately to think too, to consider some of the unpalatable facts that she had been presented with. Her mother, it seemed, had created a fantasy world about her time at Trevennon for some reason best known to herself. Perhaps she hadn't wanted to face facts either, Morwenna thought unhappily.

The young man was speaking again. 'Well, if you must rush away, then I suppose it can't be helped. But do drive carefully. A tree came down on our road tonight. Jacky Herrick was moving it with his tractor as I drove down, but there might be others.'

She smiled at him with an effort. 'Perhaps it's just as well that I haven't a car,' she said, trying to speak lightly. 'I presume there will still be buses on the main road.'

'Yes, but they're few and far between.' He studied her for a moment with undisguised curiosity, then swung towards Dominic Trevennon who had been listening to the interchange with a faint sneering smile playing about his lips.

'Dom, what's going on here? You aren't seriously suggesting that she should walk all the way back to the main road on a night like this—not when we've got half a dozen empty bedrooms.'

'Oh, please.' Morwenna intervened, alarmed. 'I really must be going. I've made arrangements....'

'Then you must let me take you in my car.' He gave her

a smile of such charm that she felt warmed by it in spite of everything that had happened. 'Where are you staying? The Towers in Port Vennor?'

'Er—no.' Morwenna thought rapidly. 'As a matter of fact, I'm staying with some friends. But you really don't need to put yourself out.'

'I'm not. Dom, don't just stand there. Tell her that she's not putting us to any trouble. What's the matter with you? You surely weren't going to let her simply trudge off into the night, for God's sake?'

Dominic Trevennon raised his eyebrows coolly. 'Frankly, it didn't seem to be any of my concern,' he said offhandedly. 'In any case, Miss Kerslake has already impressed me as a young lady more than capable of looking after herself.'

'Miss—Kerslake?'

Dominic Trevennon nodded. 'You heard me correctly—and your assumption is equally correct. And as introductions now seem to be in order, Miss Kerslake, this is my younger brother Mark.'

His handshake was warm enough, but Morwenna already sensed a faint air of withdrawal in his manner. The younger brother had an easy forthright charm which his elder totally lacked, she thought, smouldering.

She said very sweetly and politely, 'If after my dire identity is disclosed to you, the offer of a lift is no longer forthcoming, I shall quite understand.'

'What? I mean—oh, no.' Mark Trevennon looked hot with embarrassment. 'I'll take you wherever you wish to go—just as soon as you're ready.'

Without another word or glance in Dominic Trevennon's direction, she walked into the hall. After a moment Mark joined her and they walked together to the front door.

A battered-looking Mini was parked in the shadow of the outbuildings. Mark unlocked the passenger door and helped her in punctiliously, stowing her rucksack on the back seat.

As he got into the driver's seat, Mowenna said rather awkwardly, 'I'm sorry about all this. I had no idea until I arrived here this evening that there'd been any kind of rift.'

He smiled tightly. 'It must have been a nasty shock for

you,' he said, turning on the ignition.

'The thing is,' Morwenna gripped her hands together in her lap, 'I still don't know what it is my mother is supposed to have done. Mr Trevennon—your brother—was talking in terms of misery and ruined lives. I can hardly believe we're talking about the same person. I was only a child when my mother died, but I just don't remember her as—a destroyer. She was a very warm, creative person. She drew people to her.'

'Perhaps that was the trouble.' Mark peered forward through the windscreen frowning a little.

'What do you mean?'

He shrugged uneasily. 'Oh, forget it. I honestly don't think anything will be gained by going over old ground. I'm sorry if Dom gave you a tough time, but things haven't been exactly easy for him, either. Your arrival on the scene must have seemed the last straw in many ways. Why did you come, by the way?'

Morwenna bent her head and stared down at her clasped hands. 'I wanted your brother to store some paintings for me,' she replied tonelessly.

He gave her a sharp sideways look. 'You mean some of your mother's work?' When she nodded, he gave a short explosive whistle. 'My God, that would really have put the cat among the pigeons!'

'And yet I'm never to know why.' Morwenna gave a mirthless smile, and then paused, pressing her hands against her whitening face. 'I'm sorry—please, can you turn the car round? I have to go back to the house.'

'Why, for heaven's sake?' Mark braked and brought the Mini to a halt by the side of the road. He sent her an impatient glance. 'I really don't advise it.'

'I don't need your advice,' Morwenna said tautly. 'Believe me, if I had any choice I would never go near the place again, but it so happens I've left the paintings there—in the study on your brother's desk. He—he was looking at them, and later—when all the fuss began—I simply forgot all about them. I just wanted to get out of the house as quickly as possible.'

Mark paused, his brows drawn together in a sharp frown. Then he gave a little sigh. 'Look, love, I think we'd better stick to the present plan and get you to your destination. Dom will deal with any problems at Trevennon, and we'll bring the paintings over to you first thing in the morning. How's that?'

Morwenna shook her head. 'I'd prefer to fetch them now.' Her voice was flat. 'But it seems that I have no choice.'

'This way is best, believe me.' Mark gave her a placatory smile as he set the car in motion again.

'Again, I'll just have to take your word for it.' She could not keep a note of bitterness from her voice. 'I didn't realise I was such a—pariah.'

'You're not. It's nothing to do with you personally at all —oh, hell!' Mark made a ferocious gear change, revealing that he was not using the necessary concentration. 'Look, do you know anything about boats?'

Morwenna shook her head. 'Nothing at all. I'm not a sailor.'

He sent her a guarded look. 'Well, did you ever hear the *Lady Laura* mentioned when you were a child?'

Morwenna stared at him. 'Of course not. My mother was Lady Kerslake, not. . . .'

'No,' he shook his head impatiently. 'You don't understand. The *Lady Laura* wasn't a person. She was a boat, although admittedly she was named for your mother. She was a very new, almost revolutionary design for a sailing dinghy, and Uncle Nick designed her. He'd been in the Navy during the war, and when he came back to Trevennon when it was over he persuaded my father to go in with him and buy a small boatyard in Port Vennor. I won't bore you with all the details, but eventually after a number of setbacks they started to do quite well. But you may know all this already?'

'No—definitely not. My mother told me a lot about this area, but she never mentioned anything about a boatyard.' She could not prevent the instinctive wistfulness in her voice. 'She made Trevennon sound wonderful. All her memories were happy ones.'

'Is that a fact?' Mark raised a wry eyebrow. 'Then she must have had an endless capacity for self-deception as well.'

'As well as what?'

'As well as the ability to deceive other people.' Mark's voice was hard. 'I'm sorry if you don't like it, but you did want to know, remember. Laura Kerslake—Laura Warrender as she was when she came to Trevennon—had an amazing ability to win people over—fascinate them, accept their affection and their love and then use it against them. See how much I know about her, and I wasn't even born when she came to Trevennon. She made—a deep impression on everyone here. We're still recovering from the effects of it, psychologically and financially.'

Morwenna stared at him, her lips parted. 'I can't believe we're talking about the same person,' she murmured, half to herself.

'Oh yes, we are,' Mark said almost savagely. 'She grew up here and she watched the boatyard grow too. When she went, she left Uncle Nick a broken man and the business in ruins.' He flung his head back. 'Did you know she was going to marry Uncle Nick?'

'No!' Morwenna was aghast. 'I thought—I always believed my father had been the only man in her life.'

Mark shrugged. 'Maybe he was. But she had Uncle Nick on a string as well. The *Lady Laura* was to be his wedding present to her. Everyone knew that, just as they knew that once it went on the market it would make the fortune of Trevennon Marine. But then your father came on the scene. He was spending a holiday locally and they met. He came to the house regularly—he was a visitor and a welcome one. No one realised there was anything going on until they ran away together. They didn't even have the courage to stay and face the music, but that wasn't all. We soon found out why—or Uncle Nick did when he went down to the yard. The design and specifications for *Lady Laura* had vanished from his office.'

'And you think my mother—oh, I don't believe it!'

'Uncle Nick didn't want to believe it either. He insisted that they must have been mislaid, but he soon discovered his mistake when he went to the Boat Show and saw *Lady Laura*. Oh, she wasn't called that, naturally, and the crowd who'd made her—a big concern on the south coast—had used cheaper materials, but it was Uncle Nick's boat. It went into mass production shortly afterwards. Legally, of course, Trevennon Marine hadn't a leg to stand on. Uncle Nick couldn't prove that his design had been pirated, but he knew and so did the sharks who'd bought it. Their sales manager was laughing all over his face. All's fair, he told Uncle Nick, in love and business. Said he ought to be more choosy about his lady-friends.'

'Oh, God!' Morwenna was appalled. 'So—what happened?'

Mark sighed. 'Trevennon Marine nearly went bankrupt. We'd invested heavily on the strength of the *Lady Laura*, bought up the adjoining properties so that we could expand, taken on more men. It all had to go. And there were bank loans to be repaid. My father had to sell off some of our land. But the hardest thing for Uncle Nick to bear was that this whole mess had been perpetrated by the woman he loved. He's never really got over it. So now you can see why your arrival at Trevennon wasn't exactly greeted with open arms.'

Morwenna was silent for a long time. Then at last she said, 'I don't believe it. You never knew her—you've admitted as much. She wasn't a—guilty person. She couldn't have borne a load of mischief like that for all those years without letting something show. Unless you're trying to suggest my father was her accomplice and that they both managed to cover up what they'd done.'

Mark looked uncomfortable. 'We never really knew what part he played in it. To make matters worse he was on the point of becoming engaged to someone else—a local girl, a friend of the family. You can imagine the scandal this whole thing caused in a small community like this.'

'Yes.' Morwenna felt numb. The situation was swiftly assuming nightmare proportions, but she made herself hang on to what she believed to be the reality in spite of anything she had been told. 'I've heard everything you've said, Mark, and I've tried my best to take it in.' She shook her head helplessly. 'But it's no use. I can't equate the woman I remember—or my father either—with such sly, needless cruelty. Perhaps they did elope—people can't always help their feelings, after all—but they would never have compounded the injury by selling out Trevennon Marine. There would have been no need.'

Mark made a small defensive gesture. 'The evidence suggests that they—or rather she—did,' he said quietly.

'Then the evidence is wrong,' Morwenna said fiercely. 'Did anyone ever contact my mother—ask her for an explanation?'

'No.' Mark gave her a surprised glance. 'As you can imagine, no one in the family ever wanted to speak to her or hear from her again. Uncle Nick wouldn't even allow anyone into the room she had used. He locked it up and took the key away and none of us have been in there since. I think he may have been in there sometimes—until he became ill, of course.'

'What's the matter with him?'

'He had a slight stroke. There was some paralysis at first, but fortunately it wasn't too serious and he's been recovering with physiotherapy. But you must understand that Dom couldn't allow you to see him. We couldn't risk making him ill again after all this time.' He halted the car at the main road. 'Now then, you said you were staying with friends.' He gave her an uncertain look. 'Was that the truth or just a face-saver?'

Morwenna bit her lip. 'I have somewhere to go,' she said shortly. 'I'll get out here.' She hesitated. 'When I have a permanent address, I'll let you know and perhaps you could send the pictures on to me.'

'Glad to,' Mark said a shade too heartily. He paused. 'I'm sorry it had to turn out like this.'

'I'm sorry too,' she said flatly. She found her case and rucksack and stood watching until the car's tail-lights disappeared back down the lane. Then she gave a little shiver. She was really on her own now, and somehow she would have to find her way to St Enna and trust to luck that the friendly Biddy would put her up for the night.

She stood irresolutely at the bus stop for a few minutes, then shouldered her rucksack and picked up her case. It wasn't warm enough for her to stand around for too long, and it wasn't that far to St Enna. She would walk.

Or at least it hadn't seemed that far on the bus, if her arms and legs hadn't already been aching, and the suitcase hadn't seemed to weigh a ton. She stopped every now and then, transferring the weight of the case from one hand to the other, flexing her protesting muscles.

Any moment now, she thought pessimistically, the bus would pass her. It was important to concentrate on minor hardships of this nature, because she couldn't let herself think about what Mark had just told her. It was too painful and incredible, and she had all the pain and uncertainty that she could handle just at the moment. And to think she had worried over Biddy's warnings about the kind of reception she could expect in Trevennon! She shook her head bewilderedly. The half hadn't been told to her.

She heard the sound of an engine behind her and tensed, but it wasn't the bus. It was a car, travelling at a moderate speed. Instinctively, Morwenna dropped her case at her feet and stuck out her arm. The car went past, but she saw its brake lights go on, and her heart lifted. The occupants were a couple, middle-aged and obviously married. The woman wound down the passenger window. 'How far are you going?'

'Just to St Enna.' Morwenna swallowed. 'I know it isn't far, but I've done quite a lot of walking today, and my case is getting very heavy.'

'Oh, we can manage that.' She turned to her husband. 'Open the boot, Ronald.'

He was just about to close the boot again when another car came round the corner, headlights full on, catching them in the glare. Morwenna closed her eyes for a moment, dazzled, and when she opened them again, she saw to her surprise that this car had also stopped just a little way past them. Then she saw who was walking back towards them, and she wasn't surprised any longer, just frightened. She grabbed at the startled Ronald's arm and said urgently, 'Oh, can we go, please?'

But it was too late. 'So there you are.' Dominic Trevennon, his hands thrust deep into the pockets of a black leather car coat, confronted them. 'And just where do you think you're off to, young woman?'

She stared at him dazedly for a moment, then: 'As if you cared,' she began roundly, but he was ignoring her and speaking to Ronald and his staring wife.

'I'm sorry if this troublesome brat has been bothering

you. I'll take her off your hands and get her home where she belongs.'

His hand fell on her arm and she wrenched herself away furiously. 'Are you quite mad?'

Her glance fell on Ronald, who, obviously embarrassed, was moving away. 'Oh, please don't go,' she appealed. 'I don't know why he's saying these things. I don't live with him. He's a stranger to me. You must believe me.'

'Stop behaving like a silly child and get in the car,' Dominic Trevennon said crisply. 'Just because we had a misunderstanding earlier, you don't have to make a stubborn scene.'

Morwenna had never felt murderous before, but she knew now what it was like to experience that blind all-encompassing rage.

'How dare you call me a silly child!' she raged. 'You turned me out of your house and wild horses won't drag me back there!' She saw him turn towards Ronald and give a slight rueful shrug, as if to imply, 'These youngsters,' and she could have screamed with anger and frustration.

'He *is* a stranger to me.' She swung desperately towards Mr Ronald, who was observing these goings on open-mouthed. 'I won't go with him. Why, he doesn't even know my Christian name,' she added with sudden inspiration. 'Go on—ask him. Ask him what it is and I bet he won't be able to tell you.'

'It seems reasonable,' Ronald mumbled, staring down at his feet. 'Er—do you know this young lady's name?'

Dominic Trevennon paused and Morwenna met his eyes triumphantly. This, she thought deliriously, is going to take some explaining, even by the uncrowned king of Cornwall.

'Her name,' Dominic Trevennon said quietly, 'is Morwenna.'

'But you don't—you can't know!' She stared at him robbed of her triumph, her lips trembling suddenly in reaction. 'I didn't tell you. I didn't even tell Mark, so how can you know?'

It was all over. Ronald was already unloading her luggage from the boot and shouting with laughter at some murmured remark Dominic had made to him. She could guess the subject of the joke and her slim body quivered with humiliation. He came back to her, and his fingers fastened round her arm. She went with him to his car, her head high. He opened the passenger door and put her into the front seat without gentleness. As he got in beside her, she said, her voice shaking with rage, 'You won't get away with this. You're abducting me. But you won't get away with it, I promise you that. I'll make you sorry, if it's the last thing I ever do!'

'I'm already sorry,' he said wearily. 'Sorry I ever set eyes on you. I'm taking you back to Trevennon not because I have the slightest wish to have you there, but because your clever little ploy with the pictures worked and my uncle wants to see you.'

'Your uncle? But you said....'

'I know quite well what I said.' He leaned forward and started the car, lifting his hand in salute as the other car overtook them and disappeared into the night. 'I never intended that my uncle should know that you existed, let alone that you had come to the house, but I underestimated you, Miss Kerslake. You're a bright girl, leaving those pictures behind on my desk so inadvertently. And you summed Inez up pretty well too.'

'I'm sorry.' Morwenna pressed a hand against her aching forehead, as he turned the car back towards Trevennon. 'I'm not in your league for cryptic remarks. What has your housekeeper to do with all this?'

'And I'm not in your league for assumed innocence,' he said grimly. 'Are you trying to pretend that Inez didn't pick up your resemblance to your mother—and that when she saw those pictures it wouldn't occur to her who you were?'

'Frankly I never gave it a thought,' she said tiredly. 'Besides, leaving the pictures behind was a genuine mistake. I was upset, can you believe? Didn't Mark tell you....'

'Oh, Mark told me. But then he's still impressionable, easily influenced by limpid eyes and feminine curves. You must have found him an easy touch. I'm afraid you'll find me a little more difficult to convince.'

'Fortunately, I don't have to try.' She lifted her head and straightened her shoulders. 'As I've said, I have no intention of spending any more time under your roof. I suppose it's too much to hope that you've brought the pictures with you. If so, you could drop me at the bus stop, and I'll make my own way from there.'

His lip curled. 'That, my sweet innocent, is what I've been trying to convey to you. I no longer have your damned pictures. My uncle does, and he wants to see you.'

Morwenna felt as if she was trying to fight her way out of a maze.

'But I thought that was the last thing you wanted,' she began, but he cut ruthlessly across her stumbling words.

'Precisely, but as I've been trying to make clear, Inez found the pictures when she came in to collect your tray and she took them straight upstairs to Uncle Nick's room.'

'But why should she do that?'

'Meaning you didn't put the idea into her head yourself? Inez is a law unto herself and always has been. Your mother was a great favourite of hers and once Inez gives her devotion it's generally for life. It's a pity that in your mother's case she couldn't have found a more worthy object for her affections.'

'Damn you,' she said slowly and distinctly.

'I'm sorry.' It was the merest token of an apology. 'But, after all these years, to be suddenly faced with the re-opening of all these old wounds....' His hands tightened on the steering wheel as if he wished it had been her neck.

Morwenna made a deliberate attempt to let the tension drain out of her and leaned back against the seat.

'I'm sorry too,' she said, trying to speak normally. 'If I'd had the slightest idea of any of this, I would never have come here. You must believe that. I—I hope that seeing the pictures—being reminded of my mother hasn't—worsened your uncle's condition.'

'Fortunately, no.' His voice was harsh, totally disregarding her tentative extension of the olive branch. 'But of course he wants to see you.'

There was a long silence, then she said, 'Please—no. I'd rather not.'

'Why not? This is what you wanted, isn't it? What you came all these miles to achieve? You can't just expect to back out because the going's got rough.'

'But then I didn't know,' she began haltingly, her eyes

fixed on the dark face beside her, willing him to understand.

'And because Mark has filled you in on our family history, that's supposed to make a difference?' he asked bitingly. 'I'm sorry, Miss Kerslake. This situation is entirely of your own making. You've tactlessly blundered in and you're going to have to live with your mistake for a while. If my uncle wants to see you, then I think you owe him that.'

'Because I happen to be my parents' daughter?' she challenged.

'If that's how you want to read it.'

She looked down at her hands, clasped tightly together in her lap. 'You could always tell your uncle that you couldn't find me, that I'd disappeared.'

'I could,' he said, 'if I was prepared to lie for you—which I'm not. My uncle is an elderly man and for some reason of his own he has set his heart on seeing you for a few minutes. You will indulge that whim.'

She did not speak again until the car drew up on the broad gravel sweep that fronted the house. Then she said, 'How did you know my name was Morwenna?'

He looked at her, his mouth twisting sardonically. 'Let's call it an educated guess,' he said. 'Morwenna is a Trevennon name. It seemed a reasonable bet that Laura Kerslake would have stolen that too.'

She got out of the car and went blindly ahead of him into the house.

Inez was standing in the hall, her broad face crumpled into lines of anxiety. As soon as she caught sight of Morwenna, she came forward.

'Oh, Miss Laura's girl! How come I didn't know you, my dear?'

Morwenna found herself clasped against a capacious bosom, her hair being stroked by a rough but kindly hand.

Behind them Dominic Trevennon said with ice in his voice, 'Save the transports of delight until later, Inez. And I shall be wanting a word with you as well.'

Morwenna was released and Inez gave the master of the house a defiant stare and a sniff.

'T'wasn't right, Mr Dom. Miss Laura's girl coming here, and Mr Nick not knowing about it.'

'Well, he knows now, thanks to you.' Dominic Trevennon flexed his shoulders wearily. 'You'd better take her up to him.'

'She can't see him now. He's asleep. It'll have to be the morning.'

'Asleep?' Dominic Trevennon's face was like thunder. 'It can't wait until morning. Miss Kerslake will be catching a train back to London in the morning.'

Inez shrugged. 'Can't be helped. He was getting himself in a proper old state, so I gave him one of his tablets. Sleeping like a baby he is now.'

He gave her a long, level look. 'I see. So I needn't ask, of course, if you've got a room ready for Miss Kerslake?'

'No, you needn't,' Inez said severely. 'And she needs it too, by the look of her, poor maid. Out on her feet she is. You come along with me, my dear.'

Morwenna knew she should have stood her ground, protested, insisted on being taken to a hotel in Port Vennor, but she was too tired. Besides, it seemed clear that anyone prepared to argue the toss with Inez would need all their wits about them. So she obediently allowed herself to be led away upstairs to a large room. The sheets and pillowcases on the big carved bedstead might have been darned, but they were linen and fragrant with cleanliness. A fire blazed in the hearth, and when she drew back the blankets it was to find an old-fashioned-looking chiffon nightdress wrapped somewhat incongruously round a large stone hot water bottle.

Morwenna lifted up the nightdress and stared at it stupidly, then held it against her cheek. Suddenly and silently, enormous tears began to spill down her cheeks and there was nothing she could do to prevent them. Inez was there at once, enveloping her in another warm hug.

'There now, my lover, don't take on so. A good sleep, that's what you need. Then it will all seem better in the morning.'

But when she was alone, in spite of her bone-weariness, sleep was a long time in coming. And her last coherent thought before she drifted at last into an uneasy doze was that everything in the morning might well seem a great deal worse.

CHAPTER FOUR

WHEN she awoke, it was to find a pale and watery sunlight filtering in the room through a gap in the ancient brocade curtains. She lay very still for a moment, confused, wondering where she was. Then memory came flooding back and she rolled over on to her stomach with a faint groan. She had slept the previous night because she was frankly exhausted, but her rest had done nothing to relax her or clear her mind. She felt as tense as a coiled watchspring, and the thought of the coming interview with Nick Trevennon sent her stomach churning.

She sat up in bed and looked around her. Someone had brought up her case and rucksack, so at least she had a change of clothes to put heart into her. The bathroom, just a little way down the corridor, was large, old-fashioned and chilly, its fixtures built for their staying power rather than any transitory elegance. But the water which gushed with disconcerting thoroughness from the large brass taps was reassuringly hot, and she lay and soaked for quite a while.

She still could not understand why Nick Trevennon wanted to see her. Under the circumstances that Mark had described the previous night, she would have thought she was the last person in the world he would want to see and while she could not accept this, she could understand it to a certain extent. Nor could she imagine what he was going to say to her when they did meet. She bit her lip. She did not think she could bear any more accusations against her parents—accusations that she was at the moment totally unable to refute. Not that she believed one word of them. Perhaps Laura and Robert Kerslake had hurt the feelings of people close to them by their elopement, but that was hardly a crime.

Morwenna sighed. If only she hadn't been quite so young, she would have observed more, perhaps—even been able to form a judgment from what she remembered of her mother's statements or reticences. As it was, all she could remember was the tone of utterly affectionate reminiscence, the weaving of everyday incidents into a fairytale web. But no guilt. She would have staked her life on that.

She put on a pair of dark green corded jeans and a white sweater with a roll collar. She brushed her hair thoroughly and left it hanging loose around her shoulders, acting on an impulse she only barely understood. She hesitated over disguising some of her pallor with cosmetics, eventually deciding against this. She had nothing to hide, she told herself defiantly.

It was almost ten o'clock when she descended the stairs. She was very hungry, but she supposed she was expecting too much to be offered breakfast. All the doors round the hall were closed, and she had no idea what lay behind any of them with the exception of Dominic Trevennon's study, and she had no intention of going anywhere near there.

She stood on the bottom step, looking around her uncertainly and totally unprepared for what happened next. The front door swung open bringing with it a flood of cold air, and two large dogs came dashing in. They caught sight of her immediately and began to bark, their ears laid back menacingly. Morwenna froze where she was, recalling the half-joking warning she had received the previous evening.

She said placatingly, 'Come on, boy. Good dog.' But her voice sounded high and unnatural in her own ears and it had no effect whatsoever on the dogs, except to make them bark all the louder.

Surely someone would hear all the noise and come, Morwenna thought nervously. She was not normally afraid of dogs, but these seemed particularly aggressive. And then, through the front door, in the wake of the dogs, came a girl. She was tall and slim with very dark hair, cleverly cut to show off the shape of her head, and she wore camel trousers with a matching tunic top over a white silk shirt with a casual elegance that made Morwenna more than usually aware that her own jeans and sweater had seen better days.

She stopped when she saw Morwenna, her eyes flicking over her with a surprise she made no effort to conceal. The dogs ran back towards her still barking and she hushed them impatiently and quite effectively.

'Who are you?' she asked coldly.

It was tempting to reply that it was none of her business, but Morwenna resisted the temptation. It was too risky an assumption for one thing. The newcomer seemed quite at home at Trevennon and quite probably had every right in the world to breeze in as if she owned the place and ask what questions she pleased. But at the same time, Morwenna thought, she was damned if she was launching into any more long and detailed explanations of her presence for yet another complete stranger. The Trevennons could do that after she had departed, if they so wished.

'I'm Morwenna,' she returned with equal shortness, and was surprised to see the other girl's head jerk up at the information and find herself subjected to an even more searching head-to-toe scrutiny.

'Are you trying to be funny?' she asked at last.

'If so, I've made a pretty poor job of it so far,' Morwenna said wearily. 'Are the dogs safe now?'

They didn't appear particularly safe. True, they were standing quite still and they were quiet, but as she looked at them, one of them lifted his lip back from his teeth in an unmistakable snarl.

'They won't hurt you,' the other girl said indifferently. 'They can just sense that you're frightened and an outsider.'

'Oh, I'm that all right.' Morwenna felt her temper rising. 'That makes the consensus of opinion round here pretty well unanimous. Now if you'll be kind enough to direct me to Mr Trevennon's room, I'll accept his condemnation too and then be on my way.'

'Mr Trevennon?' the other enquired, her well marked brows drawn together in a swift frown. 'I don't really see what....'

'It's all right, Karen,' Dominic Trevennon's voice broke levelly into the interchange. 'I'll deal with this.'

He had emerged from his study and was standing there, his hands resting lightly on his hips. It occurred to Morwenna that this was the first time she had seen him in broad daylight and her eyes went to him with frank curiosity. He was wearing a suit today, the pants belted low on his lean hips, and a white shirt, and she thought that the formal clothes seemed somehow alien on him. Doublet and hose, she thought, and tall Spanish leather boots and a gold earring in one ear. Then she realised that he was looking back at her and a hot tide of crimson raced up over her face to the roots of her hair. It was a stupid reaction, she castigated herself mentally. He could not possibly have guessed what she was thinking, and if he had, what odds? She would soon be away and gone from this place and it could not be too soon.

'Good morning, Miss Kerslake.' His voice was very smooth, very courteous. 'I hope you slept well. Have you had your breakfast yet?'

'Er—no.' She was furious with herself for stammering. 'I thought I would be too late....'

He raised a sardonic eyebrow. 'You didn't really imagine we intended to starve you, I hope? If you go into the dining room, I'm sure you'll find Inez has everything ready for you.'

He strolled across the hall and opened one of the doors. Almost reluctantly Morwenna left her sanctuary on the bottom step and joined him.

'Thank you,' she said without looking at him.

'When you've had breakfast, Inez will take you up to my uncle,' he added.

'I see.' She moistened her lips. 'How—how is your uncle this morning?'

'He seems well enough. He asked for you as soon as he woke up. I think he was afraid that I might not have been able to persuade you to come back here with me.'

Her sweet smile was tinged with acid. 'I'm sure he doesn't realise just how persuasive you can be,' she said.

'One last thing,' he said softly. 'I'd be grateful if you would keep your interview with him as brief as possible.'

'Don't worry.' Her own voice was equally quiet. 'I'm just as keen to leave here as you are to see me go.'

She walked past him into the dining room and heard the door close behind her with something approaching a slam. But not before she had heard the girl Karen say in puzzled tones, 'Darling, who on earth ...?'

Darling, Morwenna thought, as she walked to the single place laid at the large table. That betokened a girl-friend at the very least, maybe even a fiancée. She tried to remember whether she had seen a ring on the girl's hand and thought that there had not been one. Not that it mattered. She had not taken to the undeniably beautiful Karen, and she and Dominic Trevennon were welcome to each other.

The door opened and Inez bustled in carrying a large tray.

'So there you are, my lover. Come on now, before it gets cold.'

Unlike the dining room which shared the same faded grandeur as the rest of the house, the breakfast she was served made no concessions to economy. A large piece of grilled ham was flanked by a pile of fluffy scrambled eggs and there was an ornate silver rack of toast to follow, accompanied by a choice of honey or home-made marmalade. Inez hovered around while she was eating, observing her progress with evident satisfaction.

'That's better,' she remarked as Morwenna laid down her knife and fork. 'You could do with a bit of weight on you. I don't hold with all this old dieting—not for a moment, I don't.'

Stealing a glance at Inez's own Junoesque proportions, Morwenna thought wryly that no one would ever have thought otherwise. This morning she presented a truly amazing spectacle, her ample lines girded in an exotically flowered overall and her thick greying hair escaping from a hasty bun contrived at the nape of her neck. She wore a pair of man's slippers on her feet and an inch or more of pink petticoat hung down below her skirt, yet Morwenna knew instinctively that no one had ever laughed at these minor eccentricities and that no one ever would. In spite of her inner turmoil, she managed a shy response to the other woman's beaming smile as a fresh pot of coffee was placed beside her.

'It's been a long time since we had a maiden living in the house,' Inez continued, and Morwenna realised with a pang that she was referring to her mother.

She bit her lip. 'And I shouldn't be here either,' she said quietly. 'I—I realise you did what you thought was right, but I wish you hadn't taken those paintings up to Mr Trevennon.'

Inez gave an almighty sniff as she began to clear the used dishes. 'And why not, may I ask? There's too many things been left unsaid in this house that should have been brought out into the open years back. Grow up with bitterness and you could carry it to your grave. Why, there's Mr Nick sitting up in that room of his, grieving for the loss of something that was never his, and neither chick nor child to call his own. 'Tidn't right.'

Morwenna stared up at her. 'You were fond of my mother?'

The other's rather harsh features softened. 'That I was, and a proper turn it gave me when I saw her face looking up at me from Mr Dom's desk. Why I didn't know you the moment you walked in I'll never understand.'

Morwenna forced a smile. 'Perhaps it would have been better if you had. Then I might just have been ordered off the premises and all this would never have happened.'

'Well.' Inez prepared to leave the room with her tray, 'mebbe so, mebbe not. For my part, I think it was all meant, and you can't fight against fate, my dear.'

As she poured out her coffee, Morwenna reflected that it wasn't a battle with fate that was her chief concern at the moment, but the battles she had already engaged in with Dominic Trevennon. She sighed and pushed her hair back from her face. It had been an unequal contest, with all the advantages on his side, including a few that he probably hadn't even been aware of. And now she had to face his uncle, the source, from what she could gather, of all the bitterness against her parents. She stirred a spoonful of sugar listlessly into the fragrant brew. Once again she would be forced to take up the cudgels in her mother's defence. Not that she was unwilling to do so. In her heart, she knew that Laura Kerslake had not been capable of the kind of deceit the Trevennons attributed to her, but this was all so new to her, while they had some twenty years of prejudice to lend weight to their arguments.

She picked up her coffee cup and walked over to the window, standing looking out into the garden. A few roses still bloomed, sheltered from the gales by the high wall which surrounded the garden at the rear of the house, but otherwise the empty beds had a bleak uncared-for look

Morwenna tried to tell herself that the same thing could be said for most gardens in late November, but she knew it wasn't true. Nor did it explain why the house looked very much the same. As if everything had been let slide a long time ago and no one since had ever bothered to call a halt.

She replaced her empty cup on the table and stood looking round her rather irresolutely. She wondered if there was a telephone anywhere so that she could call a taxi which would be waiting to take her away from here as soon as her interview with Mr Trevennon was at an end. They might want to be rid of her, but they weren't making any great effort to speed her on her way, she thought rather bitterly.

She opened the door and looked out into the hall. A curious hush prevailed everywhere as if everyone in the house had suddenly departed leaving her in sole occupation. The quiet was emphasised by the deep reverbatory tick of the tall grandfather clock standing at the foot of the stairs.

Moving her feet with the utmost reluctance, she started up the stairs. Inez had not told her which room was Nick Trevennon's, so she would have to rely on instinct. She paused at the head of the stairs and looked along the gallery from left to right. All the doors were closed with the exception of the second door on the left which stood ajar. Morwenna took a deep breath as she trod along the gallery. She hesitated briefly, then knocked, lightly but resolutely. A deep voice called with some impatience:

'Yes, who is it? Come in!'

It was a large room, able to accept the furniture of both bedroom and study without any sense of overcrowding. It was light too, with large windows looking out towards the sea cliffs, and beside the windows a man was sitting in a high-backed wing chair, a rug thrown over his knees.

Morwenna swallowed, then she walked forward. 'Mr Trevennon?'

He turned his head and stared up at her. She didn't know what she had been expecting. Perhaps an older version of the man downstairs, but certainly not this weary-faced stranger, his grey hair streaked with white, his eyes filling with a new pain as they focussed on her face. There was a small table set beside his chair and on it were piled the pictures she had brought, the painting of her mother lying on the top.

She said very quietly, 'Mr Trevennon, when I came here first, I didn't know what the situation was. No one had told me. But I know now, and I'm sorry I ever forced my way in here.'

He said gruffly, as if she had not spoken, 'You're very like her. But of course you know that.'

'Yes, my father always said so.' Oh God, another blunder!

He had not appeared to notice. 'You don't remember her very well?'

'I was eight when she died. I remember some things, not others.'

'Tell me what you remember.'

She was silent for a while, then she said with difficulty, 'That she was loving and happy—even when she became ill. And that she always remembered this place—Trevennon and all the people in it—with joy and affection.' She shook her head. 'Under the circumstances I suppose that sounds rather ridiculous.'

'No.' He closed his eyes and leaned his head back against the chair. 'It confirms what I've always hoped and believed about Laura.' He too was quiet for a time. Morwenna stood quite still, not knowing what her next move should be. One part of her mind was prompting her to pick up the paintings and leave, while another was telling her that this would be the act of a coward.

At last he opened his eyes and looked at her again. 'Will you sit down?' He indicated a chair behind her. 'You must forgive the fact that I didn't get up when you came in.' He gestured at a walking frame close to his chair. 'I'm having to learn to walk again, and it's a damned nuisance. It all happened at a time when I least wanted it to.' He turned slightly in his chair to indicate the littered desk which stood at one side of the room. 'I'd started writing a history of the Trevennon family, and I've had to shelve it more or less. Your—mother will have told you of some of the family stories and legends.'

'Not a great deal,' she said. 'She told me more about her own childhood.'

'But she called you Morwenna,' he said. 'She always said

if she had a daughter she would call her that. Then, of course, I always imagined it would be my daughter.' He sensed that she had moved uneasily in her chair and held up a placatory hand. 'I'm sorry, I didn't mean to disturb you. You have heard, no doubt, what happened—all those years ago?'

'Yes.'

'I loved your mother,' Nick Trevennon said reflectively. 'Almost from the moment that she entered this house as a child. But she didn't love me. Oh, she was fond of me and I told myself that this would be enough, that I would make it enough. And for me it would have been. But not for her, although it's taken a lot of time and bitterness to recognise this.' He looked across at Morwenna. 'Almost until this moment when you looked at me with your mother's eyes.' He smiled sadly. 'I'm sorry if that sounds sentimental, but this frankly is a sentimental moment for me.'

'Mr Trevennon——' Morwenna began again.

'Nick,' he interrupted her. 'Call me Nick. Everyone does. Except Laura, of course. She always called me Dominic because she liked the name. But that's how my nephew is known and it might cause confusion....'

'Yes,' Morwenna said tautly. 'I've met him.'

'And disliked him, evidently.' The smile reached Nick Trevennon's eyes. 'I think you've had a rough passage with us, my dear. But that's over now.'

'Yes, it is,' she said steadily. 'I came here to ask you to look after the pictures for me. Then I was told—what my mother was supposed to have done and I decided it was an impertinence. But now that I've met you, and you've been so kind, I would like you to have the paintings—for your own.'

He shook his head. 'From what I've heard, that wouldn't be right,' he said. 'I'm told they are all you have left of Laura—of your home, in fact. Won't you listen to what I have to suggest first?'

'The thing is,' Morwenna said a little desperately, 'I don't have a lot of time. I have to get the train back to London today and start looking for work.'

'You can spare me a few moments more,' he said calmly. 'I've waited long enough, heaven knows. I always hoped in a way that it would be Laura who would come into the room, but I suppose that was too much to ask under the circumstances.'

Morwenna stared at him. 'She would hardly have been welcome here.'

'No,' he said heavily, 'that's true enough.' There was another long silence.

Morwenna moistened her lips. 'I really must be going.'

'No, wait.' He put a hand out to detain her and Morwenna sank back into her chair. 'I'm sorry, child. You're puzzled, and you have every right to be. You're wondering why when everyone in this house speaks of your mother with bitterness, I should refer to her with regret—especially when I was the one most deeply wronged.'

'I suppose so.' Morwenna's voice was constrained. 'Although I don't believe my mother wronged anyone. I think there must have been some dreadful mistake.'

'Oh, there was no mistake,' Nick Trevennon said slowly. 'My design for the *Lady Laura* was sold to another company before we could build her. But whether your mother had anything to do with it is the debatable point.'

Morwenna looked at him incredulously. 'Then you don't believe it,' she cried. 'But if you don't, why does everyone else? Surely you could have convinced them?'

Nick Trevennon shook his head wearily. 'At the time this happened, my dear, I was a hurt and an angry man. I did love your mother and I wanted her to become engaged to me. She wouldn't give me a definite answer, but I felt sure I would win in the end. So I let it be known that she was my future wife. And then she met your father. When she told me that they had fallen in love, I was furious. I said he would never be allowed to come to Trevennon again. They ran away together the following night, and I never saw her again.'

'But the design,' said Morwenna. 'What happened to it?'

Nick sighed. 'The drawings were missed almost at once from the yard,' he said. 'For a while, I thought Laura had taken them with her by mistake, then when I saw Lackingtons' new dinghy at the Show, I knew it had been deliberate. Laura was immediately blamed by everyone. My brother was alive in those days, Dominic's father, and he was convinced of her guilt. I think my sister-in-law had a hand in that. She had always disliked Laura and her elopement with Robert Kerslake set the seal on that dislike.'

'But why didn't you stop them?' Morwenna persisted. 'If you didn't believe it. . . .'

'I did believe it at first. I would have believed anything of her for a time. I couldn't believe, you see, that she'd gone. I'd been made a fool of, and I couldn't forgive that. People don't make fools of the Trevennons, or live to boast about it. We've had a proud, violent and not always admirable history, my dear, and I behaved quite true to type. Even when her letter came, I said nothing about it to anyone. Inez knew because she brought it to me, but she's never mentioned it and neither have I.'

'She wrote to you?'

'Yes.' Nick Trevennon put a hand to his face as if he found the light from the window troublesome. 'She wrote to ask my forgiveness and to tell me of her happiness with Robert. She said she was sure that one day I would see we would have been quite wrong for each other and that I would find happiness in my turn. It was then I knew for certain that it could not have been Laura who sold us out to Lackingtons. I'd had my doubts for a long time. It was so completely out of character, and besides, she must have known that the finger of suspicion would point straight to her. She wasn't stupid. And if she had done such a despicable thing, her conscience would not have allowed her to write to me as she did.'

'But why didn't you try to put matters right?'

Nick Trevennon shrugged and his face grew harsh under the lines of strain. 'Expediency,' he said simply. 'If Laura was innocent, it meant that someone else was guilty, and such a limited circle of people knew of the design's existence, and our hopes and plans for the *Lady Laura*. I thought then it would be better to remain silent and allow her to take the blame rather than open a new line of enquiries with possibly disastrous results. I felt then I would rather not know who hated Laura enough to do this thing to her. I thought in time the bitterness would die down, but my brother kept it going, urged on by his wife. There were others involved too. And our losses were considerable. I'd gambled on expansion, you see, and it didn't happen. So, all in all, I needed a scapegoat.' He stared down at the carpet. 'Long after, when my initial bitterness began to subside, I was sorry, more than sorry for what I'd done. My only comfort was that your mother would never know about it. When I didn't reply to her letter, I knew she would never risk a second rebuff.'

He looked up and regarded Morwenna steadily. 'My dear, if you want to revenge yourself on me on your mother's behalf it would be very easy. You could just take up your paintings and go out of this house and out of my life without another word. But I'm hoping very much that you won't do that.'

There was a silence, then Morwenna gave a short, unhappy sigh. 'No, I shan't do that,' she answered. 'I think there's been too much bitterness already, and in a way I can understand why you acted as you did, although I don't condone it.'

'So you'll stay?'

She was startled by the eagerness in his voice. She spread her hands in a negative gesture. 'Well, only for a little while longer. I have a train to catch and. . . .'

'No, no.' Nick Trevennon dismissed trains and their timetables with a testy shake of his head. 'You misunderstand me. I want you to stay here, child. You have nowhere to go, no definite plans—you admitted as much to my nephew last night. I want you to consider Trevennon as your home.'

'Oh, no!' Morwenna's hand strayed to her cheek in pure horror. 'I couldn't possibly do that.'

'Why not?' The weariness and pain had gone from his eyes now. They were keen and piercing beneath the grizzled brows.

'For all sorts of reasons.' She tried to steady her voice. 'For one thing, your nephew dislikes me. He wouldn't want me here, I know.'

Nick Trevennon laughed. 'One of the compensations of being an invalid is that one's whims are pampered in a way that never happened when I was well,' he said. 'If I want you to stay, there will be no arguments from Dominic. If his attitude has upset you, you must make allowances. His opinion of Laura was much influenced by that of his parents.'

'But that's not all,' Morwenna said hastily. 'I—I really do need to get a job. I have to support myself. I'm not a charity case, however well-meant the offer might be.'

'Who's talking about charity?' Nick Trevennon barked. 'And there is a job for you. I need an assistant to help me with my Trevennon chronicles.'

'But I have no secretarial experience whatsoever,' Morwenna protested.

'You can write, can't you? That's all I ask.' He lifted his right hand from his lap with difficulty. 'I'm recovering some use in my hand, but I can't hold a pen yet, and my attempts to write with my left hand have been ludicrous. I need someone to write to my dictation, and you would be more than capable of that. The typing of the manuscript is immaterial at the moment. If and when the book is finished it can go to a woman in Port Vennor who does typing at home. Now, what do you say?' He saw her hesitation, and added, 'My dear, you would be helping me so much. Not just in a practical way. But don't you see, I could begin to put right the wrong I did Laura all those years ago. Be generous, Morwenna. Help me to live at peace with myself, after all these years.' He paused again, and when she was still silent, added, 'Perhaps it still isn't too late—even now—to put things right, and find out the truth.'

It was blackmail, and she knew it, but blackmail of the most potent kind. If it could only be possible, she found herself thinking, to clear her mother's name and see the Trevennons grovel in apology when the truth came out. Or one Trevennon at least, if she was totally honest with herself.

She said quietly, 'Very well, Nick, I'll stay. But only until the chronicles are finished. Then I must go, whether the truth has emerged or not.'

'Agreed.' He extended his left hand and she put hers into it.

After a moment he said gruffly, 'Don't imagine this is going to be a sinecure, child. I don't take kindly to being almost helpless, as you'll find. This is one of my better days. You'll find me a hard taskmaster.' He cleared his throat. 'Now send Inez to me, so that I can tell her the change in arrangements. I shall rest until lunchtime, but come here to me once you've had your meal and I'll start you off on some background reading.'

She was halfway down the stairs when she suddenly thought, 'My God, what have I done?'

And as if to lend emphasis to her misgivings, Dominic Trevennon came out of his study and stood at the foot of the stairs, looking up at her.

'As soon as you're ready, Miss Kerslake,' he said, 'I'll drive you to Penzance.'

'I'm not leaving,' she said, and was amazed to hear how steady her voice sounded. Thank heavens he would never know that her insides were churning and her legs felt like jelly.

'I beg your pardon?' His tone was blank, but his brows were already drawing together in one of those thunderous frowns.

'Your uncle has asked me to work for him—in a temporary capacity,' she said. 'He needs someone to get his notes on the family history into proper shape for the typist. So I shan't be leaving just yet.'

'My God,' he muttered, his voice sinking almost to a whisper. 'You scheming, conniving little bitch!'

She shrugged with an insouciance she was far from feeling. 'Sticks and stones, Mr Trevennon,' she said. 'After all, this interview with your uncle was your idea, don't forget.'

'I'm not likely to forget—anything,' he said. His eyes skimmed over her contemptuously. 'Well, you've seen the house, Miss Kerslake, and no doubt in the next few weeks you'll see what's left of the estate and the boatyard. I'm afraid you won't find the pickings quite as good this time around. I can't think of anything you'll be able to take with you when you leave.'

There was her mother's good name, she thought, and the reflection brought a confident smile to her lips.

'Can't you, Mr Trevennon? I can.'

He looked at her incredulously for a moment, then his head went back and his brows lifted in the sneer she detested so much.

'So that's it? You're like a chameleon, Miss Kerslake. I

can't keep up with all these changes of role. From waif to old man's darling in a few easy lessons.'

For a moment she looked at him uncomprehendingly, then his voice went remorselessly on: 'You really mean to begin where your mother left off, don't you? An elderly man's loneliness—sentiment for the past—anything's grist to your mill, isn't it? Tell me, Miss Kerslake, will you too jib at the actual wedding ceremony, or don't you have any qualms about selling your body to a man old enough to be your father?'

She took two shaking steps down the stairs and her hand lashed out to meet the side of his face in a stinging slap with all the weight of her arm behind it.

As soon as she had done it, she stood stricken, half expecting that he would retaliate. Oh, why had she let his taunts get to her? When her mother's memory was vindicated, she could have made him eat every one of them instead of losing her temper like a silly schoolgirl.

The marks of her fingers were already reddening on his cheek, she noticed. Wretchedly, she made her eyes meet his.

'I'm sorry,' she said, aware how inadequate the words sounded.

'You will be,' he said very softly, in a way that was somehow more alarming than plain anger would have been. 'Oh, yes, Morwenna, you'll pay dearly for that, and for everything else. And that's a promise.'

He turned on his heel and walked away down the hall. The front door slammed behind him, and after a minute or two Morwenna heard the sound of a car engine being revved and then fading in the distance as he drove away.

She expelled a long trembling breath, then sank down on the bottom stair, resting her cheek against the carved newel post. And again a voice inside her asked, 'My God, what have I done?'

CHAPTER FIVE

The next few days passed in such a fever of activity that Morwenna was left little time for introspection, and for this she was grateful.

Nick Trevennon had not been exaggerating when he had described himself as a hard taskmaster. After the solitary lunch that Inez had served to her in the dining room that first day, she had plunged willy-nilly into the past of the Trevennon family, a subject which she found much easier to contemplate than the immediate present. She was amazed at the amount of background research that Nick had managed to carry out prior to his stroke. Photographs of ancient church records, reference books and original documents from various periods jostled for attention on the big littered desk and Morwenna decided that priority must be given to getting this mass of material into some sort of order. Nick, she discovered quite early on, had a habit of demanding a particular book or document and reacting sourly if it did not immediately come to hand.

Much of the earliest family history—and there had been Trevennons in that part of Cornwall, she learned, since early Tudor times—had already been chronicled by succeeding generations and many of these records still existed in crumbling leather-bound books with fading and almost indecipherable brown writing. But many of the best known legends, Nick informed her, had been handed down by word of mouth, and had lost nothing in the retelling.

And among these, apparently, was the story of her namesake Morwenna, but when she asked Nick, intrigued, to tell her more, he merely looked mysterious and murmured that she would hear it 'all in good time'.

In many ways, she found, life at Trevennon seemed to revolve round two different households, the only link between them being Inez and to a smaller extent her husband Zack. Morwenna had frankly dreaded the idea of having to meet Dominic Trevennon at mealtimes, and was thankful that this proved unnecessary. The Trevennon brothers seemed to breakfast at a very early hour. At any rate they were always finished and gone by the time she came downstairs. Generally she lunched with Nick, and had her supper on a tray in her room. Inez had made no demur about this when Morwenna had tentatively asked if it could be so. Indeed, she rather embarrassingly seemed to enter into the spirit behind the request, telling Morwenna confidentially that she was 'not to worry her head. Mr Dom would come round in time.'

Morwenna had toyed with trying to assure her that she had no desire for 'Mr Dom' to be reconciled to her presence in any way, but it seemed more dignified to pretend that she did not understand what Inez meant.

Each evening, when she was sure that Nick did not require her any more, she went down to the big shabby sitting room at the front of the house, where Inez had kindled a fire in the big stone hearth and read or listened to the radio. Once Mark had joined her and she had welcomed his presence, especially when the initial awkwardness between them had worn off. He was only a few years older than she was and much younger than Dominic, and he said frankly that he had been an afterthought on the part of his parents.

'But they say second thoughts are always best, don't they?' he added, grinning cheerfully.

Dominic, she was glad to notice, never came near the sitting room in the evenings. He spent his free time in the study where she had been taken on that first evening. She wondered sometimes if this had always been his practice, or whether it was something new, adopted since she had come to stay in the house, but she told herself that it was no concern of hers. As long as Dominic Trevennon kept away from her, he could spend his time as he pleased.

On the fourth morning she made her way to Nick's room after breakfast to be told rather brusquely that he wouldn't need her that morning. A physiotherapist was coming from Penzance to check on the progress he was making and put him through various exercises. He grimaced as he said this and Morwenna guessed that he was in for an uncomfortable few hours.

He gave her a keen look. 'You look peaky,' he opined.

'I've been working you too hard. It's not raining today. Go for a walk, get some air.'

It was far from an uninviting prospect. The weather over the past few days had been uncertain, with grey skies and squally showers predominating, but today the sun shone and there was the crispness of frost in the air.

'And keep away from the beach unless you check with someone about the tides,' he called after her. 'The sea comes into Spanish Cove like a millrace.'

She promised to be careful and went downstairs feeling positively lighthearted, like a child who has been unexpectedly let out of school. She was filled with self-reproach at the thought. She knew she would only have had to drop the slightest hint to Nick that she was becoming jaded and he would have called a halt to their labours at any time. But she had not done so because she was enjoying their work together, although it was altogether different from anything she had ever tackled before. She felt a curious sense of involvement, of kinship even with these early Trevennons with their quarrels and their feuds and their carefully arranged marriages with local heiresses that in some cases, Morwenna thought, were little more than abduction and rape. Nick, it seemed, was prepared to reveal the whole picture of the family's past, warts and all.

She had collected a sketching book and a box of pencils from her room on her way downstairs, and Inez, on her knees wrestling with a recalcitrant plug on an elderly vacuum cleaner, gave her an approving stare as she went past.

'Going out, then? That's right. If you're anywhere up near Jacky Herrick's you could bring me back a dozen eggs and tell Jacky I'll see him for the money.'

Outside the house, Morwenna stood irresolute for a moment or two, wondering which way to go. But the lure of the sea was irresistible and eventually she turned up the track which led away from the house towards the cliffs.

The wind was fresher and stronger up on the exposed headland, dragging at her hair and whipping it across her face. She raked it back with impatient fingers and looked about her. The tide was at its height, sucking and roaring at the cliff-face below her and sending up damp fingers of spray which seemed to hang in the sunlight. Away to her right, she saw the deep gracious curve of the bay with the huddle of roofs that was Port Vennor almost at its centre. A few feet ahead of the spot where she stood, the ground fell away almost sheer into Spanish Cove where generations ago Trevennon men had scrabbled after the wreckage of a proud galleon driven on to its rocks by the storms that had scattered the Armada fleet. Its beach could be reached by means of steep and precarious steps cut into the face of the cliff, but few people ever went there now, Nick had told her. Instead it had become a haunt for seals who used it in the early autumn as a breeding ground.

Morwenna's eyes keenly scanned the tumbling waves and foam-capped rocks, but she could see no sign of sleek, grey bodies, somewhat to her disappointment. The seals would be back, she knew, to moult early in the new year, but would she still be at Trevennon to see them? It seemed unlikely.

She began to walk along the edge of the cliff, skirting the massive granite boulders with which it was littered and keeping a wary eye open for old mine workings. Although she had spent most of her life living in the country, she felt an alien in this wild, desolate-looking world. There was an untamed, brooding quality about the landscape that disturbed and exhilarated her.

She found a convenient rock, at last large enough to give her shelter from the ubiquitous wind and with a shelf which she could perch on. She sketched in the contour of the bay with clean swift strokes and merely suggested the houses and breakwater at Port Vennor. An inquisitive gull came and perched on the rock beside her, but it soon flew away when there were no titbits forthcoming. Morwenna wriggled her shoulders inside her sheepskin jacket. It wasn't ideal weather for sketching out of doors. The wind seized at her sketchbook pages as if it was trying to tear them and there was no real power in the winter sun. The year was running down, she thought. It had been a melancholy time for her and she was glad to see it go. But the prospect held out by the coming months did not seem any too bright in comparison. Moodily, she added some shading to a rock in the foreground of her drawing. Would she still be here at Trevennon, taking refuge in the past lives of other people, living the life of a semi-recluse, ignored by one part of the household altogether?

With a sudden burst of irritability, she snatched the page out of her sketchbook, crumpled it up and let the wind take it, whirling out of sight over the cliff. If only things could be wiped out as speedily and completely, she thought wryly as she got to her feet. She thrust her pencils into her pocket and tucked her book under her arm. She felt chilled and out of sorts. The virtue had gone out of the morning for her. She might as well find her way to Herricks' farm, collect the eggs that Inez wanted and get back to the house.

She wasn't completely sure how to get to the farm, but guessed she would have to walk up to the main road first. She was about halfway up the lane she had trudged down that first stormy night when she heard the sound of a car engine behind her and a horn tooting a warning. Deliberately, she did not look round. She was keeping close to the hedge, not blocking the road at all, and the unknown motorist had plenty of room to pass, she told herself, trying to regain some control over suddenly hammering pulses.

But when the car drew level with her, its horn tooting again rather plaintively, she saw with an odd feeling of deflation that it was Mark's Mini.

'Hullo.' He leaned across and opened the passenger door. 'Have you been given time off for good conduct? Hop in and I'll give you a lift.'

After a brief hesitation she complied. 'I'm only going to Herricks' farm to collect some eggs for Inez,' she told him as she settled herself in the seat.

'Is that all?' He sounded unimpressed. 'I'll drop you there.'

There was still a slight awkwardness between them, but she thought she was probably as much to blame for this as he was. Whenever she encountered either of the Trevennon brothers, her guard rose instinctively.

'How's the great history going?' Mark asked lightly after a few minutes.

'Slowly,' she admitted. 'There's a lot of sorting out to do.'

He sighed and pursed his lips. 'That's not so good.'

She gave him a long level look. 'Why? Because it will mean my remaining at the house for longer than your brother thought?'

'Good God, no.' Mark's eyebrows shot up. 'You are touchy, aren't you? No, my anxieties are purely for Nick's sake. He's been a very sick man—you know that, don't you? We tried to keep from him how strong the possibility of another stroke was, but I think he guesses. At first, he used to try and push himself to get better. At least now he seems to take each day as it comes.' He gave her an uncomfortable glance. 'If you can help in that, I don't need to say we would be very grateful.'

'We?' She gave a brittle little smile.

He sighed rather wearily. 'Yes—even Dom. One of the main objections to your arrival in the first place was that he thought it would upset Nick and perhaps precipitate another attack. Now, of course, he knows differently.'

'But it hasn't altered his attiude one iota,' she said.

Mark sighed again. 'Have a heart! Did you really think the prejudices of a lifetime were going to be swept away in a few hours or even days? Don't forget that all the main burden of our financial struggles in recent years has fallen on Dominic.'

'And these in turn are blamed exclusively on my family,' Morwenna said coldly. 'I haven't forgotten.'

The road to Port Vennor wound along the edge of the coast, affording frequent glimpses of the sea and occasional views of rubble and fallen chimneys where former mineworkings had stood.

'The Trevenonns mined tin once upon a time,' Mark commented at her side. 'Made a lot of money from it too. But it didn't last, of course. I reckon we probably made more out of smuggling and such ventures than we ever did out of our respectable business endeavours. The boatyard is a case in point.' He hesitated. 'But perhaps the tide is going to turn for us at last, even there.'

Morwenna longed to ask him what he meant, but she knew that under the circumstances this was quite impossible.

He brought the car to rest at the side of the road. 'Herricks' place is down there. Just follow the track down. And there's a short cut back if you don't want to go round by road—ask Molly Herrick to show you.'

Morwenna found the farmhouse without difficulty, and the negotiations over the eggs were accomplished without delay. Mrs Herrick was friendly, but with an obvious penchant for gossip, and when her questions about Morwenna's unexpected presence at Trevennon became too pointed, Morwenna made an excuse that Inez was needing the eggs and said a hasty goodbye.

Following the directions Mrs Herrick had given her, she walked across a field, avoiding the more obvious patches of mud, then went through a gate into a copse of trees. On the other side of the copse, she had been assured, she would find the yard at the back of Trevennon.

When she emerged from the trees, she was confronted by the high wall at the back of the house. The catch on the tall white gate was stiff, and the creaking of the hinges as she pushed it open indicated how little it was used. She turned to push it shut, and as she did so she heard the dogs barking excitedly quite close at hand. Her heart sank. This was something she hadn't bargained for. She had not seen them since that first day and Inez had assured her that they were usually kept outside. Clutching the boxes of eggs awkwardly against her chest, she managed to latch the gate securely. There were a number of outbuildings all around the yard, including a former barn and a disused stable block, so Morwenna began to pick her way cautiously round the edge of the yard, keeping a wary eye open for the dogs. All was silent for a moment or two, then suddenly the barking broke out again with renewed frenzy and coming in the direction of the yard.

Forgetting everything she had ever been told about standing her ground, Morwenna fled into the nearest shelter. This was where Zack kept his gardening tools and other implements, and she picked her way hurriedly between forks and rakes and a rusty-looking lawnmower, seeking a dark corner. There was a ladder leaning rather precariously against one wall and when she glanced up she saw that it led to some kind of loft. Still clutching the eggs against her, she scrambled uneasily up the rungs and swung herself into the loft. It smelled musty and unpleasant, and there were vague rustlings that Morwenna decided it might be better to pretend she had not heard. She peered cautiously down, just as one of the dogs reached the bottom of the ladder and began to jump up and down barking uproariously.

Morwenna sat down on the dusty floor, carefully depositing the eggs beside her, and considered her predicament. She felt incredibly foolish. She liked dogs, for heaven's sake, and they had always liked her. She was just letting this terrible unwelcoming atmosphere at Trevennon get to her. After all, even Dominic Trevennon was unlikely to have trained his dogs to actually bite her. She giggled weakly at the thought, and glanced down over the edge of the loft, only to be greeted by renewed and even more furious barking and growls. Both dogs were there now. Having cornered their quarry, they were now apparently prepared to wait for as long as it took.

Morwenna groaned inwardly. The obvious course was to climb back down the ladder and risk being bitten, but she didn't like the way they kept jumping at the ladder and shaking it. And the floor below her was far too littered with prongs and sharp edges for her to risk any kind of fall.

The best she could do would be to sit out her vigil and hope it would not be too long before she was missed.

She shifted herself into a more comfortable position on the hard wooden floor and looked at her watch. Her mouth felt parched, but there was still a good hour and a half to go before lunchtime which was the first time that any enquiries as to her whereabouts would be made. And even then no one would have any idea where to look unless curiosity led them to find out why the dogs were making such a row.

And of course, out of sheer contrariness, they had gone quiet. She peeped out again and Whisky leaped up at the ladder, snarling. Well, not all that quiet.

'Stupid animals,' she muttered crossly, and paused listening intently as she caught the sound of footsteps approaching over the cobbles outside. Her heart lifted. Ideally, it would be Inez, but she could even tolerate Zack's undoubted malicious enjoyment of her plight just as long as she got out of this loft before the horrors that she was sharing it with actually manifested themselves.

The dogs had heard the approach too and were off like greyhounds with eager whines. But they'd be back if the new arrival was simply passing through the yard on the way elsewhere.

'I say,' she shouted, 'can you hang on to those dogs while I get down from here?'

There was a silence, then she heard the footsteps gingerly picking their way across the floor below with the dogs snuffling excitedly in attendance. She peered over the edge and her eyes met Dominic Trevennon's.

Her lips moved but no sound came out as her brain searched feverishly for some totally reasonable explanation for her presence in a disused loft at the top of a rickety ladder when his question came as it inevitably would. And did.

'What the hell are you doing up there?'

'Escaping from your damned dogs!' Morwenna glared down at him, silently daring him to be amused. One glimmer of a smile, one twitch of the lips and she would throw both boxes of eggs at him.

'That's utter nonsense,' he said flatly, plainly not at all amused. 'They wouldn't hurt you.'

'Don't tell me. Tell them,' she returned tersely. 'If you'll keep them away from the bottom of the ladder, I'll come down.'

The dogs, she noticed disgustedly, like the hypocrites they were, had taken to fawning round their master's feet, their plumy tails waving in devoted eagerness, all friendliness and slavish adoration as if the idea of taking a lump out of anyone could not be further from their minds.

She found the top rung with her feet and began a cautious descent, only too conscious of Dominic Trevennon's watching eyes. She found she was shaking and told herself that it was pure reaction, but her nervousness under his regard was her undoing. She was about halfway down when her foot slipped. She cried out as her shoulder jerked painfully, taking her weight, and the egg boxes tumbled from her slackened grasp. Then strong hands gripped her waist and swung her to the floor, deftly missing the sad little heap of crushed cardboard and egg yolk at his feet.

He was shaking too. She could feel it, and she knew, now that there was nothing left to throw at him, that it was suppressed laughter.

'Are you practising for some kind of obstacle race?'

'No.' She was angry to discover that her voice was trembling too and that she was close to tears. 'Just everyday life in your rotten household. And Inez *wanted* those eggs!'

He grimaced slightly, glancing down to where the dogs were having a field day. 'Inez is welcome to them. And there are plenty more where those came from.'

She realised suddenly that he was still holding her waist and she wanted to move away, but there were few places to move to without stepping on a garden rake and fracturing her skull. He wasn't even holding her very tightly, but she was as conscious of him as if his fingers had been touching her bare skin. The thought was a disturbing one and she felt a betraying warmth begin to spread upwards over her face.

'Your dogs hate me,' she said lamely.

He shrugged slightly. 'You're still a stranger to them. They'll get used to you—in time.'

'It's your fault,' she accused. She knew she was being childish, but was totally unable to stop herself. 'You hate me too. You resent my being in your house and the dogs can sense it.'

Now what, she wondered hysterically, had made her say that? Why couldn't she just have thanked him quietly for his assistance, disengaged herself with dignity and gone on her way? She felt tension close round her like a cloak. And felt, unbelievably, his hands tighten on her, drawing her towards him.

'Is that really so?' he drawled. 'Then perhaps we'd better confuse the vibrations.'

As his dark head bent towards her, she lifted her hands in sudden panic, pushing at his chest, but she might as well have tried to thrust away a piece of Cornish granite. Only he wasn't rock. He was bone and muscle and lean warmth under her suddenly paralysed fingers.

He kissed her slowly and very thoroughly with a lingering and slightly brutal insolence. Her legs seemed to be dissolving into jelly and her heart felt as if it was fluttering in her throat like a frightened bird. No one, certainly not Guy, had ever kissed her like this and she was terrified of the response he was so expertly evoking, a response that made her want to press herself close to him, feel his hands caressing her body. A long wild tremor ran through her, and then suddenly his arms were no longer holding her and his mouth was no longer moving, warm and hard and sensually demanding, on the softness of hers.

Their eyes met, and there seemed to be little devils dancing at the back of his.

'Perhaps that will solve some of your problems,' he said gently, but Morwenna had the strangest feeling that he was angry, and this intuition sparked off her own temper.

'With the dogs, undoubtedly,' she said rudely. 'I didn't realise I would also have wolves to cope with.'

His eyebrows rose in cold mockery. 'No? But I seem to remember that one of your ploys was going to be "to get the king of Cornwall to fancy you". I would have thought your success would have pleased you. Because I do fancy you. Or do you require further proof?'

He reached for her again, his hands sliding down her waist to her hips and pulling her against his body in intimate, insolent demand.

'Now do you understand?' he murmured against her ear, his lips teasing its lobe and sensitive hollows.

'You're vile!' She jerked her head back violently. 'I hate you!'

He smiled cynically down at her. 'Where there's no love, hate can often make a very adequate substitute.' He brushed a lazy finger across her indignantly parted lips. 'I could prove it to you to the undoubted satisfaction of us both if our surroundings were—er—slightly more propitious.'

'My God, you flatter yourself,' she whispered. 'As if I'd let you....'

'As if you could stop me if I once made up my mind.' His mouth twisted. 'But I won't force a confrontation here and now. As I've indicated this is hardly the ideal time or place.'

'Thanks for the warning.' Temper came to her aid. 'I'll make sure I remain strictly out of your way from now on— and I shall lock my bedroom door.'

'How very conventional of you, Morwenna. I should make sure first that there's a key—and remember too that a locked door never stood in the way of a really determined man. And what you've learned of our family history so far should have told you that the Trevennons were all—really determined men.'

He was no longer holding her, so it should have been the easiest thing in the world to turn and walk away. Yet it wasn't, in spite of all her brave words. Oh, she could control her mind, but she had learned in one sharp disastrous lesson just how little control she had over her senses. All she could do was salvage what she could—make some attempt to get back to normality, whatever that was.

'It must be nearly lunchtime,' she said faintly, cringing inwardly at the banality of the words. 'Will—will you explain to Inez about the eggs?'

'I'll do better than that. I'll drive round to Herricks' later and get some more.'

'Thanks,' she said helplessly. She felt gauche and inadequate, as if this was the first time that a man had ever kissed or touched her. She had thought briefly that she wanted Guy, but now she knew she had not even known what wanting was and the knowledge was a torment to her.

'Well?' he said after a moment or two, and his voice seemed to come to her from a distance. 'What are you waiting for?'

She looked up at him, but his dark face was remote and enigmatic, giving her no clue as to what he was thinking.

'Nothing,' she said tonelessly. 'Absolutely nothing.'

It was colder when she got outside and as she walked across the yard, she turned her coat collar up against the encroaching wind. But there was a cold and bitter truth that she had no shield against, and it had been her own words that had brought it home to her. And the truth was that not even Nick's affection and the possibility of restoring her mother's good name could ever compensate for the knowledge that, without Dominic's love, there was nothing for her here at Trevennon.

CHAPTER SIX

LUNCH was a predominantly silent meal. Nick appeared preoccupied and Morwenna was thankful in many ways as she forced herself to make an attempt at least at eating. Her mind was seething with the events of the morning and she badly needed to think over what had happened, especially the unwelcome illumination about her feelings which had come to her.

She gave a little half-suppressed sigh as she pushed the remains of the cheese and bacon casserole round her plate, then stole a swift glance at Nick to see if he had heard her. Up to now he had always been solicitous for her wellbeing, aware, seemingly, of her every change of mood, as if this was all part of his recompense for the past. But he seemed to be sunk deep in his own abstractions. He looked tired, she thought with a swift feeling of compassion, and older than she had ever seen him look. The physiotherapist's visit must have wearied him more than he had expected.

So she was utterly bewildered when he announced rather abruptly just as Inez was bringing in the plates of apple tart and cream that they were going out that afternoon.

'Going where?' Morwenna asked rather helplessly.

'Into Port Vennor.'

Inez snorted. 'We'll see what Mr Dom has to say about that,' she said grimly. 'You don't want to go running afore you can walk, Mr Nick.'

'God damn it, woman, who said anything about running?' Nick banged his walking stick on the ground with frustration. 'Do you think I want to live and die in this room? Just because I'm no longer in charge at the yard it doesn't mean I've relinquished all interest in it. I'm not written off yet, you know.'

'No one ever said you were,' Inez said soothingly. 'All I'm saying is that you want to go easy.'

'Mrs Lane told me that I should take more exercise,' Nick muttered, his face mutinous.

'But she didn't say you were to go down to that yard crawling and clambering around a lot of old boats,' Inez said calmly and unanswerably. 'A little walk round the gardens and maybe down to the beach later on. That's what she meant.'

When they were alone again, Morwenna said gently, 'She's right, you know.'

Nick scowled down into his apple pie. 'Are you on her side too?'

'No.' She smiled at him. 'On yours. And is this a taste of the Trevennon temper you were telling me about the other day?'

Nick gave her a wry glance, his face relaxing. 'Just a taste.' He smiled back unwillingly. 'To hell with it, Morwenna. I need to go down to the yard. There's something there I want.'

'Couldn't one of your nephews bring it for you?'

'They could if I asked them,' he said abruptly. 'But I'd rather keep it to myself for various reasons.' He gave her a narrow look. 'But you could fetch it for me. It's quite simple. It's a folder—a green one, coded PY/33, and it's in the top drawer of the filing cabinet in the inner office.'

'Nick,' Morwenna gasped, 'I can't go into the office and start rooting round in the filing cabinets. Supposing someone saw me?'

'Then naturally you tell them the truth—that you're removing the folder with my authorisation,' Nick said rather testily. 'But if you take ordinary care, no one need see you. It's a busy place you know, especially at this time of year when all the repairs for next season are being done.'

He waited for a moment rather impatiently and when she didn't speak said, 'Well, if you won't do it, Morwenna, then there's nothing else for it. I must go myself.'

'No.' Morwenna put out a detaining hand. 'I don't want you to do too much on your first outing. I—I'll go. Only how do I get to Port Vennor?'

'Mark will take you in. He usually goes back about two o'clock. Tell him you want to do some shopping.'

'At the boatyard?' Morwenna asked sceptically. 'All right, I'll think of something.'

She fetched her sheepskin jacket from her room, and as

an afterthought, picked up her rucksack. She would need something to put her imaginary shopping in, she thought, and somewhere to conceal the folder.

When she arrived downstairs she found that her timing was almost perfect. Mark was standing at the front door, apparently giving Zack some instructions, and he agreed readily to give her a lift.

'Why didn't you say this morning that you wanted to go into Port Vennor?' he asked as he settled her in the car. 'I could have driven you in there and then and we could have had lunch together.'

She smiled at him. He was very attractive and pleasant and a different Morwenna at another time could quite have enjoyed a brief romantic attachment without strings with someone like Mark Trevennon. But not now. The Marks and the Guys of this world were totally in the past. Only what did the future hold instead?

She dragged her painful thoughts away from the vision of bleak emptiness that instantly presented itself and forced herself to respond to Mark's cheerful conversation.

Port Vennor lay, she discovered, in the curve of a small bay, and the road fell away steeply downhill running through its houses and shops down to the quay which at one time, she supposed, would have been the hub of the town's activities. In fact, in the season, it probably still was, but now, with a few bare weeks to go before Christmas, the harbour was quiet and almost deserted.

Mark pulled up near the lifeboat station. 'A lot of places are closed at this time of year,' he said. 'But there's a newsagent's and a chemist, and rather a good coffee shop where they also have books and gifts. Come along to the yard when you've finished looking round. Someone's bound to be going back to the house.'

Morwenna sighed a little as she watched him drive away along the quayside towards the sprawl of buildings which constituted Trevennon Marine. It would have been so much easier to have said, 'I need to go to the yard to collect something for Nick.' To have been open and above-board about the whole thing, but Nick wanted the secrecy and as he'd said, the whims of a sick man were usually indulged.

She wandered desultorily up the steep main street, glancing in shop windows, killing time until she could reasonably expect to present herself at the boatyard. She soon found the coffee shop that Mark had mentioned and decided to go in. It consisted of a few tables set in a room leading off the gift shop. There didn't seem to be anyone around and Morwenna went in and seated herself at one of the tables to wait. She could hear a murmur of voices beyond a curtained doorway and guessed this led to the kitchen and office premises. She was just glancing at the menu when the curtain was pushed back and a familiar figure in a long cape came through into the café.

'Hello,' said Biddy, and grinned cheerfully. She was carrying a large raffia basket filled with lumpy objects wrapped in newspaper. She indicated this. 'Samples,' she explained. 'Miss Penruan has been giving me an order.'

'That's good.' It was lovely to see a face that was friendly without reservations. 'Have you got time for a coffee or are you tearing off somewhere else?'

'Always time for a coffee.' Biddy put the basket down and took the opposite seat. 'I was telling Greg I'd met you and we were wondering how you'd got on at Trevennon and whether we'd see you around.'

Morwenna looked down at the red and white checked tablecloth. 'Oh, I'm still at Trevennon. I'm working there in a way.'

'Working?' Biddy almost gaped. 'For Dominic Trevennon?'

'Oh, no,' Morwenna said hastily. 'For his uncle. He's writing a family history and I'm helping.'

Biddy whistled. 'Wonders will never cease,' she muttered, half to herself. In turn, she picked up the menu and stared at it as if it was written in a foreign language. Then in a voice that was just too nonchalant, she said, 'And how's Mark Trevennon?'

'Fine.' Something about the tone of Biddy's voice struck Morwenna as odd. 'I didn't know you knew Mark?'

'Oh, I knew him.' Biddy gave a little bitter laugh. 'With the accent on the past tense. Big Brother didn't approve of our association, so that was that. Struggling potters aren't his idea of a suitable connection for the mighty Trevennons. I should have thought one wealthy and eligible lady in the family would be enough without Mark having to follow suit.'

Morwenna's heart skipped a beat. 'What do you mean?'

'Are you saying you've been at Trevennon nearly a week without running into Karen Inglis?' Biddy gazed at her. 'Dark, glamorous and a bitch, but as Dominic's the male equivalent, I don't suppose he notices.'

'Oh, yes, I've met her,' Morwenna said steadily. 'Is he going to marry her?'

'If she has anything to do with it, he will,' Biddy said with a shrug. 'And of course her aunt will be delighted. She's got money of her own, but she works as company secretary at Trevennon Marine and she'd welcome anything that linked the two families further. Funnily enough....' she paused and reddened slightly. 'Look, I ought not to gossip like this. The Trevennons are obviously friends of yours and....'

'I wouldn't put it quite like that,' Morwenna said drily. 'What were you going to say?'

'Well——' Biddy paused until Miss Penruan, a tall rather gaunt figure in a flowered smock, had emerged from the back premises and taken their order. 'It was Mark who mentioned it to me originally. He was joking, I suppose, but he said that Barbie Inglis was trying to push Karen at Dominic because she'd failed to get Nick for herself.' She gave an uncomfortable laugh. 'I don't suppose it's true. Mark said something about them both having been disappointed in love years ago and that everyone had thought they would end up consoling each other. Only it never happened, so the next generation will fill the breach instead. Cosy, eh?'

Morwenna agreed bleakly. Something that Biddy had said was nagging away at the back of her mind, but before she could recall what it was, Miss Penruan had returned with their coffee and the moment was lost. She was silent for a moment or two, the image of Dominic with Karen Inglis at his side very vivid in her mind, then dragged herself back to reality with a determined effort.

'I'm sorry that it didn't work out for you and Mark,' she said rather awkwardly.

Biddy shrugged. 'Just one of those things,' she said.

'And maybe it was for the best, anyway. Mark's good-looking and terrific company, but if he hasn't got the guts to stand up to Brother Dominic, then he's no use to me.' She drank some of her coffee. 'And if he had cared anything about me, then he would have stood up to him—wouldn't he?' she ended a little uncertainly.

Morwenna shook her head. 'I don't know. He—Dominic—has a very strong personality, and he's much older than Mark, of course, and his boss as well. It's a pretty formidable combination,' she added unhappily. Just how formidable, she was only too well aware.

Biddy stared broodingly at her coffee cup. 'Maybe,' she said abruptly. She was silent for a few minutes, then she said, 'How long do you expect to be at Trevennon? Perhaps you could come over to St Enna for a meal some time.'

'Oh, I'd like that.' Morwenna was eager.

Biddy smiled back. 'So would I. I'll be in touch.' She finished the remains of her coffee, and got to her feet.

Morwenna detained her. 'You wouldn't like me to give Mark any kind of message?'

Biddy shook her head decisively. 'Thanks, but no, thanks.' She paused. 'If there's going to be any kind of move, then it has to come from him. At least that's how I feel right at this moment.' She gave Morwenna a lopsided grin and a wave and disappeared.

Glancing at her watch, Morwenna decided it was time that she moved on too. She picked up her patently empty rucksack and eyed it with misgiving. She stopped in the bookshop on her way out and bought a guide book on local walks. On the way back down towards the quay, she replenished her stock of tights, and visited the chemist for more toothpaste and a luxurious bar of her favourite toilet soap, but she was still very much aware as she walked along the quayside towards Trevennon Marine that none of her purchases amounted to very much and hardly justified a trip to Port Vennor.

Her steps slowed as she approached the entrance to the yard. She could see Mark's Mini parked outside and beyond it was Dominic's car. She bit her lip and made herself walk up to the entrance. She found herself inside a large shed with a high roof made predominantly of glass. There were several boats, pleasure craft and the fishing boats used for shark expeditions, undergoing repair, and the air was filled with the pleasant aromas of wood, paint and varnish. In the distance she could hear the whine of machinery. In the far corner of the shed, a door with a painted sign and an arrow indicated that this was the way to the offices.

These, she found, were housed in a small complex of fairly new prefabricated buildings situated on some waste ground at the rear of the boatsheds. A concrete path led to them and a rough shelter with a corrugated iron roof protected those using the path from the vagaries of the weather. Morwenna trod along the path as if she was skirting her way through quicksands. The first door she came to said 'Reception' and she made herself steady her breathing as she pushed it open.

It was a narrow room, bisected by a counter, behind which two girls sat typing. There were a number of filing cabinets round the walls, and a small switchboard on one of the desks.

'I'm looking for Mr Mark Trevennon,' Morwenna said.

'Everyone's in a meeting, I'm afraid,' one of the girls rose and came forward. 'Is he expecting you? Do you want to wait?'

Morwenna hesitated. The coward's way out would be to refuse politely and catch the next bus back to Trevennon, but instead she found herself nodding.

'Oh, all right, then.' She was conscious that both girls were studying her with thinly disguised curiosity. They were both young and attractive, and she found herself wondering whether Biddy might not have been the sole subject of Mark's attentions.

Mark's office turned out to be a cubbyhole, just large enough to accommodate his desk and two chairs. Morwenna sat there for a few minutes, getting her bearings and trying to remember the precise instructions Nick had given her before she set out. When she was sure that the receptionist had returned to the front office, she got up and quietly opened the door. She had noted what Nick had described as the inner office as she went past, and her heart had jolted uncomfortably when she noticed a neat sign reading 'D. Trevennon' fixed to the door. Nick hadn't mentioned that it was also Dominic's office, she thought. But the door had been open and the room obviously unoccupied, and she would never have a better chance than now while everyone was in a meeting.

As Nick had said, there was only one filing cabinet. For a moment she thought it might be locked, but the top drawer opened easily enough when she tugged at it. There were several green folders there, but none of them bore the code number that Nick had mentioned. Perhaps he had made a mistake. With a feeling of frustration she closed the top drawer and tried the second one, but it was not there either, and it was with increasing desperation that she tried, unavailingly, the third drawer and then, on her knees, the fourth.

'Looking for something?'

If there had ever been a moment in her life when she wanted to die, to simply let the floor open and swallow her up, this was it. She gulped and looked over her shoulder at the door. He was leaning in the doorway, his hands thrust into his pockets with the air of someone who had been there for some considerable time.

She got to her feet, brushing off the knees of her jeans. 'I was, but I haven't found it.'

He said very silkily, and she could not meet his eyes, 'Perhaps I can help.' He walked over to the big desk, took a bunch of keys from his pocket and unlocked one of the deep drawers. A green folder came skidding across the polished surface towards her. She did not even have to check the coding.

'Well,' he said, 'That's what you came for, isn't it? Take it.'

There was a kind of weary anger in his voice.

She had to explain, to say something to justify her behaviour. 'I don't think you understand.'

'Oh yes, I do,' he said cynically. 'I do understand, my Lady Morwenna. I've been expecting it, in fact, ever since you arrived on the scene.'

That hurt, and she knew she had flinched openly. He sighed quickly and sharply. 'I knew it would only be a matter of time,' he said, half to himself. 'But I must admit I didn't think it would be quite so soon.'

She took two quick steps forward, picked up the folder and thrust it into her rucksack, fastening the straps with hands that shook.

'Right,' he said. 'Now perhaps you'd be good enough to get the hell out of here, before any more harm is done.'

But as he spoke, a door opened somewhere close at hand and there were voices and footsteps approaching. Dominic swore long and elaborately, just under his breath. He turned to face the corridor, filling the doorway with his body as if he wanted to block the knowledge of Morwenna's presence from the newcomers.

From outside, Morwenna heard Mark say cheerfully, 'Hey, Dom, have you seen Morwenna? Di told me she'd arrived, but she's vanished.'

Dominic said wearily, 'She's here.'

Mark pushed past him into the office. He gave Morwenna a smile, apparently unaware of the tension in the atmosphere. 'That didn't take long.'

'My own sentiments entirely,' said Dominic, watching them from the doorway.

She felt a deep, painful flush wash over her face to her hairline. She said hurriedly to Mark, 'Can we go now? I don't want to keep Nick waiting.'

'Sure thing,' Mark agreed amiably. He slid a hand through her arm. 'How did you find the bustling metropolis of Port Vennor? All human life is there, you know. It just takes a bit of finding at this time of the year....' His voice tailed away uncomfortably and Morwenna realised that someone else had joined them.

She was a small slender woman with elegantly blue-rinsed hair waving back from her forehead. She was wearing clove pink—a woollen dress with a matching jacket and black patent shoes. Morwenna had never seen her before, but she knew with a strange instinct that this was Barbie Inglis. And she knew too with the same instinct that Barbie Inglis had recognised her instantly.

'Another girl-friend, Mark?' Her voice was light and teasing, but Morwenna knew she had not imagined those few seconds when the blue eyes had narrowed and sharpened as they saw Laura Kerslake in her face, and two bright spots of colour had stood out on the woman's cheekbones.

Dominic said drily, 'Not this time, Barbie. Allow me to introduce Morwenna Kerslake, a young friend of Nick's who is spending some time with us. Morwenna, this is Barbara Inglis, our company secretary and very good friend.'

Barbie Inglis's hand was very cold as it touched Morwenna's. 'My dear,' she said, and paused. 'What a pleasure!' She laughed. 'And what a shock, frankly, after all these years to enter a room and see Laura standing there. It's the hair, of course, and the bone structure. Quite unmistakable.' She turned towards the two men, smiling radiantly. 'My dears, please don't look so embarrassed. It was all a very long time ago, you know.' She glanced back at Morwenna. 'I knew your mother very well, of course, but one loses touch over the years. How is she?'

Morwenna said very steadily, 'My mother died when I was eight years old, Miss Inglis, and my father and brother were killed earlier in the year in a car crash.'

'So naturally you came to Trevennon for sanctuary.' There was nothing but warmth and sympathy in Barbie Inglis's voice. 'Heavens,' she gave a low laugh, 'how history does repeat itself!'

The folder seemed to be burning a hole in Morwenna's rucksack. Barbie Inglis had no means of knowing about that, of course, but in the nicest possible way she had represented Morwenna as a leech and a parasite, and that was bad enough. Morwenna did not look at Dominic Trevennon. She already knew of the contempt that she would read in his eyes.

Suddenly it seemed very warm in the small room, and the neck of her sweater seemed tight and choking.

She said almost pleadingly, 'Mark, I really must get back....'

'Of course,' Barbie said almost soothingly. 'And I shall look forward to renewing our acquaintance this evening. Did Nick mention that we have a weekly game of chess? No? Well, no doubt he's had a great deal on his mind. And we'll have to arrange a little party of some kind very soon. A "welcome home" party for Laura's daughter.'

It was all so warm, so kind, so eagerly said. There was

nothing to which anyone in the world could have taken exception, but the blue eyes held the cold, hard glitter of sapphires.

Morwenna knew that her smile would seem forced, but there was nothing she could do about that. She said very politely, 'I shall look forward to that too.'

She was thankful to be out in the fresh air again. Glad too of Mark's hand under her arm. Behind them, she could hear Barbie laughing and talking to Dominic as they followed. Laura Kerslake's daughter, she thought, being shown off the premises in style, but very firmly and definitely all the same.

She told Mark, 'I met a friend of yours today—a girl called Biddy who runs a pottery at St Enna with her brother.'

He said, 'Oh, really?' and his voice was too casual. 'How was she?'

'She seemed fine.' Morwenna matched him for casualness, and no matter how she strained her ears she could not hear what Barbie was saying so confidentially to Dominic just a few steps behind them. She hesitated. 'Is it all right, my dragging you away like this? Your receptionist said something about a meeting—I haven't broken things up by my arrival?'

'Certainly not.' He sounded a little abstracted. 'It was just a routine discussion—nothing very exciting. Of course, I suppose all this is new to you. I never thought to ask you if you wanted to see round the yard.'

'It's all right,' she assured him emphatically. 'Another time, maybe. I really do have to get back to the house.'

He helped her into the passenger seat of the Mini and slammed the door shut, and went round the car to get into the driver's seat. Morwenna leaned forward, putting the rucksack down by her feet before adjusting the seat belt. She looked back at the building and saw that Dominic was standing in the doorway watching her go. Barbie was at his side and Morwenna saw her raise her hand in a brief farewell salute. She made herself wave back as the car drew away. And found herself thinking, ' "Our very good friend." And my enemy.'

*

'Calm down,' Nick said pacifically.

'Calm down!' Morwenna nearly exploded. 'I've never been so humiliated in my life. He caught me red-handed, my fingers in the till, and never even gave me a chance to explain.'

Nick grimaced slightly. 'Believe me, child, that was not what I intended,' he said grimly. He sighed. 'I should stick to my chronicles of the dead, and not try to manipulate the living. I'm sorry, Morwenna. I implicated you quite deliberately in an experiment that failed, but you don't have to worry about your part in it. I'll provide all the necessary explanations—to Dominic or anyone else.'

'An experiment?' Morwenna gave the green folder, lying on the table beside his chair, a despairing glance. 'Then you don't want this file? It was all a pretence?'

'No,' Nick said firmly. 'I do need the file, and I had my doubts as to whether Dominic would co-operate if I asked him to bring it to me. He's determined that I shan't start overdoing things and making myself ill again.' He smiled wryly. 'He doesn't realise that you can become ill sometimes through sheer boredom and frustration. That's why I started on the family history—but I'm no historian. Boats have always been my life, and I'm too old to turn my back on them now.'

'I can understand that,' Morwenna said quitely. 'But not why you involved me as you did. Surely there were other ways?'

'Oh, plenty.' Nick leaned his head against the high back of his chair. He looked tired and strained. 'Forgive me, child. I used you as if you were a pebble I could fling into the middle of a pool to watch the ripples spread. But I see now that I was unfair not to warn you in advance.'

Morwenna stared at him, her mind working feverishly. She said almost hoarsely, 'Dominic wasn't meant to catch me, was he? It was someone else—that woman—Barbie Inglis. You wanted her to find me in his office with a folder I had no right to in my hand. But why?'

The look of strain deepened. 'You've read your *Hamlet*, haven't you, child?' He quoted softly, ' "The play's the thing wherein I'll catch the conscience of the king." But it was a stupid idea. I know that now.'

Morwenna spread her hands helplessly. 'What are you saying? That it was Miss Inglis who sold the design for the *Lady Laura* to Lackingtons?' She managed an unsteady laugh. 'For God's sake, Nick, what did you think she would do when she found me? Scream and faint and confess everything in broken tones?'

'Something of the sort, perhaps. I don't know.' Nick closed his eyes. 'Over the years I've given her every chance, God knows, to tell me the truth. I've no real proof that it was her, just a gut-certainty that's stood between us like the Berlin wall.' He gave a grim laugh. 'For almost twenty years people have been asking themselves why Barbie and I didn't cut our losses and settle down together. I've asked myself the same question, a hundred times or more. But the answer is always the same—not with this question always hanging between us. How can there be love where there's no trust?'

Morwenna stared down at her hands twisted together in her lap.

'I can hardly believe it,' she murmured, half to herself. 'Why would she do such a thing? Why? Was—was it because she was in love with you? Because she was jealous?'

Nick sighed. 'She was jealous, yes. Laura was always more popular locally, because she was warmer, more outgoing. Barbie relied too much on the Inglis family name and dignity. I think it was the affront to that dignity that prompted her to this ultimate piece of malice.'

'Affront?' Morwenna echoed bewilderedly. 'I don't see....'

'Of course not. You don't know. How could you?' He laid his hand over hers. 'Barbie had hoped to marry Robert Kerslake—your father.'

Morwenna gazed at Nick in silence, open-mouthed.

'Oh, no!' she said after a moment. 'Oh, God, Mark told me Daddy had been on the point of getting engaged to a local girl, and then Biddy said something too—but I never realised. What a fool I've been!'

'If we're talking of fools,' said Nick, 'then I must be the biggest. It took me a long time to realise the truth, and even then I didn't want to accept it.'

'What made you suspect?' Morwenna asked.

'A number of things,' Nick answered, frowning. 'She was so eager to make amends—uncharacteristically eager. She invested money in the boatyard when things looked black for us. And she couldn't quite hide her relief when Laura's guilt was accepted, apparently without question, by everyone. And of course, she didn't know about the crack that Lackingtons' man had made to me about my lady friends.'

'But you never tackled her about it,' said Morwenna. 'Even when you were sure, you kept silent. You let my mother take the blame instead.'

He made an abrupt movement. 'Yes—because by then it wasn't as simple as you imply. I pitied the unhappiness which had driven Barbie to do such a thing. I could even understand it up to a point. And there was another thing. We'd become—close, and I believed then that it would only be a matter of time before she told me of her own accord what she had done. Put things right between us, so that we could both start again, I didn't want an apology, or even an explanation. I only wanted the truth.' He smiled faintly. 'I didn't realise how long it would take.'

Morwenna felt tears prick at the back of her eyelids. 'Oh, Nick, what a waste of a life—of two lives!'

'I'm not dead yet,' he reminded her with some asperity. 'And nor is Barbie. So she'll be over for her chess game.' He smiled and shook his head. 'She plays a good defensive game, but I have a feeling that this time—this time she may be going to lose. And in the meantime'—he picked up the folder and opened it—'I'll renew my acquaintance with my other love.'

She could see drawings, pages of figures and notes. 'Another boat?'

He nodded. 'But not another racing dinghy like the *Lady Laura*. This one will travel the oceans of the world when she's built. She'll challenge Cape Horn and the Roaring Forties and win. People will talk of her as they talk of *Gipsy Moth* and *Lively Lady*. And she'll be built at Port Vennor.' He looked ironically at Morwenna. 'Do you think I'm fantasising? Slipping into early senility? I'm not, you know. Two years ago, when I first got the idea for her, I talked about it to Alan Hewitt-Smyth. You've heard of him, I suppose?'

Morwenna had indeed heard of him. Hewitt-Smyth was one of the younger generation of lone yachtsmen, and his sometimes hectic adventures had made most of the newspapers and colour supplements in the country.

'And he was interested?' she asked rather doubtfully.

'He was more than interested,' Nick returned forcefully. 'About a month ago I had a letter from him reminding me of the project, and suggesting he might be able to get sponsorship for it. They're talking of another big race and he wants to win it with the *Lady Morwenna*.'

'Oh!' Morwenna pressed her hands against suddenly burning cheeks. 'But that's what he—Dominic—called me when he found me in his office. My Lady Morwenna.'

Nick gave a short laugh. 'Did he now? Well, he's no fool, my nephew, and he knew I'd be looking for these specifications as soon as I got my strength back. Although I never told him I'd heard from Hewitt-Smyth,' he added with some satisfaction. 'That's a little surprise I'm keeping up my sleeve for the time being.'

'But why *Lady Morwenna*?' Morwenna asked rather doubtfully. 'I know it's a family name, but....'

Nick nodded again. 'It's that all right, and it's a name for courage as well. Or did Laura never tell you the story of Morwenna Trevennon? I can understand her reticence. It isn't a bedtime story for a child, after all, but it always fascinated your mother, so it's no wonder that's the name she chose for you.'

'No wonder at all,' Dominic Trevennon said from the doorway, and Morwenna had to resist an impulse to shrink back in her chair. He came forward, his eyebrows lifted, and looked down at his uncle. 'What's this, Nick? More family history?'

Nick grunted, 'Past, present and future, I hope.' His hands almost caressed the folder in his lap.

Dominic glanced at it, his dark face sardonic. 'You employ strange messengers for your errands at times, Nick. Why all the mystery?'

Nick lifted a shoulder. 'I have my reasons.'

'I hope so.' Dominic's voice was grim. 'I won't even try to guess what they are. But you do realise that you put Miss Kerslake in a damned difficult position this afternoon?'

'She's forgiven me,' said Nick. 'She may even forgive you in time. And why so formal? Her name's Morwenna, remember.'

'I'm not likely to forget,' Dominic said not quite under his breath.

Morwenna's chin went up in defiance. 'I suppose my appropriation of the family name must seem like adding insult to injury to you, Mr Trevennon.'

'Well, don't lose any sleep over it, Miss Kerslake. Not at this late stage.'

'Oh, I shan't.' Her smile was cool, even slightly provocative. Anything to conceal the truth—that because of this man with his dark, taunting smile, it might be many a moon before she closed her eyes in peace again.

She turned slightly desperately to Nick. 'Isn't anyone going to tell me my namesake's story at last?'

He leaned back in his chair, closing his eyes as if to aid his concentration. 'It doesn't take long to tell. She was the only daughter of Matt Trevennon who ruled the coastline hereabouts in the name of Elizabeth the First, but for the greater honour and glory of Matt Trevennon. His wife had borne him several sturdy sons, but Morwenna was the last of the brood and the sole girl, and he—like many another strong man—worshipped her from the moment she was laid in the cradle. When at last she came to her teens and it was time to think about her marriage, there wasn't a match good enough for her.' He gave a slight chuckle. 'Hardly to be wondered at, I suppose. As well as being a considerable heiress, she was a lovely thing, even taking artistic licence into account.'

Morwenna stirred in her chair. 'Is there a portrait of her somewhere?'

'A portrait exists,' said Dominic Trevennon. 'Although it hasn't been seen for some considerable time.'

Nick grunted something and sat hunched irritably in his chair with his lips pursed. Then, with an obvious effort, he took up the story again. 'At last a betrothal was arranged, with the son of an earl high in favour at court, and Matt crowed over this the length and breadth of the Duchy. But the marriage itself was postponed because England was on the brink of war with Spain. In fact, it was said a great fleet had already been dispatched to invade England and all thoughts of weddings and celebration had to take second place to the national emergency.' He shrugged. 'What happened next is history, of course. Various factors, including the weather, contributed to the downfall of the mighty Armada and its ships were scattered. One of them came to grief on the rocks not far from this house.'

'Spanish Cove,' Morwenna breathed.

Nick nodded. 'And on the morning tide, clinging to a spar, came the only survivor of the wreck, as far as we know—Don Esteban de Aldobar y Vaga. It was Matt Trevennon that found him, and that probably saved his life. Anyone else would probably have quietly knocked him on the head and put him back in the sea after emptying his pockets, but Matt knew from his clothing that this was no ordinary Spanish sailor and he had him taken up to the house.'

He sighed. 'He saw the lad was young, dressed like an aristocrat and with gold in his pockets, and the thought of ransom filled his mind to the exclusion of all else. What he'd forgotten was that waiting in his house was his daughter, his own flesh and blood, as wild and wilful in her own way as he was, facing a loveless although brilliant marriage with a man she'd met about twice.' Nick grinned from Dominic to Morwenna. 'It must have been like setting a match to a fuse. Particularly when news came that young Matt, the son and heir, had been wounded aboard one of Drake's ships and was lying at Plymouth, and Madam Trevennon together with the old nurse, who was still technically in charge of Morwenna, went flying off to look after him and bring him home as soon as he was well enough.

'So she fell in love with this young Spaniard? Even though he was her country's enemy?' Morwenna could not keep a note of surprise out of her voice.

Nick smiled faintly. 'She was Cornish, remember, and it's a moot point whether the Cornish have ever genuinely regarded themselves as part of England. It's been suggested that a number of sailors from the Armada made their way ashore and settled down quietly, intermarrying with the locals and never a word mentioned to the authorities. Certainly Don Esteban's presence at Trevennon was kept mighty quiet from the powers that be. If any benefit was to accrue from it, it would have to be for Matt Trevennon alone. So in the absence of her mother and the nurse, Morwenna looked after the lad herself and, of course, the inevitable happened.'

'But didn't her father notice?'

'Apparently not.' It was Dominic speaking. 'But her mother did as soon as she returned with her convalescent son in tow, and she recognised what her husband had taken for an attack of ague as the early symptoms of pregnancy.' He shook his head. 'It's not difficult to imagine the scene that ensued—Matt shouting and blustering and Morwenna defying him, swearing that the earl's son could end in perdition and that she'd marry Don Esteban or no one. As if the choice was ever going to be hers.'

'So what did they do?' Morwenna prompted.

He gave a faint shrug. 'They were cruel times. Don Esteban's fate was sealed even though the ransom from Spain had not arrived. But they fed the girl a tale. Matt appeared to capitulate—to accept that the grand London wedding would never take place. But he imposed a condition: Don Esteban must go back to Spain to ensure that his family would receive his bride with honour and consent to the marriage. Later Morwenna would be sent to him.'

'And she believed him?'

'He was her father and she had always been his spoiled pet. She had no reason to believe he would deny her the wish of her heart. When you've only ever looked for one side of a person, it's hard to realise that another may exist that you've never glimpsed. So Morwenna said goodbye to her beloved.'

'And she never saw him again?' Morwenna asked soberly.

'Indeed she did. Heaven only knows how she was tipped off. Perhaps one of her brothers dropped a hint. Maybe she overheard a snippet of conversation not intended for her ears. Perhaps a servant told her the truth. It seems that none of the Trevennons wished to soil their hands with Esteban's blood. They reasoned that as the sea had brought him, the sea could take him again. So they trussed him up and left him in Spanish Cove for the tide, and that's where

Morwenna, flying to the rescue, found him, just before high tide at midnight.'

'So they escaped after all.' Morwenna was surprised at the outcome. The story up to now had been told on a sombre note which had suggested otherwise.

'No,' Dominic shook his head, 'they didn't. The ropes that had been used had swollen in the damp and she could neither cut them nor free him. In the end, so the legend had it, when she saw it was no use, she lay down on the sand beside him and let the tide take them both.'

'Dear God!' After a pause, Morwenna moistened her lips. 'That's quite a story. No wonder my mother never told me. It's hardly fairytale material.'

'You've come to the wrong place for fairy tales, my dear.' Dominic's voice was suddenly harsh. 'The Trevennons don't go in for happy endings. Haven't you heard enough of the family history to know that by now?'

Their glances met and locked. She said, keeping her voice very steady, 'You make that sound almost like a warning—Mr Trevennon.'

'Perhaps it is at that,' he said quietly. He laid a hand momentarily on his uncle's shoulder, then turned and went out of the room.

She watched him go, a pain like a sword stabbing at her heart. She needed no warning, she thought achingly. She already knew that loving him could guarantee her nothing but heartbreak, not when Karen Inglis moved at his side with her tall dark beauty in all the confidence of possession.

She realised Nick's eyes were on her, filled with anxiety, and resolutely fought back the tears that were threatening to overwhelm her. She could not cry now, not without giving herself away, and she could not do that if she was to leave Trevennon with the rags of her pride intact. So she would cry later, when she was alone. And it was the prospect of that loneliness, she knew, that would be the hardest to bear.

But the day was not finished with her yet. They worked for the remainder of the afternoon, largely in silence. Morwenna did not have to speculate what occupied Nick's thoughts as he pored over his drawings and figures. Her own musings followed much the same complex lines, she thought as she sat at the desk staring at the notes she was supposed to be transcribing with sightless eyes.

Somehow she had to come to terms with this new pain, this new yearning which had beset her. She lifted a hand and brushed it against the softness of her mouth as if her fingertips were capable of recapturing his kiss, but at the same time she despised herself. Hadn't she learned sufficiently from that transitory experience with Guy of the deceit of physical passion? She knew without conceit that she was attractive and desirable, so there was little wonder that Dominic should have taken advantage of their proximity for a little casual lovemaking. More than that, she had practically invited the situation by her own foolish remarks at their first meeting, although she had believed the provocation, the attraction she had dimly sensed between them even then had been cancelled, neutralised by the anger and antagonism since.

And Dominic was wrong. Hate was no substitute at all for love. Passion on those terms might be momentarily beguiling, but it would leave a bitter taste. It was strange how she knew this even though she had never given herself and tested the truth of her reasoning. She loved him, but that would have to remain a secret in this house where too many secrets had been nursed in bitterness and regret.

From the other side of the room Nick said abruptly, 'I shall have dinner downstairs this evening.' He looked across at her with something of a challenge in his eyes. 'Well, nothing to say?'

She smiled with an effort. 'Would any comment from me really affect the decision either way?'

'Not really. I've remained passive too long. It's time I took a hand in my own affairs.'

She said wryly, 'Well, you started today when you sent me to the boatyard.'

'That was only a beginning.' His smile crinkled the corners of his eyes. 'Now go and tell Inez the good news. She mentioned something earlier about roast duck. We can have a little celebration feast to mark my return to the land of the living.'

His tone was bland, but she was not deceived. She said:
'What are you planning, Nick? I have to know.'

'You'll know soon enough.' His eyes glinted at her, then he transferred his attention deliberately back to his papers. 'Now do as I ask, there's a good girl, and then go and pretty yourself for this evening.'

Inez received the news that there was to be a party tranquilly enough. She was sitting at the table peeling apples.

' 'Bout time there was summat to look forward to,' she remarked rather cryptically. 'I'll get Zack in to clean up the good silver.'

'I could help,' Morwenna offered.

'No need for that. Though if you'd finish these apples for me, I'd be grateful. I'll see about something special in the way of a pudding.' Inez pushed the remaining fruit and the paring knife over to her. 'Whatever is it, maid? You look a bit down in the mouth.'

Morwenna concentrated on the apples. 'I suppose I'm a little worried about Mr Nick,' she said at last. 'Worried that he'll overdo things.'

'I reckon Mr Nick knows where he's to, better'n you or I,' Inez said serenely. 'You let him bide, my dear, and give heed to yourself. You've got something different to put on than they old trousers, I hope. Miss Karen'll be here tonight and she always comes dressed up like Lady Fan Todd.'

'I've got a long skirt,' Morwenna admitted weakly, wondering why she did not deny any wish to compete with Karen on any level.

'That'll do,' said Inez. 'And watch what you'm doing with that knife. You're about as 'andy as a cow with a musket.'

'I'm not that bad,' Morwenna protested. 'Look, I've got all this peel off in one piece.' She held it up triumphantly.

'And most of the apple with it,' said Inez, unimpressed. 'Still, seeing as you've done it, us might as well make use of it. Say the words after me, then throw the peel over your left shoulder. "St Simon and St Jude, may I intrude and tell me the name of my lover...."'

'No.' Morwenna looked down at the length of unbroken peel in her fingers. 'No, I'd rather not.'

'Go along with you,' Inez urged robustly. ' 'Tes only an old bit of superstition. It can't hurt you.'

'I suppose not,' Morwenna muttered, capitulating. But

she felt ridiculously nervous and self-conscious as she repeated the words of the old charm and tossed the apple peel over her left shoulder.

'Dear life,' Inez remarked blankly, and Morwenna knew before she even turned what initial letter the peel would have formed on the kitchen floor. She steeled herself to laugh it away, but the smile froze on her lips as she turned and saw Dominic standing silent in the kitchen doorway, the betraying apple peel at his feet.

'Teaching our visitor old wives' tales, Inez?' he asked, his mouth curling sardonically.

' 'Tes just an old custom, my dear, and where's the harm in that?'

'None.' He pushed the peel aside with the toe of his shoe. 'As long as no one makes the mistake of taking it seriously.'

Morwenna would have given anything she possessed to prevent that all-too-betraying blush from spreading over her face, but it was beyond her control. She swallowed as she rose to her feet. 'I'll clear that mess away,' she began, but he cut sharply across her words.

'Leave it, Miss Kerslake. Inez will see to it. I'd like a word with you in private.'

She walked stiffly after him, wiping her sticky hands unobtrusively down her jeans like a naughty child.

'Is something wrong?' she asked haltingly as he led the way into the study and closed the door behind them.

'Do you know why my uncle has taken it into his head to dine downstairs tonight?' He was frowning.

She shook her head. 'Does there have to be any particular reason?' she asked lamely.

He sent her a narrow-eyed look. 'Everything Nick says or does these days seems to have the same basic motivation,' he said coldly. 'He seems determined to re-open old wounds, and I'm quite aware whom we have to thank for that.'

She moistened her lips. 'I think you overestimate my influence, Mr Trevennon.'

'I don't.' His eyes were fixed on her face. 'Oh, I acquit you of any desire to become an old man's darling, but the charge of being obsessively single-minded about gaining your own ends still stands.'

She wanted to tell him then that it was no longer she that was single-minded. That if it was left to her, she would go no further with her attempt to clear her mother's name. Laura herself would not have cared, she thought achingly. Her generous affection would have wanted Nick's happiness, whatever the cost. She had expected him to be happy. Perhaps even then she had suspected that once she was out of the way, he and Barbie Inglis would arrive at an understanding then undreamed of.

'I don't think you understand,' she began, but he interrupted remorselessly.

'I understand only too well. You're quite determined to drag this whole mess out into the open once again, and you don't care who you may hurt in the process.'

Karen Inglis? she wondered. Was that whom his concern was for? Any sort of disgrace to her aunt would be bound to affect her even peripherally. She felt her face stiffen.

'There's nothing I can do,' she said quietly.

His laugh was short and harsh. 'All that golden innocence and charm on the surface, and complete and utter ruthlessness underneath, my Lady Morwenna.'

'Please don't call me that.'

'Why not?' He raised his eyebrows. 'She was ruthless too, in her own way, and look where it led her.' He walked over to her, so close that their bodies were almost touching, and looked down at her. 'Morwenna,' his voice was low and it tingled across her senses. But he wasn't making love, he was making war, and she must never let herself forget that. 'Give this thing up now. I'm asking you.'

She could feel the power emanating from him, a sensual dynamic power that turned her bones to water and which he was using deliberately to bend her to his will. But it was not her decision, it was Nick's, and she wasn't even certain how much he wanted Dominic to know, if anything. If he wanted to tell him, wouldn't he have been in his confidence already?

She whispered, 'I'm sorry.'

He did not move, but suddenly he was light years away from her. Then he said very quietly, 'You will be.'

She turned away from him, biting her lip until she tasted blood. She walked very calmly out of the room and shut the door behind her, then she ran like the wind for the stairs and she did not stop running until she was safely in her room. Then she lay across the bed, her fingers gripping the worn quilt, and cried until she had no more tears left.

CHAPTER SEVEN

LATER, when she looked critically at herself in the mirror, there was no sign of that storm of weeping. True, she was a little pale and her eyes looked larger than usual, but that could be because of the cosmetics she had used. She had twisted her hair into a soft coil on top of her head, allowing a few soft tendrils to escape around her ears and the nape of her neck. Her skirt was black velvet with contrasting panels embroidered in gold thread and she wore a simple black silky top with a scooped neck. Around her slim throat she tied a gold locket on a piece of black velvet ribbon. She looked good, she thought. Not dramatic or sensational, but good.

The sitting room door was open as she approached the top of the stairs and she could hear voices and laughter. So the evening's guests had arrived. She walked slowly down, lifting her skirt carefully. Morwenna Trevennon, she thought wryly, descending the stairs to face whatever wrath was to come.

They were all assembled, she realised as she stood in the doorway. She was the last one down. She hadn't planned on making an entrance, but if one had been thrust upon her she would make the most of it.

'Good evening,' she said clearly and sweetly into a lull in the conversation.

'My dear child.' Nick smiled across the room at her from where he was ensconced by the fire. 'What a picture you look! Dominic—someone—give Morwenna some sherry.'

It was Mark who brought the glass to her. 'Wow!' he murmured under his breath, his eyes travelling over her in undisguised appreciation. She laughed back at him, lowering her eyes in mock demureness. This was the sort of reaction she was used to and could cope with. It took her across the room on Mark's arm to the sofa where Barbie Inglis was sitting. She was wearing green, impeccably cut, but a harsh colour for her. Or was she just ultra-pale that evening? Karen's dark beauty was triumphantly stated in flame coloured chiffon. Lady Fan Todd, Morwenna thought, and the glimmer of a smile caught at the corners of her mouth, making her look mysterious and mischievous at the same moment. The conversation which had been at a standstill since her appearance re-started with a jerk.

They had been discussing holidays, it seemed, past, present and to come. Karen was in her element, as flame-like as the dress she was wearing, overdoing the enthusiasms slightly perhaps, but who would notice that when she was such a pleasure to watch. She was talking about surfing, arguing the merits of the local beaches and comparing them with those of California where she had spent a year. Of course, Morwenna thought cattily, and was ashamed of herself. She had never surfed, so the talk was of little interest to her. Nor to Nick, who sat shading his face from the heat of the fire, his eyes hooded enigmatically. Looking at him, the proud head, the fine bones, she knew what Dominic would be like as he grew old and the knowledge that she would not be here to see it or share it with him slashed at her like a knife.

And she was not the only one who was silent. Beside her, Barbie Inglis sat as if she was supported on invisible wires, her carefully applied lipstick turning her mouth into a straight gash of crimson without humour or tenderness.

Morwenna felt her sense of compassion growing. Laura Kerslake had been loved and cherished. She had been compensated a hundred times over for any loss of affection she had suffered from her adopted family. But this quiet tense woman sitting next to her had gained nothing from that despairing act of spite. Even the happiness that could have been hers had been denied her because of it.

She wanted suddenly, desperately to turn to her and take her arm and tell her that they knew what she had done and that there was nothing, nothing to be gained by concealment any longer, and put an end to this thing once and for all, but she had no right. She had walked into the situation unknowingly, but the protagonists were Nick and Barbie and they had to find their own salvation.

She sipped her sherry. It was a good one, but it might as well have been gall and wormwood, and there was a little pain throbbing dully in her temple. She wanted to press her fingers against it, but when she looked up she saw that Dominic was watching her and she could not afford to show any sign of weakness, even a slight one like an incipient headache.

The meal was delicious. The dining room was lit by candles which concealed the shabbiness, and emphasised the beauty of the polished table and the old-fashioned silver, glowing thanks to Zack's unwilling ministrations. Clear soup preceded the duck, which was followed by a creamy syllabub.

Morwenna made a pretence of eating, but in reality she did little more than push the food round her plate. Her throat felt tight suddenly and she was on edge all the time, although she could not have explained why. It was like the feeling that one got before a thunderstorm, she thought, that feeling of tension that made one glad when lightning eventually ripped the sky apart and cleared the air.

Nick was in his element, she noticed. Karen was no longer permitted to monopolise the conversation, which had turned to purely local matters, and had a frankly reminiscent flavour. Nick was turning to Barbie more and more, destroying the web of silence she seemed to have created about herself, drawing her into the talk with shared memories and requests for her opinion. And she was beginning perceptibly to relax. There was more colour in her face, and she was beginning to smile naturally.

So in a way this made what happened next all the more startling. They had finished dinner and were back in the sitting room having coffee. Inez had brought in a trolley and Karen had jumped up immediately and gone to it, busying herself with the pouring out as if she was already the hostess. As she might be, Morwenna reminded herself. She would hardly have taken so much upon herself without some positive encouragement from Dominic.

When the cups had been handed round and Morwenna realised that hers was still empty on the trolley, she decided not to say anything. Her headache was getting worse and she did not want any coffee anyway. Karen was moving over to Dominic, cup in hand. She was smiling, her head thrown back provocatively, her voice lowered as she said something for his ears alone. And perhaps he was smiling back with a look in his eyes that he kept for her alone. Morwenna felt her nails dig into the palms of her hands and it took all her self-control to stop herself from getting up and running out of the room.

But that might be what Karen wanted. She knew all the pressure points—exactly when and how to make Morwenna feel a complete outsider. The coffee was just a final pinprick.

Nick said gruffly, 'Karen, I think you've forgotten someone. Morwenna has no coffee.'

All eyes were turned on her immediately and she felt herself flush and heard her voice say almost beseechingly, 'It's all right. I really don't want any.'

'Oh—I'm sorry.' Karen's voice was effusive. 'What a dreadful mistake! I saw there was an extra cup and thought that Inez had miscounted.' She gave a little theatrical laugh. 'I get so used to there just being family at these little gatherings.'

The silence after the smiling words had been spoken was suddenly electric. There had been no mistaking the insolence, the desire to wound that underlay them. Morwenna felt as if she had been struck in the face publicly.

Dominic was the first to move. He walked across to the trolley, filled the remaining cup with coffee and brought it to her. She muttered a confused word of thanks as she took the cup from him, and stole a look at his dark face. It told her nothing, but there was an air of icy control about him as if he was keeping a tight rein on his temper. He would not be pleased with Karen for her lack of courtesy, but he could not be too angry with her when her words had simply reflected his own feelings.

Nick's voice was a rumble of anger, however, and she jumped slightly, slopping a little of the coffee into the saucer.

'To me, my dear Karen, Morwenna is as much a member of this family as anyone else in this room.'

Karen saw she had made a bad mistake, but didn't know how to recoup it.

'But of course.' She spread her hands in front of her,

placatingly. 'I see that I've totally misread the situation. I understood that Miss Kerslake was employed here as some sort of secretary. It never occurred to me....'

'Well, let it occur to you now.' Nick could not have been more brusque, his face harsh with displeasure. Morwenna saw Barbie Inglis make a slight movement as if she was in pain and wanted to cry out to Nick to drop the whole thing now. There was nothing to be gained by hurting Barbie through this attack on her niece, or by setting herself at odds with the woman Dominic loved.

'I have never regarded her as an employee,' the angry voice went on. 'She has become as dear to me as the daughter I never had. As dear to me as her mother was before her.'

'Nick!' Morwenna protestingly pressed her hands to her burning face, but he went on remorselessly:

'I want no one left in the slightest doubt about my regard for this child.' He got to his feet clumsily, reaching for his stick. Dominic went to his side, grasping his arm.

'Steady.' The warning sounded bleak.

Nick shook him away imperatively. 'I'm all right, damn it. Morwenna, come here, girl, and give me your arm. I have a surprise for you. I hadn't planned it for this moment, but events have overtaken me.'

As they went towards the door, she said in a desperate undertone, 'Nick, what are you doing?'

'It's all right,' he silenced her authoritatively. 'It's for the best, believe me.'

She said no more. He was shaking with anger, and she was terrified that another attack might be prompted by his outraged emotions. The others were following them, she realised, in a bewildered procession. She caught a glimpse of Barbie's face and saw that she was as white as death.

They turned right at the top of the stairs. Nick was breathless, but his grip on her arm was as firm as ever. He marched her along the gallery until they reached a door at the far end, and then he released her, searching in his pockets.

Dominic said, his voice cold with fury, 'Nick, for God's sake. There's no need for a big dramatic gesture.'

His uncle made no reply. He had brought out a bunch

of keys and was fitting one of them into the lock. The door was opening before them and Nick was urging her forward. She didn't want to go into the room. She knew what it was. This had been her mother's room, the one that had been locked up ever since she went away. She didn't know quite what to expect—something out of *Great Expectations* perhaps, but she stepped forward with numb obedience as Nick's hand pressed her arm and looked round her.

And, after all, it was only a large and quite beautiful bedroom. There wasn't a cobweb in sight or a speck of dust either. There were long curtains brocaded in green and gold at the tall windows and a matching quilted bedcover with a valance that reached the carpeted floor. The furniture was walnut with an elegance that did not belong to the present century. There was even a fire of apple logs and pine cones waiting in the marble fireplace, and fluffy towels hanging on the rail of the washstand. It had an air of waiting as if the usual occupant had been away on a journey and was expected back at any minute. There was no feeling that it had been shut up for over twenty years.

'This is to be your room, child,' said Nick. He threw the words out as if they were a challenge, daring anyone to object. He turned and pointed to a large painting on one of the walls. 'And there she is, your namesake, Morwenna Trevennon.'

Morwenna was shaking inside, not so much with what had just happened, although that was disturbing enough, but because as Nick spoke she had caught sight of Dominic looking at her. He wore an expression of black rage and frustration that terrified her. She had the craziest impulse to fling herself at his feet and cry out, 'I'm sorry. I'm sorry. I didn't know this was going to happen.'

Only he wouldn't believe it. He would think the whole thing had been planned in advance, and that she'd persuaded Nick to establish her position in the household so that there could be no argument about it.

She wanted to be happy about this. She wanted to thank Nick for this gesture of affection and faith and be sincere in her thanks, but she felt totally miserable inside. Karen was there, staring round the room, looking daggers at the furnishings which still had a pristine quality sadly lacking in the rest of the house. Her eyes seemed to linger on the bed, which was enormous, a wide double bed, far too large for just one person.

Morwenna thought, 'But this wasn't intended for just one person. This is a room designed and intended for a couple.' She turned to Nick, the question forming on her lips, but he forestalled her.

'Yes,' he said quietly. 'Your mother decorated and furnished this room. It was, I hoped, going to be our room eventually.'

Barbie Inglis, who had stood like a stone, suddenly spoke. 'Laura's room,' she said, and her eyes were bright and fierce with tears. 'My God, after all these years! I hope you realise how honoured you all are to be allowed to set foot in—Laura's shrine.' She gave a little harsh laugh, then turned on her heel and walked out.

Karen gave a little gasp and went after her. Mark, obedient to a swift gesture from Dominic, followed. The three of them were left alone, confronting each other.

Dominic said tautly, 'I hope it's given you satisfaction— this act of gratuitous cruelty.'

Nick shook his head wearily. 'I didn't intend it to happen like this,' he said. 'My plans were very different. I lost my temper, that's all. But it may all turn out for the best, even yet.'

'You can say that?' Dominic demanded, his voice vibrating with scorn. 'How can you even contemplate the future when you're so hung up about the past?'

'Oh, stop, please!' Morwenna clapped her hands to her ears. 'Don't let's talk about it any more tonight.' She knew she was near to tears.

'Why not?' Dominic swung towards her, his eyes blazing. 'Can you think of a more appropriate time—or place? She was right, you know, when she said this was a shrine. The locked and sacrosanct room with its bitter-sweet memories. God in heaven!' He stared around him appraisingly. 'I can only say it seems in remarkably good order. Your work, Nick? I can't actually picture you with duster and broom, but I suppose everything is possible in this truly amazing world.'

Nick moved his shoulders tiredly. 'Of course I didn't do

it,' he said irritably. 'Inez has been cleaning it regularly for years on my instruction.'

'You kept that very quiet,' Dominic accused.

'Is that so surprising?' Nick asked with a gleam of humour. 'Locking the room in the first place was the big dramatic gesture you mentioned just now. Having it springcleaned regularly hasn't nearly the same muscle. Frankly, I was ashamed of the whole business. It's a beautiful room—one of the best in the house. It was madness to keep it shut up and I knew it, but it's hard to back down once a gesture has been made.'

'Then why make the same mistake again?' Dominic glared at him. 'You may not find this one so easy to get out of.'

'Please.' Morwenna interposed herself between them. 'The question of gestures doesn't arise. I'd prefer to stay in my own room. I can't possibly sleep here alone in that enormous bed.'

Dominic's smile was slow and insulting. 'Is that an invitation, my Lady Morwenna? Because if so you've badly misjudged your sense of timing.'

'Dominic!' Nick almost roared. 'You'll apologise for that.'

'It doesn't matter.' Morwenna put her hand on his arm. Her head was aching badly now. She wanted to get away from the tension in the atmosphere and escape to the peace of her own room. 'Please, let's get out of here. I don't think I can stand any more.'

'Any more?' Dominic Trevennon gave her a long contemptuous look before he turned away. 'Believe me, lady, this has barely begun.'

The door slammed shut behind him. Nick lost his rigid look. There was a small brocade chair close beside him and he made his way to it and sat down heavily.

'Oh, God,' he said quietly, and stared down at the floor.

'Why did you do it?' Morwenna demanded. She swung round, her hands spread despairingly, indicating her surroundings. 'I don't want all this—you know I don't. It's a room for a couple.'

Nick sighed deeply. 'As I said, I lost my temper. It doesn't happen very often, and perhaps that's been my biggest mistake. Perhaps I should have lost it long ago and dragged this whole issue kicking and screaming into the light of day. But instead I did what I thought was right.' He bent his head. 'I'm sorry,' he said lamely.

Morwenna went over and knelt beside him, putting her hand on his knee.

'Don't be sorry.' Her voice was gentle. 'We'll make it right.' She made herself smile. 'It has to come right.'

And not just, she thought achingly, to clear away the shadows and bring back the joy to this old house, but to feed the vain hope that one day Dominic might look at her without hating or despising her.

She said hesitantly, 'You—you haven't told your nephew —the truth. About Barbie, I mean.'

'No,' he shook his head. 'The fewer people that know, the better. I've always felt that, as you know.' His eyes sought hers. He looked older suddenly and oddly defeated. 'Can you bear this burden with me for a little longer, child?'

'Yes,' she said at last in a low voice. They were silent for a little while, then Nick roused himself.

'I'd better return downstairs and see what's happened,' he said ruefully. 'Will you come with me?'

Morwenna shook her head. 'I think I'd rather go to my room.'

'This is your room,' he said almost sharply. 'I meant what I said. This is the room you are to occupy while you remain at Trevennon.'

'But I can't sleep here tonight,' she protested. 'The bed won't be aired for one thing—and all my things are in the other room.'

Nick stuck his chin out mulishly. 'Inez shall air the room tomorrow,' he declared. 'And I'll tell Zack to move your things along.' He got to his feet, reaching for his stick. 'There are still some of her things in the drawers,' he said abruptly. 'The nightdress you wore the first night you were here was one of them. She left some trinkets in the dressing table too which you may care to have. It's all yours, to do as you want with.' He gave her a strained smile as he moved to the door. 'And you won't be completely alone, anyway. You'll have Morwenna Trevennon to keep you company.'

She felt very cold when she was alone. She turned round, still on her knees and gazed up at the big oil-painting Nick had indicated earlier. Elegantly dressed in the fashion of a bygone age, Morwenna Trevennon sat in her high-backed chair in the classic repose that portraiture demanded, a small pet monkey nestling in the folds of her skirt. But that representation of demure restfulness was totally misleading, Morwenna knew instinctively. As soon as the artist laid down his brush for the day, the great chair would have been kicked backwards and the small velvet cap tugged off, allowing the mass of golden hair it confined to tumble over her shoulders and down her back. The girl's mouth was set in prim enough lines, but there was something about its curve which suggested that an unladylike grin would never have been too far away. But it was her eyes that were the biggest give-away. If it was true they were the mirrors of the soul, then Morwenna Trevennon's soul had been wild, wilful and full of life, as unpredictable as the sea which had been her doom.

If I was going to draw her, Morwenna thought suddenly, that's what I would aim for. I'd paint her as part of the wind and sea, daring them to do their worst to her.

She gave a little impatient sigh, realising how little her painting had meant to her since she arrived at Trevennon. She'd managed that one brief sketch on the cliffs above Spanish Cove and nothing more. If things continued like this she would have nothing to show Lennox Christie when she saw him again. But did it really matter when all she really wanted with all her heart and mind and body was here in this house? In this brief time at Trevennon, her life had changed completely. She was no longer the same girl who had come from London to ask a favour and remained to bestow one on an elderly man at the expense of her peace of mind. Why hadn't some warning voice at the time whispered to her that it was her attraction to Dominic, unwilling and unconfessed though it had been, which had prompted her to agree to stay with Nick? Why hadn't she run while she still had the chance?

She got slowly to her feet. But she hadn't run. She had stayed, and she had to accept that it was an impulse which she might well end up regretting for the rest of her life.

One thing was certain: she would not still be here when Dominic married Karen Inglis.

Even if she had been able to like Karen as a person in her own right, she could not have borne that. She looked round the room. This was how this room had been planned—as a bridal chamber, although it would probably not suit Karen. She would want to change it all, to alter the decor and choose other furniture. She would exorcise the ghosts of the past with wallpaper and paint and billowing new curtains, and relegate Morwenna's portrait to the head of the stairs.

Dominic was probably with her now, she thought flatly, placating her, wooing her back to a good humour, making amends for the hurt her aunt had suffered at his family's hands.

She shivered, trying to close out of her mind the tormenting image of Karen in Dominic's arms, her dark head pillowed against his chest, her mouth raised invitingly towards his. Her whole attitude towards him was an invitation, she thought miserably, remembering the possessive hand on his arm, the intimate way her body swayed towards him when they were standing close together. And it was no act, designed to inspire jealousy in the breasts of any onlookers. It was just the way Karen would normally behave when the man she wanted was near her. Her claim had been staked long ago, and she was making no bones about stating the fact. She was probably Dominic's mistress already and quite content to bide her time until she was mistress of Trevennon as well. The pattern had been prearranged long before Morwenna came to Cornwall—the aunt with the uncle, the nephew with the niece—until her intervention. No wonder Karen had not been able to resist the impulse to fire a few barbs at the girl whose arrival had thrown a spanner into the works of this orderly progression.

Now she might well be regretting her impetuosity, and certainly its repercussions would do nothing to endear Morwenna to her.

Morwenna walked out of the room and closed the door quietly behind her. She went along to the head of the stairs and stood listening for a moment. She could hear the sound of voices, but all the tones she could discern were masculine, so it was clear that both the Inglis women had gone home, and who could wonder at that?

She went into her own room, and undressed and got into bed. Although she had been using this room for a comparatively short time, it felt like home and the bed cradled her comfortably as if it were fond of her. Tomorrow night, she would feel like a very small pea in a very large pod, she thought ruefully, wrinkling her nose. But to please Nick she would make the move as planned.

She turned over, pillowing her cheek on her hand. Now that Nick had rediscovered his first love of boat designing, she wondered whether he would want to continue with the family history. That was something they would have to discuss, because if his interest in it was waning, it gave her an excuse to leave.

It would soon be Christmas, and the thought of spending it alone in some small bed-sitter was not an appealing one, but what else could she do? She would not be wanted here. Christmas was a family time, a time for reconciliation, and her presence would only be a barrier to this.

For a moment she considered swallowing her pride and returning to the Priory for Christmas, but she soon abandoned that idea. The thought of Cousin Patricia's air of forbearance and Vanessa's knowing smile was altogether too much to take. People said, didn't they, that half a loaf was better than no bread at all, but she was not at all sure that was true.

Money was going to be a problem, but if she left soon she might be able to get some kind of work in a department store until at least the January sales were over. Shops did look for extra personnel at times like this, she told herself, trying to feel optimistic. She would find some way of keeping herself occupied during the daytime and in the evenings she would paint until she had enough canvases to show Lennox Christie and convince him that she deserved to join his class at Carcassonne.

It was good to take hold of herself and make plans that would fill her working hours. But what she could not plan for, as the grandfather clock in the hall below signalled the passing of the night, was how she was going to be able to stop herself thinking.

She awoke from a troubled sleep very early the next morning. There had been a sharp frost during the night and the earth and trees outside her window glinted and sparkled in the sun. She knew there was no point in trying to get any more rest. She had dreamed fitfully. At one moment she seemed to be outrunning the tide in Spanish Cove, weighted down by and stumbling over the heavy skirts of her farthingale. At the next, the door to Trevennon seemed barred to her and as she beat impotently upon it with her fists, Karen Inglis, vibrant in flame coloured chiffon, laughed at her from an upstairs window.

No one else was stirring. If she got up now, the beauty of the morning would be hers alone to enjoy in peace before the inevitable problems of the day rose to engulf her.

She washed and dressed and slipped on her sheepskin jacket, winding a long woollen scarf round her head and allowing the ends to hang over her shoulders. Then she went quietly along the landing and down the stairs towards the front door. She reached up to unfasten the massive bolt at the top of the door and discovered to her surprise that it was already drawn back. So she wasn't the only early bird after all. She let herself out of the house and began to walk along the gravelled sweep which fronted it towards the cliff path.

She turned, naturally enough, when she heard the sound of the car engine, shading her eyes against the sun's dazzle. It was Dominic's car and as she stood watching as if she was rooted to the spot, it pulled up in front of the house and he got out. He was wearing the same clothes he had been wearing the previous night, only his tie was loose and the top button of his shirt unfastened. She could see the dark line of stubble on his chin.

She understood then why the bolts had been drawn—because Dominic had gone out the previous night and not come back, and it did not take the least imagination to surmise where he had spent the night. And by some ill-chance, she had to be there to witness his return. She felt the hot embarrassed colour flood her cheeks, and turned away abruptly, her booted foot scrunching the gravel. His head had been bent but at the sound he looked up sharply and saw her.

'Morwenna—wait a minute.' His voice was low-pitched, but it reached her quite distinctly in the crisp air.

For a moment she hesitated, then she hurried on as if she hadn't heard, hoping against hope that he would go indoors. But the hope was a vain one, because she could hear him coming after her, and coming fast. She felt a sudden panic rise in her and before she could regain control of herself, she took to her heels and fled. The moment she had done it, she was cursing herself inwardly for being an idiot. Just where did she think she was running to? And she hadn't bargained for how slippery the ground was in the frost. At every step, her balance was threatened so there was no way she was going to outrun him.

She stumbled on, her boots slipping and sliding on the short turf, praying that he would give up the chase and go back to the house. She would have to face him later, she know that, but not now, please not now.

But her prayer went unanswered. She slipped and went sprawling to her knees, and in that instant he caught up with her. His hands went under her armpits and she was dragged unceremoniously back to her feet and turned so that she faced him.

He looked thoroughly ill-tempered, as well he might, she supposed. His eyes were faintly bloodshot and there were deep shadows underneath them, and it was acute pain for her to have to contemplate what had caused this look of sleeplessness.

'Don't pretend you didn't hear me call to you,' he said icily. 'Why did you run away?'

There was no point in denying that she had done any such thing. She had made sufficient fool of herself already.

'I should have thought that was quite obvious,' she said, staring down at her feet.

'Not to me. You must have known I would want to talk to you.'

'There is nothing you have to say to me that I want to hear,' she said, still staring at the ground.

He gave a short angry laugh. 'I can believe that. Nevertheless, there are things that must be said. And the first is, I owe you an apology—from last night. I was damnably rude. I can only plead that I lost my temper.'

She lifted a shoulder. 'It doesn't matter.'

'Oh, but it does.' His hand reached out and gripped her chin, turning her unwilling face up to his. 'You forgave Nick for his loss of temper. Why must I be condemned to outer darkness for the same fault?'

She jerked herself free and stepped back. 'Of course I forgave Nick. I'm very fond of him.'

'And of course, you're not fond of me at all, are you, Morwenna?' He laughed softly, but his laughter held no amusement. There was an odd note in it, but she was too disturbed and confused to be able to spend time on deciphering what it might be.

'Do you really expect me to be?' Her voice trembled. 'You apologise for insulting me, but your entire attitude since we first met has been one long insult. I thought for a moment that you might be going to apologise for kissing me as you did, but I suppose as an arrogant Trevennon, you'd think any woman would be flattered by your attentions.'

Her heart was beating so thunderously she thought it must have been clearly audible as she waited for his reply. It was a long time in coming.

'Not flattered, perhaps,' he said slowly. 'But I didn't think you were completely indifferent either. Maybe we both need to refresh our memories.'

He pulled her against him so hard that the breath jerked out of her body in a startled gasp. Then his mouth crushed hers, parting her lips with cold, sensual ruthlessness, the bristles on his face rasping her soft skin. His lips explored her mouth, teasing, caressing, probing, arousing feelings and desires she had never dreamed she was capable of. Her hands, raised in last-minute panic to push him away, were trapped against his chest and the warmth of his skin through his shirt seemed to scald her palms. She tried to twist her head, to drag her mouth away from his. Her senses were reeling, screaming at her that kissing was no longer enough. She struggled to free her hands and his shirt buttons parted under her frantic efforts, allowing her fingers to spread across his bare flesh.

She could hear herself moaning softly, deep in her throat, as the relentless kiss went on and on. She couldn't breathe. She couldn't think. She was all sensation. Her arms slid slowly upwards round his neck, her fingers tangling in his dark hair, holding him to her with a new, all-encompassing possessiveness. The only barrier between them now was the clothes they stood up in and even these seemed unimportant as her slim body moved against his, her small breasts arched against the hard muscularity of his chest in a silent invitation more potent than any words.

His hands went up, wrenching her arms from around his neck, then descended to her shoulders, pushing her away, holding her literally at arms' length while he studied her face with eyes suddenly cold and unsmiling. She knew how she must look—her eyes blurred with the passion she could not control, her parted lips reddened and swollen. And in that moment she could have died of shame.

'No,' he said sardonically. 'Hardly indifferent, my Lady Morwenna. And this is one insult I have no intention of apologising for, now or ever.'

He let her go so abruptly that she almost staggered and strode away towards the house without a backward glance.

One shaking hand crept up and covered her mouth as she watched him go. She stood very still for a long time because she was afraid that if she tried to move she would fall down. Her pulses pounded and there was a throbbing ache deep inside her unsatisfied body.

When at last she was capable of movement, she turned like an automaton and continued along the path to the cliffs. The wind from the sea stung at her face and she lifted her head to it with a kind of gratitude. A voice within her seemed to be crying out in disbelief at what had just transpired, but her senses and quivering nerve endings told her that it had all been only too true.

She tried to tell herself that she only had herself to blame for the incident. She had provoked him to anger, and had brought the results of that provocation down upon herself.

'It means nothing,' she whispered. 'He was just punishing me, that's all.'

But she had known that from the moment he had taken

her in his arms, so how could she defend or excuse that shattering, trembling response to that calculated insult of a kiss? Why hadn't her pride come to her rescue? Why hadn't she been able to conceal from him the emotions that declared her his on any terms he chose to dictate? And she could have no illusions as to what those terms would be. She shivered, and automatically drew her coat further round her body, although her coldness was more mental than physical. Her body had betrayed her utterly, she thought numbly, and God alone knew what he had seen in her eyes when he had scanned her face with that cold, derisive glance.

The sound of the sea was loud in her ears and almost without being aware of what she was doing, she found her way down the steep stone steps that led to Spanish Cove, her fingers gripping the rickety wooden handrail to steady herself. The steps were slippery from the frost and normally she would not have attempted such a precarious descent, but for some inexplicable reason she knew that the beach was where she wanted to be.

The tide was well out today and she walked down over the broad band of shingle to the water's edge. She stood watching the water as it creamed and eddied only inches from her booted feet. It looked placid enough, but it was brown and cold and it hissed and gurgled over the stones and pebbles as if it was issuing a sibilant warning.

Morwenna turned and looked back up the shelving beach. In spite of the intervening years—the family picnics, the shouts of playing children searching for crabs and limpets among the rock pools—there was a brooding air about the place that spoke of unforgotten tragedy and violence. Other ships had been wrecked here beside the Spanish galleon, she thought, and there had been other deaths under these overhanging cliffs besides those of Morwenna and her lover. She shivered again and dug her hands deep into her pockets, her fingers closing round a familiar shape. She'd forgotten her sketch pad. She took it out and stood for a moment, irresolutely flicking over the pages, looking at some of her most recent work. So much had happened in the intervening period since she had made these sketches, she thought, including her own transition from girlhood to womanhood. She looked at the familiar scenes from home that her pencil had captured and felt as if she was seeing them with a stranger's eyes. They no longer seemed to have meaning or relevance.

Almost unwillingly, her fingers closed round the pencil in her other pocket. She needed something, she thought, something to keep for the rest of her life as a permanent reminder of this strange tormented morning. She crouched down out of the way of the wind in the shadow of a rock and began to draw with quick jerky movements. The lines began to form on the page as if her fingers were moving beyond the control of her brain. There was a rock—a boulder eroded into crags and pinnacles by centuries of fierce tides, and clinging to this rock was the figure of a girl, half woman, half mermaid, her hair flying behind her on some wild wind. Her shoulders hunched desperately, Morwenna Trevennon stared her last defiance at the storming sea, and as she looked at it, she realised with a sudden chill that the face she had drawn was her own.

It was one of the best pieces of work she had ever done, and how had she been capable of it when she was physically and emotionally drained? She snapped the book shut and thrust it back into her pocket. This was one piece of self-revelation that she would never dare show anyone.

Inez was waiting for her when she eventually returned to the house.

'So there you are,' she greeted her rather reproachfully. 'Mr Nick's been getting 'isself in a right old stew wondering where you were to.'

'I went for a walk and took longer over it than I intended.' Morwenna shrugged off her coat.

'Well, it's given you a bit of colour, I'll say that.' Inez studied her for a moment with embarrassing shrewdness. 'Breakfast's ready now, and Zack will be up for your bits of traps when you've finished. I'm real glad Mr Nick has opened that old room at last. Wicked waste it was, all shut up like that with no one but me to see it.'

'It's a beautiful room,' Morwenna agreed quietly. 'But it's much too large for me. I'd rather remain in my old one.'

'Never.' Inez looked at her with open scepticism. 'Why,

it don't compare with t'other one. You take it, my lover, and think yourself lucky. Besides,' she added with rather ponderous roguishness, 'mebbe it won't seem that big for too long. Mebbe there'll be someone to share it with you before you'm much older.' She nodded and moved off towards the kitchen, leaving Morwenna to gaze after her. It occurred to her that she and Dominic must have been in full view of the house while they were kissing, and the thought brought the hot blood racing into her face. It would be unbearable if Inez in her innocence started dropping broad hints that she had designs on Dominic. She would have to do something to convince her that this was not the case, and quickly.

It took a lot of courage to push open the dining room door and walk in, but Mark, to her relief, was the only member of the family present.

'Oh, hello,' he said rather awkwardly. 'How are you this morning?'

She slid into a seat. 'Average,' she remarked lightly. 'And you?'

He shook his head. 'Completely out of my depth. Just what was the purpose of all that last night?'

Morwenna shrugged. 'You'd better ask Nick,' she replied shortly. 'It was his idea, not mine.'

Mark grinned faintly. 'I can accept that. You looked as shattered as the rest of us, or even more so.' He shook his head. 'But I felt sorry for Barbie. If Nick had slapped her across the face, she couldn't have been more shocked. Karen had to drive her home—she simply wasn't capable of handling the car herself. I really thought she was going to cry at one point, and I've never ever seen her shed a tear in all the years I've known her.' He sighed. 'I'm afraid Nick is going to regret that piece of hastiness.'

Morwenna bit her lip. 'Not nearly as much as I do,' she said half to herself.

'Well, no one blames you,' said Mark, trying to be consoling. 'And I've got a piece of news to cheer you up. How would you like to go out to supper tonight?'

'With you?' Morwenna was surprised.

'Would it be such an unheard-of thing?' he asked a little defensively. 'Yes—with me, although that's incidental.

We've been invited to St Enna. Biddy rang up last night to invite you, only you were in your room and I didn't like to disturb you under the circumstances. And as I took the message, she invited me as well.'

'I'm sure that wasn't the sole reason,' Morwenna said drily, and he flushed.

'Well, maybe not.' He looked down at the table, fiddling with his knife. 'If you'd like to go, it might be as well not to mention it around the place.'

'So what do we do?' Morwenna raised her eyebrows. 'Steal out of the house separately under cover of darkness?'

'No,' Mark said impatiently. 'I'll just say I'm taking you out to dinner. If—people think we're going to the Towers in Port Vennor, so much the better.'

'By people, I suppose you mean your brother.' Morwenna gave him a long look, and after a moment he nodded. She chose her words carefully. 'It's none of my business, I know, but perhaps if you're so—conscious of his opinion you should let me go to St Enna on my own this evening.'

Mark's lips tightened as he poured himself more coffee. 'It's not as simple as that. I suppose Biddy must have told you that we were—seeing each other.'

'Yes, she did.'

He stirred sugar into his coffee. 'I don't know what else she told you. In many ways I'd rather not know. She could be bitter, but then if she was she would never let me see it. She sounded the same as ever on the phone. A little quiet when she realised she was speaking to me, that's all.'

'I know that you were seeing her, and Dom—and your brother put a stop to it.' Morwenna tried to keep her voice free of censure, but she saw Mark wince slightly.

'And you're wondering how I could have been so weak-kneed as to let him?' He gave her a wry glance. 'I can understand that. I've often wondered myself. It's just that all my life I seem to have been surrounded by quarrels and bitterness. I didn't want my relationship with Biddy to start off in the same way, so I decided to take the line of least resistance—to go along on the surface with what Dominic said, yet try and win him round over Biddy over a period of time.' He gave a short laugh. 'It didn't work. Even Biddy couldn't see what I was trying to do. I hurt her,

I know I did. I went round there to try and explain and she showed me the door.'

'But didn't you discuss it with her beforehand?'

'No,' Mark admitted. 'It all happened rather suddenly. I wasn't even aware Dominic knew I was taking her out. But someone had told him.' He frowned. 'I don't have to guess who.'

'Karen Inglis,' Morwenna suggested.

The frown deepened. 'Right. I don't know what she said, but she poisoned his mind against Biddy. You see, before they came to St Enna, Greg, her brother, used to belong to an artists' commune near St Ives. I don't know the whole story, but there was a drugs raid and a lot of them were charged with possession and other things. The commune broke up after that. Greg's pretty tight-lipped over the whole business, so I can't say how much he was involved, but I've never seen any trace of pot smoking or anything else at St Enna. And Biddy was never at the commune at all. She was still at art college in London when all this happened. I can only think Karen got hold of some distorted version of the facts and repeated them to Dominic. He's pretty down on the whole drugs scene anyway, and he'd already clashed with Greg over some planning permission for an extension at the pottery, so there was no love lost there. And he also said with a fair amount of justice that so far I hadn't shown a great deal of staying power in my romantic attachments, and that my main attraction to Biddy was the fact that she was—different from the girls I usually took out.'

He smiled ruefully. 'I was a great one for surface glamour, and that's not Biddy. But there's warmth and a peace about her that I need. I tried to explain this to Dominic, but he wouldn't listen. He just took it for granted that I'd become infatuated with some kind of hippy and that because of her I would drop out and start taking drugs or some weird thing.' He sighed. 'I can see his point in a way. The Trevennons have always had a reputation for wildness. As you've no doubt discovered from working with Nick, there are a lot of question marks hanging over the past, and a lot of skeletons in the family cupboards. Dominic's worked damned hard—and Nick and my father before him—to redeem that image. Communities like this have long memories. We have to convince everyone that we no longer wreck boats—we build them instead.'

Morwenna shook her head. 'I had no idea the sense of the past was so strong.'

He shrugged. 'Why should you? After all, you don't know us very well yet.'

His words suggested that she would be at Trevennon long enough to make all the discoveries that were needful, and she was grateful to him for that. She could see that in many ways it would have been this sense of the past that had fascinated Laura Kerslake and kept her looking back nostalgically to her childhood. But Laura had recognised that there was also a world of reality as represented by Robert Kerslake and the calm safety of his love, and she had opted for this in the end.

And what will happen when I leave here? Morwenna asked herself. Will I too be always looking back over my shoulder, remembering the dark cliffs and the wild sea and the arrogance of men who built a house to stand for hundreds of years in the teeth of the wind?

And even as she formulated the thought, she knew that above and beyond everything else she would remember one man all her life and the hot, sweet danger of his lovemaking that held no love at all.

She ate the food Inez put in front of her because in some ways it was less trouble to do that than to argue about it, although she had no appetite. When she had finished her meal, she went listlessly upstairs to transfer her belongings back into her suitcase so that they could be moved to Laura's room. That was how she thought of it. There was no way in which she could relate the possession of such a room to herself.

While she was waiting for the grumbling Zack to bring her things along, she wandered round it, examining everything more closely. There were cut glass scent and cosmetic jars on the dressing table, and a pretty glass tree on which to hang rings, she supposed, only her hands were bare. She remembered Nick had said there were some trinkets in the dressing table and found them without difficulty. There was not a great deal—a small silver cross and chain, a necklace made out of shells, some coral ear-rings, and a ring to hang on her tree—a pretty thing made out of pearls. She tried it on and it fitted, and as she looked down on it she remembered that people said pearls were for tears, but surely she had cried enough.

Then the door opened and Zack entered, weighed down by a strong sense of grievance as well as her case and rucksack and an unwieldy brown paper parcel.

'Troublin' folks and botherin' 'un, and turning the 'ole 'ouse upside down,' he muttered truculently as he dumped the case down on the carpet. He produced a hammer and some picture hooks from inside his waistcoat and fixed her with a stern look. 'And now I s'pose you'll be wanting these hung up.' He indicated the brown paper parcel which he had put down on the bed.

In spite of her emotional state, Morwenna had to suppress a giggle. The more she saw of Zack, the more impossible it seemed that there could be any kind of relationship between him and the cheerful outgoing Inez.

'I'm sorry,' she apologised meekly. 'I realise I'm giving a great deal of trouble. What's in that parcel?'

'Them pictures you brought when you come here. Been at the framers in Penzance, they have, and now you'll be wanting them up.'

She pulled off the string and the layers of brown paper with fingers that shook. It was quite true, they were her mother's paintings, surrounded by antique frames which became them far better than the original ones at the Priory. She had wondered several times what had become of them, but had not liked to ask Nick, thinking that perhaps he had put them away somewhere because he found the sight of them painful still. But instead he had sent them to be framed somewhere as a surprise for her. She felt tears prick at the back of her eyelids and wiped them away with her fist as a child might do.

'Mr Nick had these done for me,' she said slowly. 'I didn't know....'

Zack snorted. 'Tidn't the only thing you don't know, by the sound of it. Where do you want 'un? I got other things to do 'sides this.'

It wasn't too difficult to decide. She got Zack to arrange them on an otherwise bare wall above a little jewel of a chest of drawers, just where the first morning light would catch them. They looked right there. They belonged, and perhaps in time they would make her feel as if she belonged too.

Long after Zack had gone, she stood staring at them, thinking of her mother and wondering what she would say if she knew where her pictures had ended up. And yet wasn't this the whole purpose of her being here? She had come to ask the Trevennons to protect her sole inheritance, and her wish had been granted.

She heard the door behind her open quietly and thought she knew who had come to see how his gift had been received. She took a long, trembling breath, aware that there were tears on her face.

'Nick, you're so good to me. I can never thank you enough....' As she turned to face him, her voice faltered and died. It was Dominic. He took a half step forward, then halted, his face like a dark mask as he saw how she instinctively recoiled from his approach.

'What's the matter?' he asked abruptly. 'Why are you upset?'

'It's nothing. No, that's not true—it's everything.' She spread out her hands in an all-encompassing gesture. 'It's this room—and her ring—and now Nick's even had her pictures framed for me. It's as if she were here—with me. Oh, I can't expect you to understand.'

'No,' he said drily, 'you can't, can you? I came to talk to you, but I can see it isn't the right moment.'

There is nothing you have to say to me that I want to hear. Brave words. Words of defiance, and now singularly inappropriate for some reason she could not even define to herself.

'No, it isn't,' she said, and her voice was ragged. 'There'll never be a right moment for us. Now if you have the slightest mercy, go and for God's sake leave me in peace.'

He made a half-movement and she tensed, willing him with all her strength not to approach her. If he touched her, if he took her into his arms she would break into little pieces. She had asked for mercy and peace because that was all she had the right to ask for. She could not ask for love.

She closed her eyes and waited and when she opened them at last, she was alone. And when she whispered, 'Oh, Dominic. Oh, my love,' there was no one to hear her.

CHAPTER EIGHT

MORWENNA fixed the last glittering glass bauble in place, then alighted from the small step-ladder and took a long, appraising look at the Christmas tree. She'd had to fight hard enough to get it here, so she was determined that it was going to look right in its corner of the sitting room.

Mark had taken a lot of persuading before he had agreed to tie it to the roof of the Mini and drive it home from Penzance where they had been doing some belated Christmas shopping.

'A Christmas tree.' She could recall the scepticism in his voice. 'In a bachelor household? Have a heart, love! It'll go down like a lead balloon.'

'Just a tree,' she had told him solemnly, her eyes dancing nevertheless. 'And I promise to forgo the paper chains and the mistletoe.'

'Oh, I don't object to mistletoe.' He had pretended to leer at her, and she'd laughed.

She had spent a lot of time with Mark over the past few weeks. So much so that Nick had asked her rather gruffly if she was sure she knew what she was doing.

'He likes to play the field, young Mark,' he told her, his brow furrowed, and again she had laughed and bent over to drop an affectionate kiss on the top of his head. Because she knew that Mark's days as a Lothario were past and done for ever.

Ever since, in fact, that first supper party they had been invited to at St Enna. She had sensed Mark's nervousness as they drove there. It was a low rambling building—two cottages knocked into one—and Biddy had answered the door to their knock. Morwenna had seen them look at each other and although nothing had been said, she knew that all was well.

Biddy had been her usual cheerful self, with a spot more colour in her cheeks than usual. She had served a delicious chicken casserole, piquant with herbs and wine, and they had all drunk Greg's home-brewed lager and grown steadily more hilarious as the evening progressed. Later she had helped Greg, tall, bearded and taciturn, to wash up in the tiny kitchen, leaving Mark and Biddy alone together.

Since that night she had spent a lot of her time at St Enna, even when Mark did not accompany her. It was a relaxed and undemanding atmosphere, and she was always sure of her welcome. She had even made a thumb pot under Greg's supervision, and it had been baked in the kiln with his own work and glazed, and she was proud of the way it had turned out. Biddy had said she had a natural flair for pottery and Greg had promised he would show her how to throw a pot on the wheel in the workshop, if she was interested. And she was more than interested, she was fascinated. She liked the feel of the clay under her fingers, and she loved sitting and watching the pots and utensils grow and take shape under Greg's hands. And, more importantly, it gave her something else to think about.

She told Greg and Biddy about her ambition to study under Lennox Christie and Biddy stared at her wide-eyed.

'Why go to those lengths?' she demanded. 'There are good art schools all over the place, including Cornwall. You could even get a grant. And who says you're meant to be a painter anyway?'

Perhaps Biddy might be hoping that when she and Mark were married, Morwenna might take her place at the pottery with Greg. If so, it was a vain hope. She couldn't confide in Biddy, because Biddy loved Mark and had no secrets from him, and she couldn't risk Mark finding out that she was hopelessly and desperately in love with his brother. Meaning well, he might choose to interfere, and her blood ran cold at the thought. No, her secret was safe with just herself. And if everyone thought that her heart was set on Mark, then so much the better. By the time the truth came out, she could be miles away.

Even Inez had issued a dark warning that 'Mr Mark was a rare one for the maidens', although her general attitude had suggested that Morwenna could do worse than join him in gathering rosebuds while they both might.

As for Dominic. ... Morwenna sighed as she bent to pick an errant piece of tinsel from the carpet. No one would be prepared to hazard a guess as to what he thought about the situation. It was impossible to suppose that he approved of her going out with Mark night after night, but he made no comment at all to either of them. But she noticed that no matter how late they returned from their outings, there was always a thin streak of light showing under the study door. Was he really working there alone, she wondered, or was he monitoring her comings and goings? She smiled bitterly to herself. If he silently objected to her going out with Mark, it was not hard to imagine his anger when he discovered the true state of affairs. She had little doubt in her own mind that Mark would choose the line of least resistance and take Biddy off to the nearest register office early in the New Year, presenting Dominic with a *fait accompli*.

She gave her tree a last look and prepared to leave the room. It seemed to light up the whole room, she thought, and perhaps the star she had wired to the topmost branch was a star of hope, after all, for Mark and Biddy at least.

There did not seem to be a great deal of hope for Nick and Barbie. Barbie had not been near Trevennon since the night of the dinner party, and according to a terse remark from Nick, Morwenna gathered that she had not been to work either at the boatyard, pleading illness.

But Karen, in spite of what had happened, had been much in evidence. She had obviously decided to overlook the fact that it was her own ill-natured behaviour which had triggered off the entire incident and behaved to everyone with an air of tolerance and Christian forgiveness which sent Nick limping hurriedly for sanctuary in his room whenever she appeared at Trevennon. Morwenna, she appeared not to notice whenever possible, and Morwenna was content for it to be so.

As she set her hand on the door-knob, her heart sank. She was sure she had heard Karen's voice outside in the hall. She hesitated for a moment, uncertain whether to go or stay and hope that she remained undisturbed, then pushed the door open and stepped out into the hall.

Karen was there and she was with Dominic. They were standing very close together, as if he had been just about to take her in his arms or had just released her from his embrace. Morwenna could not be sure, and she wished with all her heart that she had stayed in the sitting room behind the closed door and not been an unwilling witness of this intimate moment.

Dominic looked across the hall and their glances met and locked.

'Hello, Morwenna,' he greeted her evenly, without embarrassment. 'I'm going to find Inez and ask her to produce some coffee for us. Do you want some?'

'No, thank you.' She made a slight gesture towards the room she had just left. 'I'm just clearing up, and then I'll be out of your way.'

His lips tightened slightly. 'I wasn't aware that you were in my way,' he said tautly, and disappeared in the direction of the kitchen.

'What have you got there?' Karen gave the box of leftover tinsel and other baubles a disdainful look.

'Christmas decorations,' Morwenna returned. 'It is Christmas Eve tomorrow, you know.'

'I hadn't forgotten.' Karen smiled suddenly, a wide self-satisfied smile, like a cat who had got hold of the cream. Indeed, Morwenna thought judiciously, she was rather like a cat, with her small well-shaped head and her lean grace. A cat with sharp claws and little compunction about using them.

Karen walked past her, brushing her rudely out of the way—something she would not have done, Morwenna realised detachedly, if Dominic had been present to observe her.

'Oh, my God,' she said in tones of utter disgust. 'Whose idea was this vulgar display?'

Morwenna held on to her temper with an effort. 'Mine. Don't you like Christmas trees?'

'In their place,' Karen conceded. 'In town squares and hotel foyers. I don't think there's any place for one in a house like this. To me this room's always had a certain ambience—a quiet dignity. Whatever possessed you to cover it in tinsel and pine needles? I'm sure Inez won't thank you.'

'Inez was very much in favour.' Morwenna suppressed an involuntary smile remembering how Inez had nagged and chivvied a very reluctant Zack into finding a suitable receptacle in which to plant the tree.

'I see.' Karen smiled again, thinly. 'But then Inez has always been a little—arbitrary in her likes and dislikes. I wouldn't like any small successes you may have had with her to go to your head. She is only the housekeeper here—an employee like yourself, whatever delusions dear Nick may choose to foster in you both.' Her glance went derisively to the tree once more. 'And what prompted this? A desire to pander to poor Nick's second childhood?'

Morwenna said with commendable restraint, 'I should be careful, if I were you. I wouldn't allow Dominic to hear me talk about his uncle like that.'

'Oh, I'm sure you wouldn't—but then our positions are somewhat different. This is not going to be your permanent home, and you're not going to be the mistress here.'

'And you are?' Morwenna forced out of a dry throat. The fact that a blow was expected did not lessen its impact, she discovered. She felt sick at heart, and conscious of an unholy desire to smack the mocking triumph off the lovely face confronting her.

'Yes.' There was a wealth of quiet satisfaction in the monosyllable. 'And of course Dominic appreciates that I shall want some changes made. After all, a newly married couple will hardly want to share their home with a number of other people. And Inez, of course, is devoted to Nick. I can hardly imagine she'll want to stay on here when he leaves.'

Morwenna shook her head disbelievingly. 'You'd turn Nick out of his home? You couldn't do such a thing! He's an elderly man. He's been ill.'

Karen's lips twisted. 'He's made practically a complete recovery. He could live for years,' she said coldly. 'I don't intend to begin my married life in his shadow. He still likes to pretend he's master here, and it's a situation I'm not prepared to tolerate.'

'And—and Dominic agrees with you.'

'Dominic is in love with me,' Karen stated with finality. 'He won't deny me anything I ask for.' She gave a brief complacent smile, then her eyes swept coldly over Morwenna. 'And I'm afraid you'll have to look for a new sanctuary, Miss Kerslake, and a new sinecure. Your days here are numbered, believe me.'

'I'm already well aware of that.' The words were costing her pain, but they had to be said. 'I intend to leave anyway —in the New Year.'

'And go where?' Karen's eyes narrowed. 'Or do you propose to hang about locally and hope that Nick will take pity on you again when he moves to his new home?'

'No,' Morwenna said levelly. 'I shall go to London and work until the spring. Then I hope to go to Carcassonne to join a private painting class.'

'A private class?'

Morwenna nodded. 'With Lennox Christie.'

'My word!' Karen looked at her with suddenly sharpened interest. 'We are flying high. And how do you propose to find the fees for this little expedition? Out of your earnings as a working girl, or were you planning to inveigle Nick into unfastening the family purse strings for you?' She laughed. 'Good God, I do believe that's it! Well, you're wasting your time, my dear. Every penny they possess is invested in that decrepit boatyard. Can't you see that from the state of this house? It hasn't had anything spent on it in years, not since Dominic's parents died. There are no rich pickings for you here, I'm afraid, however much a nuisance you make of yourself. No one in this family can afford to buy you off.'

Morwenna's hands itched to throw the box she was holding in Karen's insulting face.

She said very quietly, 'Please don't lose any sleep over it, Miss Inglis. There's an old saying—where there's a will, there's a way. I'll make out, I promise.'

She walked along the hall and went up the stairs, without looking back. Her heart was thudding, and she felt slightly sick. Did Dominic know, she wondered, the depth of malice in his future wife, or was he so enthralled by her attractive exterior that nothing else mattered? The thought caused her physical pain.

Nick's door was open as she passed and he glanced up from his desk and hailed her. 'Did I hear Karen arrive just now?'

'Yes, she's staying for coffee.'

'Then I'm staying here,' Nick growled. 'Shut the door and come here. I've something to show you.'

He opened the desk drawer and produced a sheet of paper. 'This came this morning while you were out,' he said with obvious satisfaction. 'Read it.'

It was from Alan Hewitt-Smyth, and it was an invitation to Nick to submit his design for the *Lady Morwenna* to the trustees of the sponsorship fund who were backing him.

'They are already more than interested in what I've been able to tell them,' the letter ran. 'Perhaps we can arrange a meeting early in the New Year to put the project on a firm footing.' It ended with cordial good wishes to the other members of the family and was signed 'Alan'.

'Oh, Nick!' She hugged him impulsively. 'That's great news.'

He tried not to look to delighted. 'Well, it isn't finally settled. There's a great deal to discuss, and a lot of work to be done first. But if it all works out—child, it could be the start of a new era for Trevennon Marine. Because the *Lady Morwenna* is going to be only the first. Where Hewitt-Smyth goes, others will follow. We have the know-how and the craftsmanship right here. Now all we need is the opportunity.'

Morwenna gave him an affectionate smile. 'If the decision was mine, Nick, you'd have the contract now. You're a good salesman.'

He shook his head. 'That's Dominic's job, and one he's going to relish.' He threw back his head. 'God, but it feels good to have something hopeful to tell the boy. He can take over the negotiations from now on, and leave me free to work on the design and supervise the building.' He picked up the letter and replaced it in the drawer. 'I feel as if someone had given me a new lease of life.' He looked at her sharply. 'What's the matter, girl?'

'Nothing,' she lied, burdened by her knowledge of Karen's callousness. 'I—I'm just happy for you.'

'No, there's something else. Is it young Mark?'

'No!' Her denial was almost explosive and he relaxed with a faintly sheepish grin.

'Well, thank heavens for that. Then what is it?'

She bent her head. 'It's time I was moving on, Nick,' she

said in a subdued voice. 'You've got your boatbuilding now. You won't want to continue with the family history under the circumstances. I only agreed to stay as long as I could help. Well, my help isn't needed any longer, and I need to get away from here—make some sort of life for myself.'

He was silent for a few minutes. Then he said gruffly, 'I thought you had a life here, my dear. I thought you were happy.'

'Oh, I was. I am.' She was thankful that he believed this, and had never guessed at the truth which tortured her. 'But I can't stay here for ever. That wasn't part of the arrangement.'

He smiled rather grimly. 'I wasn't aware there had been an arrangement. I'd always assumed, selfishly, that you'd stay here as long as I needed you. And lately I'd thought that you would at least see the *Lady Morwenna* launched.'

Her hands tightened round each other, and she stared down at them blindly. 'Nick, I can't. Please don't ask it of me.'

There was another silence, then he said, 'And what of Barbie? That situation hasn't been resolved yet.'

'No. But if I go, she'll soon come round again. Everything will just return to normal.'

That would be the answer in some ways, she thought. Karen installed here in sole sway, and Nick moving to the square Georgian house on the hill overlooking Port Vennor which Mark had pointed out to her as the Inglis house.

'No,' he shook his head decisively. 'I gambled on her reactions to various moves of mine, and failed. Things will never be the same again, and I wouldn't want them to be.'

Morwenna smiled with an effort. 'Still hoping for her total capitulation, Nick?'

He sighed. 'I'm hoping for damned little these days, my girl. We'll see. If she comes to dinner on Christmas Eve, I'll know there's some hope left.'

'Christmas Eve?' She gave him a swift enquiring look, and he nodded.

'It's almost become a tradition. She's dined here each Christmas without fail for the past twenty years. And Karen with her, of course, once she was old enough.'

'And you think she won't come this time—because I'm here.'

'I don't know, child. And I doubt if she even knows herself.' He sounded tired and defeated suddenly, all the optimism that the news about *Lady Morwenna* had engendered now missing from his voice. He had been lonely, she thought, before she came, and he would be lonely again. And he might have some idea of Karen's plans for the future.

On her way to her own room, she encountered Mark.

'I'm going over to St Enna after dinner,' he greeted her without preamble. 'Do you fancy coming? From what I can gather, the lovely Karen is staying to dinner and giving us the pleasure of her company afterwards, and that's something I can well do without.'

She nodded. 'I'd like that. And it's Christmas Eve the day after tomorrow, so we should make the most of what time we have. It'll be difficult for you to get out to see Biddy over the next few days. They—they will rather expect us to be here, won't they?'

He shrugged. 'I can't say that Dominic has ever displayed a great deal of interest as to where I've spent my time, and how, in other years. But perhaps with romance on his own mind this year, he'll be keeping a closer eye on me.'

'Perhaps,' she said. Then, 'What makes you think he has romance on his mind particularly?'

Mark shrugged. 'Just the way he's been behaving lately. And, of course, the ring.'

'Ring?'

'Mother's engagement ring. One of the few family heirlooms we have left. Apparently, according to Inez, he's had it to the jewellers in Penzance to be cleaned and made smaller.' He gave a short sigh. 'So it looks as if there's going to be a big announcement at the Christmas Eve dinner. No doubt they're using that as a lever to persuade Barbie to come out of her seclusion as well. From what I can gather, there's been a message to say we're not to expect her, but if there's going to be an engagement party as well....'

'Yes,' she said numbly. 'Something to celebrate as a family.'

'Right,' he said. 'And it might not be the only thing.' He winked at her and went off whistling.

Dinner that evening was not the easiest of meals, although Karen was exerting herself to be charming. She had even managed to smile her agreement and murmur something complimentary when Nick had bestowed lavish praise on Morwenna's efforts with the Christmas tree. Dominic had merely slanted a sardonic glance at it and made no comment at all.

Nor did he make any remark when Mark announced at the end of the meal that he was taking Morwenna for a drive.

'Mind how you go,' Nick bade him sharply. 'The roads are icy, according to the weather forecast.'

'Oh, I'll take care,' Mark smiled easily. 'After all, why take risks just when I've so much to live for?'

The silence which greeted the laughing remark was suddenly electric and Morwenna felt her face flush as she rose hurriedly to her feet, murmuring that she would get her coat. Everyone round the table naturally assumed that Mark was alluding to his relationship with her. And the allusion, she could see, had been received with enthusiasm by no one. Karen's face wore fleetingly a mixture of surprise and hostility. Nick looked thoroughly displeased, and although Dominic's face was enigmatic, when he raised his eyes and looked at her she almost recoiled from the expression of cold anger she saw in them.

When they were in the car, she said angrily to Mark, 'What on earth possessed you to say such a thing? Now they think it's me....'

He grinned unrepentantly. 'Yes, I rather think they did. Let them stew for a bit. It will do them good. And they'll soon know differently, anyway.'

'Maybe, but you don't make life very easy for me with remarks like that,' she said unhappily. 'Dominic thinks badly of me as it is, and....'

He gave her a sideways look. 'Tell you what, my sweet, I think you're altogether too sensitive about Brother Dominic and his opinions. You're as bad as Biddy. Just play it cool and wait for Christmas Eve.'

'And what's going to happen then?' she asked wearily, her mind flinching from the possibility that Mark had already suggested.

He gave her an enigmatic grin. 'Wait and see.' And she was too dispirited to press him further.

At Biddy's there was hot punch to sample, and the first mince pies to make a wish over. Morwenna only pretended to wish. She couldn't fix her mind on the sort of festive trivialities required, and she knew at the same time that no traditional ritual could work the magic necessary to bring her her heart's desire.

Mark, however, had no such inhibitions. He made his wish aloud.

'I wish, Biddy my love, that you and Greg would come to Trevennon to dine on Christmas Eve.'

'Now that's plain silly,' Biddy said flatly.

'On the contrary.' He took her hand. 'I think the time is more than ripe to apprise the family of my intentions. And what better opportunity than Christmas, the time of goodwill. Especially as Dom will probably be announcing his own engagement at the same time. We can wish each other joy.' He grimaced. 'Seriously, love, he couldn't possibly make a scene, even if he wanted to, at such a time. And there's no reason why he should want to. He's doing what he wants to do. He can't hope to deny me the same privilege.'

Biddy's mouth set obstinately. 'I'm not going to Trevennon on sufferance—on a wave of possibly non-existent Christmas spirit,' she said bluntly. 'If your brother accepts the fact that we're going to be married, and invites us himself, that's a different matter. But I refuse to be produced at the family dinner table like a—rabbit out of a hat.'

And none of Mark's arguments that attack was the best form of defence, and that shock tactics were the best way of dealing with Dominic, affected her attitude one jot. By the time that Mark and Morwenna left, well after midnight, there was still deadlock. Mark was insisting stubbornly that he would be over to fetch them willy-nilly on Christmas Eve, and Biddy reiterating that there was no way she could be persuaded to cross the threshold at Trevennon without a proper invitation from the master of the house.

'I just don't understand her,' Mark fumed as they drove away. 'I thought she'd be delighted that I was taking the bull by the horns at last.'

'Not if she suspects that she'll be impaled on them first,' Morwenna said drily. 'Don't forget I have first-hand experience of your brother's treatment of unwelcome guests, and it isn't pleasant.'

'That's true,' Mark admitted. 'On the other hand, he wouldn't treat Biddy like that. In fact I can never remember him being quite so hostile towards anyone as he has been to you.'

'Thank you,' Morwenna said bitterly. 'Am I supposed to be flattered because I'm the exception to the rule?'

He gave her an anxious look. 'I didn't mean to upset you. I mean, sparks do tend to fly when you're near each other. In fact I've sometimes wondered. . . .' His voice broke off abruptly.

'Wondered what?' Morwenna prompted.

'Oh, nothing,' he said vaguely. 'Forget it. It's not important. Do you think we're going to have snow for Christmas? It's certainly cold enough.'

They talked stiltedly about impersonal matters until they arrived back at the house. Morwenna waited while he put the car away, then they walked together round the house to the front door. The air was clear and frosty and the stars looked very close.

'Huge, aren't they?' Mark took her arm companionably. 'I used to wonder when I was a kid how the Wise Men knew which one to follow.' He was silent for a moment. Then he said abruptly, 'If Biddy feels so strongly about Christmas Eve, I'll have to respect her wishes. I'll see Dominic tomorrow and tell him that I've invited both her and Greg to dinner, and the reason. And if he says one wrong word about either of them, then I'll pack my things and go to St Enna, not just for Christmas but until Biddy and I are married. After that we'll find somewhere in Port Vennor to live.'

Morwenna smiled at him. 'I'm sure that's the right decision. Don't delay the wedding too long, either. I—I shall be leaving here early in the New Year—in fact next week, probably—but I would like to be one of the guests.'

'You shall,' he promised. 'In fact you can probably be a witness along with Greg.'

'I should like that.' She smiled up at him as he closed and bolted the door, and he smiled back and bent to kiss her lightly on the lips.

'Bless you, love,' he said quietly. 'Bless you for everything.'

She was going to protest that she'd done nothing, but there was a noise just behind them and she turned to see what it was, as Mark's arm fell from her waist. The door to the study stood open and Dominic's dark figure stood directly in the shaft of light that spread into the hall. Morwenna couldn't see his face, but anyway it was unnecessary. She could feel his anger as if it were a tangible thing spreading across the intervening space to crush her.

Mark said easily, 'Oh, hello, Dom. I didn't realise you were still up.'

'Obviously,' Dominic said icily. 'I'm sorry if I've intruded on one of your love scenes.'

He turned on his heel and walked back into the study, slamming the door shut behind him. Morwenna felt the colour rush into her face.

Mark said, 'Oh, hell,' in a tone between resignation and exasperation. He took a step forward. 'Look—I'll go and explain now....'

'No.' Morwenna was adamant. 'He's in a temper now. It isn't a good moment. Wait until the morning when he's had time to cool down.'

Mark gave a short sigh. 'I suppose so. Damnation, why did he have to come out just then? If I'd caught him in a clinch with Karen—or anyone else for that matter—I would tiptoe tactfully away. But no, he has to make a big deal out of it. But why? That's what I don't understand.' He looked down at Morwenna's unhappy face and his own eyes were suddenly reflective. Yet all he said was, 'I think we'd better remove ourselves. Maybe we'll all see things in a clearer and calmer light in the morning.'

Lying sleepless in her bed, Morwenna doubted it. She rolled over and switched on the bedside lamp and looked at the small gilt clock on the table beside the bed. Nearly two in the morning and she hadn't closed her eyes. She gave a slight groan and buried her face in the pillow. She had never needed sleeping pills in her young healthy life, but she would have given a great deal for one to have materialised by her bedside now. Perhaps a drink would help, she thought. Something warm and milky.

She got out of bed and put on her housecoat, tying the sash securely round her slim waist, then trod barefoot over to the door. She listened intently for a moment or two, but the house was completely still. She was the only person wakeful, it seemed. She went lightly along the landing and felt her way down the stairs into the dark of the hall. She gave a hasty glance in the direction of the study door, but although it was still shut, no thread of light showed beneath it and she gave a silent sigh of relief as she made her way to the kitchen.

The door creaked slightly as she opened it and she heard the dogs, who slept on the mat in front of the Aga in winter, stir and growl slightly. She spoke to them quietly as she switched on the light, and they subsided. She had to admit that they had given her no trouble at all since that day in the barn. Dominic's solution to her problem might have been ruthless, and had certainly contributed to her current sleeplessness, but as far as the dogs were concerned it had been a success.

She found a jug of milk in the pantry and a tin of drinking chocolate, and began to heat her drink. The dogs watched her efforts, wagging their tails and grinning sheepishly at her, as if bemused by this early start to their day.

She poured the hot milk into a beaker and stirred the chocolate into it. The dogs were really restless now and she heard Whisky whine softly, and scolded, 'Lie down, you idiots.' It was then, and only then, that she realised she was no longer alone. Dominic was lounging in the doorway. One of his hands was thrust negligently into his pants' pocket. The other held a glass.

She went on stirring the chocolate although the powder had already dissolved by that time.

'Oh, hello,' she said awkwardly. 'I'm sorry if I disturbed you. I couldn't sleep. Would—would you like some chocolate?'

'Thank you—no.' He held up the glass so that she could

see the level of amber liquid it still contained. 'I prefer to seek my oblivion in other ways.'

There was a strange glitter in his eyes as they met hers and she found herself wondering rather uneasily how much he had drunk. Yet he seemed steady on his feet and his speech wasn't slurred in the slightest, so perhaps she was doing him an injustice.

She went on rather desperately, 'I—I thought everyone had gone to bed. All the lights were off and....'

'There's a fire in the study,' he interrupted. 'I had some thinking to do and firelight is as good a medium as any to do it by. Come and join me.'

'No, thanks.' She picked up the beaker rather unsteadily, praying that she would not actually spill any of it on the floor. 'I must be getting back to my room. It's late and I'm tired.'

'You said you couldn't sleep,' he reminded her. He reached out and took her arm. His fingers were firm and bruising on her flesh and he meant it. 'Come and join me.'

She lifted her chin defiantly. 'Couldn't you choose a slightly more civilised hour to torment me?'

He smiled grimly. 'No doubt I could, but I'm not feeling too civilised at the moment, and anyway it occurs to me that one of these days you may vanish as suddenly as you arrived before I've had the chance so say any of the things I mean to say to you. So I'll say them now, while you're here, under my hand.'

An uncontrollable shiver went through her as the significance of his words came home to her. For a moment she toyed with the idea of flinging the hot chocolate all over him, but even as the idea crossed her mind, he said quite gently, as if her thoughts were an open book to him, 'I wouldn't, Morwenna. I really wouldn't.' She trailed mutinously behind him across the dark hall to the study. He kicked the door shut behind them and led her over to the sofa in front of the fire.

Releasing her, 'Sit down,' he ordered, and knelt down beside the hearth, adding fresh logs to the glowing embers and stirring them to a blaze.

Morwenna clamped her hands round the warmth of the beaker, and stared at the dancing flames. They might take away the chill which had invaded her physical being, but nothing could ease the trembling within her.

'He frightens me,' she thought, and in the same moment, 'and I frighten myself when I'm with him.'

She raised the beaker to her lips and drank some of the chocolate, lowering the long fringe of her lashes on to her cheeks in case he was watching her and saw that sudden piece of self-knowledge revealed in her eyes.

'You said you wanted to talk to me,' she reminded him haltingly, as he rose to his feet, dusting his hands.

He gave her an unsmiling look. 'I hadn't forgotten.'

He looked very tall as he stood in the leaping firelight, and Morwenna had to resist an impulse to shrink back further into her corner of the sofa. Instead she took another hurried sip at her chocolate.

He said suddenly and roughly, 'You look like a child with your hair down your back like that. And that dressing gown. Did you have it at boarding school?'

She flushed slightly, wondering whether she should remind him that it had not been all that long ago that she had been at boarding school, and again as if he could read her thoughts, he said, 'But you are only a child, aren't you, Morwenna? A spoiled impulsive child who doesn't realise the damage she can do to people's feelings.'

She set the beaker down on the table behind the sofa. 'That isn't fair.'

'I'm not feeling in a fair mood. And I state only the situation as I see it. Karen told us tonight that her aunt will not be dining with us on Christmas Eve. The polite fiction is that she isn't well enough to come. The reality is that she's been in love with Nick for years, only you and he between you have revived—apparently deliberately—all kinds of unhappy memories for her. In God's name, why? So that you can justify your presence here in some strange way? Or are you still determined to prove that your mother was the victim of some dastardly plot to blacken her name? Let it go, Morwenna. Forget about it. Consider Laura Kerslake fully reinstated in the family roll of honour, if that's what you want, but don't meddle with the past any more. You don't realise how many people you're hurting.'

Her heart sank. She stared at the flames in silence, remembering how Nick had asked her to keep her own counsel still.

She said slowly, 'It isn't as simple as all that. The truth has to be told....'

'Are you sure you know what the truth is?'

'I think so. I hope so.' She looked up at him piteously. His face was shadowed and she could not read its expression, but there was a tension about the hard, lean lines of his body that was not encouraging. 'Anyway, it isn't up to me....'

He laughed angrily. 'Nick would drop the whole thing now, if you asked him to.'

She shook her head. 'You don't understand. But if it's any consolation to you, I deeply regret the impulse that brought me here in the first place.'

'It's no consolation at all,' he said bleakly. He raised the glass he was holding to his lips and finished its contents in one long swallow. Then he set the glass down on the mantelpiece, and reached down for her, grasping her arms and pulling her to her feet. 'Another impulse, Morwenna,' he said as he lowered his dark head towards hers. 'And God help us both if it's another wrong one.'

For a moment she was tense with panic, then as his mouth touched hers, she felt herself yield, blindly and helplessly. His arms tightened round her relentlessly so that she seemed to be fused with him, bone and bone, flesh and flesh.

When he had kissed her before, she had always been aware of other elements—his anger, his mistrust. Now she was conscious of nothing except the indisputable fact that he wanted her. His mouth was warm ravishment as it moved on hers and his hands held a bewitchment all their own as they slid over her shoulders and down the smooth curve of her back to her rounded hips.

'God, but you're lovely,' he whispered raggedly against her mouth. He kissed her eyes, the delicate line of her cheekbone, the hollows of her ears and the long curve of her throat, pushing aside the concealing folds of the housecoat so that he could caress the smooth skin of her shoulder. His mouth trailed fire on her body and when he lifted her and laid her among the tumbled cushions on the sofa, she made no effort to resist. He lay beside her and his eyes travelled over her in a wholly sensual regard that she tried shyly to meet, her silky hair loosely tangled on her shoulders, her mouth rose-red and slightly swollen from his passion.

He grimaced half ruefully, and brushed his fingers lightly and caressingly across her mouth and her own hands rose to clasp his and hold it captured for her kiss. He stiffened, and snatched his hand away.

'Don't ever do that again,' he ordered.

She smiled up at him, her eyes glinting with sweet provocation, aware of a new and delicious power. 'Why not? Isn't that how a subject is supposed to do obeisance to the king of Cornwall?'

An unwilling laugh was shaken from him. 'No,' he said. 'It's this way.' He drew her to him again, curving her pliant body to the warmth of his, and her lips parted with sweet abandonment under the demand of his kiss.

She felt as if she was dreaming, but her body's urgency and longing was real enough. It seemed as if her entire life had been a preparation for this moment when Dominic held her in his arms and kissed and caressed her as if she filled his mind to the exclusion of all else.

He held her away from him at last and his eyes searched hers. 'Do you know I'm nearly twice your age?'

She leaned forward and put her lips lightly on his. 'What's that got to do with it?'

'Some people might say a great deal. As I said, you're a child. You don't know what you're doing.'

'Oh, but I do,' she whispered. 'I love you.'

Dominic was very still for a long moment, then he said quietly, 'You don't know what you're saying. You've been here for less than a month, and during the greater part of that time we've fought like cat and dog. It's—madness even to mention the word love.'

The tone as well as the words disturbed her. She moved a little way from him, staring up into his face.

'Then what word would you mention?'

He swore softly under his breath. 'Do I have to spell it out for you?' he demanded roughly.

'No.' She felt suddenly very cold. Karen was the woman

to whom his commitment was made. She was simply a diversion. 'You—you want to take me to bed.'

'Is it so surprising?' he asked cynically. 'An older, more sophisticated woman would have recognised this—thing between us for what it was and not tried to build it into a love story. You've let Nick's old tales about Morwenna and her Esteban go to your head.'

Hurt, she lashed back, 'Someone older and more sophisticated, like Karen Inglis, I suppose.'

'Leave her out of it,' he said abruptly. 'She needn't concern you.'

'She concerns you,' she muttered, pleating a fold in her housecoat.

'If you're trying to convey that you're jealous, then I'm not flattered,' he said. He was plainly irritated, and something else as well that she could not define. 'God in heaven, because I'm the first man in your life, Morwenna, it doesn't mean that you have to be the first woman in mine.'

The dream was a nightmare now. Stung, 'Who says that you're the first man?' she hurled at him.

There was a little pause during which she seemed to stop breathing, then he gave a soft, mirthless laugh.

'So that's the way of it,' he said, half to himself. He reached out suddenly and jerked her back into his arms, crushing her breath from her. 'You know, you really had me fooled.' His voice was low and savage, muttering into her ear. 'You must have found my restraint under the circumstances utterly laughable. My apologies, sweetheart. I'll try not to disappoint you again.'

She began to struggle wildly, beating at him with her hands as his mouth found hers, suppressing her protests with brutal force. He rolled over on to her, trapping her kicking legs between his and imprisoning her wrists humiliatingly above her head with one careless hand so that she lay there at his mercy.

He rose to his knees, still holding her helpless, and looked down at her. Her eyes were full of tears, caused by the pain of his bruising grip as well as shame and fright, and she made a little incoherent noise in her throat as his free hand pulled open the front of the despised housecoat.

'What's the matter, Morwenna?' His voice reached her

mockingly. 'You're about to give yourself to the man you love—according to your own words. Or am I not even the first one for those either?'

His hand twisted in the demure neckline of her cotton nightdress and she knew he was going to tear it.

'Dominic, no, please!' Her voice was choked on a convulsive sob.

'What's wrong?' he gibed. 'Isn't this the way you planned it? Or did you intend to sweet-talk me into subsidising your trip to Carcassonne next year before permitting me these intimate indulgences that I intend to enjoy to the full? Well, don't worry, sweetheart. Play your cards right—be nice to me, as they say, and you might even get your trip. But on my terms, not yours.'

The nightgown was an old one and it tore easily, baring her to the waist, but she wasn't even aware what was happening to her.

She said, hardly moving her lips, 'How did you know—about Carcassonne?' Then, 'I suppose—Karen.'

'She completed my enlightenment on the subject. But my interest was aroused by a Christmas card that came today and which I opened by mistake. Frankly it never occurred to me that anyone would be sending you a card here, so I didn't look at the envelope properly. It was from someone called Vanessa. She wanted to know if you'd "managed to hook your handsome Cornishman yet, or whether you'd decided to settle for cash and Carcassonne instead".' His face was harsh as he looked down at her, not even softening at the sight of the loveliness his destructive hands had exposed. 'Who's your handsome Cornishman, Morwenna? Dare I flatter myself that it's me, or was it my susceptible brother you hoped to catch in your beguiling net? I shouldn't rely on Mark if I were you,' he went on, unheeding of her little protesting cry. 'Not long ago he was swearing eternal fidelity to another unlikely candidate for his affections. But that soon died the death when I put a few obstacles in his way to test how serious he really was.'

His voice altered, slowed. 'But I'm keeping you waiting, sweetheart. How unforgivable of me!' His hand cupped her breast, his lean fingers caressing the rosy tip and evoking a response that she neither could conceal nor control. And when his lips followed the same teasing, arousing path, a little moan rose in her throat. And she knew wildly that unless she escaped him now, she would be lost. She loved him, she wanted to give herself to him, but not like this. He belonged to someone else and she would never be able to respect herself again if she allowed him to use her for a cynical, transitory pleasure.

There was no way she could fight him on physical terms. He was still holding her so that she could not move, and his lips and hands were slowly but inexorably destroying any mental barriers she could raise in her own defence. There was only one answer.

She laughed, softly and ruefully. And when she spoke, her voice was steadier than she had dreamed possible. 'You win, Dominic, as always. I admit I did hope to persuade you to pay for my art lessons, but the price is a little too high even for me to pay. I—I'm sorry if I embarrassed you by my declaration of love just now. It's always proved quite effective in the past, but obviously I underestimated you. It won't happen again.'

'No,' he said softly, 'I don't suppose it will.' His hand released her wrists and travelled down to fasten around her throat. 'My God, I'd like to break your neck!'

'Why?' she asked coldly. 'Because I've deprived you of an hour's amusement? You can't pretend it would have meant any more to you than that.'

'I'm not pretending anything.' He let her go and swung his legs to the floor. 'I suppose I should be thankful that whatever passes for your conscience didn't prompt you to try and wheedle the money out of Nick.' His lips twisted as he looked down at her. 'Or were you waiting until the Hewitt-Smyth deal was finally settled before putting the bite on him? Oh, yes,' he went on mockingly, as her startled eyes flew to meet his, 'I know all about that. Nick told us tonight what was in the wind, but I knew before. Alan Hewitt-Smyth and I were at school together, so it was hardly likely that he'd leave me in the dark.'

His voice deepened, became almost menacing. 'I want you out of here, Morwenna, and I want you out soon. For that reason and that reason only I'm prepared to accede to your—request, and pay whatever fees for you this man in

Carcassonne is asking. It'll be worth it to get you off my back. But there is a condition.' He bent down and took her arm, yanking her up on to her feet. She gasped and pulled away from him.

'Don't touch me! Don't dare to touch me. Not now, or ever.'

He laughed. 'You flatter yourself, my scheming little witch.' Insolently he pulled the concealing folds of the housecoat around her and tied its sash tightly. 'There, sweetheart. Does that reassure you? Though you have nothing to worry about, I promise. If you climbed into my bed stark naked, I'd still turn away. Understood?'

Morwenna burned with humiliation at his touch and his words. Blindly she swung round and headed to the door. His hand caught her shoulder, compelling her to halt, and turning her to face him again.

'Don't be in such a hurry,' he said. 'You haven't heard my terms yet. You can go to Carcassonne at my expense on condition you forget all about that old business over the *Lady Laura*. I want Nick to have some peace and happiness in his life, which he won't have with you endlessly needling him to discover what if anything really happened all those years ago. It's not important, and you're going to promise me now not to go on with it.'

'I can't promise,' she said very quietly. 'I wish I could, believe me....'

'Believe you?' He was looking at her as if he had never really seen her before. 'Under the circumstances, that's— almost amusing. So be it, then, you've had your chance.'

He almost flung her away from him and she went towards the door, stumbling a little over the long folds of the housecoat.

She went up the stairs as if the devil was after her, but silence was her only pursuer. Safe in her room, she found herself fumbling for the key and listening to the reassuring click as it turned in the lock. What had Dominic once said? That no locked door could keep out a really determined man? She buried her face in her hands with a little shiver. The locked door, she knew, was just a gesture to herself. Dominic would not come. She had made certain of that because she could not face the prospect of his passion without tenderness or respect, but she hadn't bargained for the feeling of blank despair that overwhelmed her as a result.

She still had her pride, she thought bleakly, but that would be small comfort in the lonely days and nights that faced her in the future.

CHAPTER NINE

'ARE you out of your mind, girl?' Nick demanded. 'Where do you think you're going to find to live at this time of the year?' He glared at her. 'Every hotel will be full. People will be away—or entertaining. There'll be no shops open —no food, no services. It's madness even to think of leaving.'

Morwenna bent her head. 'I must go,' she reiterated quietly.

'You said you'd spend Christmas here with me,' he went on as if she had not spoken. 'I'd counted on that—particularly in view of what's happened. You'll have heard, I suppose, that Barbie will not be dining with us?'

'Yes,' she said unhappily. 'That's one of the reasons I want to leave. Nick—I'm sure she'd come round if I wasn't here. Then you could talk together and maybe make everything all right between you. At the moment I feel a—barrier to any reconciliation. She resents my being here. She resents me.'

He gave her a piercing glance. 'That's pure conjecture, and you know it, Morwenna. What makes you think she would change her mind one iota, even if you were out of the way? Whereas at the moment she can shelter behind this—alleged ill-health.' He snorted. 'I've never known Barbie ail a day in her life before.'

'Perhaps she really is ill,' Morwenna suggested gently. 'She must have had a shock....'

'Then it was long overdue,' he said harshly. 'I was a fool ever to delude myself that she cared for me sufficiently to tell me the truth. All she cares about is her own pride. It was the affront to that which got her into this mess in the first place.'

She sighed, 'Nick—I....' but he held up a peremptory hand.

'No, you listen to me, child. I have too much regard for you to allow you to rush off into the blue without even knowing whether you will have a roof over your head. When Christmas is over, if you're still determined to leave, then I won't stand in your way. I feel responsible for you, Morwenna. In some ways, you're still a child.'

He saw her wince and laid a placatory hand on her arm. 'Now, I've hurt you and I never intended to do that.'

'No,' she said, smiling in spite of her white face. 'It's not you, Nick. I was just remembering something—someone else once said to me.' She paused. 'Very well, I'll try and do as you ask. I'll stay here with you until Christmas is over. But you must promise me that you'll let me go in the New Year.'

'If that's what you really want.' His face was also slightly hurt and puzzled too. 'But I can't pretend I understand this sudden determination to be rid of us all.'

'No,' she said steadily. 'And it's nothing I can explain either, Nick—dear Nick, so please don't press me.' Abruptly she changed the subject. 'How is your hand standing up to all this new work?'

'Better than I expected or hoped,' he told her. 'All these months of exercise have really paid dividends, though I grumbled enough about them at the time.'

He was clearly keen to start work again, so Morwenna made an excuse that she still had some presents to wrap and went along to her own room. It wasn't true. Everything she had purchased was already wrapped and labelled. There were the gaily flowered slippers for Inez, and the driving gloves for Mark. For Nick she had bought a handsome silk cravat in a warm paisley pattern. Even Zack had not been forgotten, with a tin of his favourite tobacco. The gifts had taken almost all the spare cash she had, but she did not grudge a penny of it. There was only one person missing from the list. She had found it totally impossible to choose anything for Dominic and in view of what had passed between them the previous night she was glad she hadn't chosen out of desperation one of the pens or desk diaries or other bread and butter presents which had crossed her mind as she shopped. She had wanted the impossible, she thought. A gift that was impersonal enough to conceal her feelings and yet satisfied her own inner cravings to offer him the earth, moon and stars.

But under the circumstances, any attempt on her part to make him a gift of any kind would be an embarrassment to them both. All she could hope for was to behave as unobtrusively as possible over the next few days and then make her escape before any more harm or any more hurting was done.

She looked up at the portrait of Morwenna Trevennon, who had pursued her own goal with a single-mindedness that even the prospect of death could not deter, and felt a slight shiver of apprehension curl down her spine.

She said aloud and almost piteously, 'But I have to run away, you must see that?'

The painted eyes gazed down at her indifferently, and it was the purest imagination to think that the wide, generous mouth could compress itself for an instant in something bordering on irritation, at exactly the same moment as an errant draught from the window sent the brocaded curtain billowing gently into the room.

Morwenna expelled her breath in a long, rather shaken sigh. 'Oh, it's time—it's more than time that I was away from here,' she said in a low voice, and turned reluctantly away from the portrait and the strange compulsion of her namesake's gaze.

It was then she saw the envelope lying on the dressing table. She picked it up, recognising Vanessa's untidy scrawl instantly. The address was not at all clear, so it was little wonder that Dominic had assumed it was intended for the family. She read the brief message pencilled above it. 'Opened in error. My apologies.' She opened the card and read the words which had helped to torment her during the rest of that sleepless night. Vanessa couldn't have known that her piece of idle malice would be seen by anyone but Morwenna, but she must have realised that Christmas cards were generally public property and that her message would cause Morwenna some embarrassment at the very least. Steadily, she tore the card across and took it over and dropped it on the fire, watching it curl and blacken and become a breath of ash. She wished the aftermath it had left could be disposed of with equal ease, but that was impossible.

There was a knock on the door and she started out of

her uncomfortable reverie. Hesitantly she called 'Come in' and knew a sense of relief when Mark's head came round the door.

'I'm going into Port Vennor,' he said. 'Have you any last-minute shopping you want to do?'

'Not really,' she shook her head.

'Well, come anyway,' he mouthed. 'I want to talk to you.'

She was not really in the mood for Mark's confidences. She felt all too raw and bruised herself, but she agreed, finding her coat and winding a long woollen scarf over her hair and round her neck.

Mark was waiting for her somewhat impatiently, the car engine running, when she got outside. He drove off almost before she had settled herself.

'What's happened?' she asked apprehensively.

'I don't know.' He gave an uneasy laugh. 'I don't really believe it. I went into the study this morning just after breakfast to have it out with Dominic and it was as if he was waiting for me. He was obviously in a filthy temper and I almost chickened out, I don't mind telling you. I don't know if you've ever seen Dominic when he's good and mad, but....'

'Yes, I have,' she said. 'What happened?'

'Well, as I said, I could see he was gunning for me about something, so I thought I'd better get in first. So I told him. I said that I loved Biddy, and that I always had and always would in spite of his objections which had no foundation anyway. I told him we were engaged and that it was my right to have my fiancée and her brother join us for dinner on Christmas Eve as part of the family.' He shook his head as if it was incredible. 'And he agreed.'

'But that's wonderful!' Morwenna gazed at him with parted lips.

'Yes, it is,' he said rather wryly. 'And I haven't stopped wondering since. I even told him that she'd refused to come to Trevennon without his invitation and he said he would drive over there this morning and deliver it in person. He was still angry. I could sense it simmering away there, just below the surface, but somehow it wasn't directed at me any more. God, I can hardly believe it!' He laughed again, but on a note of jubilance.

'You'd better.' She could be happy for him in spite of her own pain.

It was all working out for Mark and that was the way it should be. Biddy would have no further qualms now that he had learned to stand up to Dominic and any lingering trepidation that she might feel when she entered Trevennon the following evening would soon be dispelled by the certainty of his love and support.

And Dominic would be there with Karen. It was odd how the previous night, the thought of Karen and the effect that Dominic's infidelity might have on her had barely occurred to her. Would Karen ever be able to wear the same certainty as Biddy, or would she even want to? She and Dominic were both sophisticated people and each understood what the other would expect from marriage. Karen wanted Trevennon, that was clear, perhaps in some twisted way to prove that the Inglis women were not lightly set aside. To obtain it, she might be prepared to settle for less than his wholehearted devotion.

So tomorrow night there would be two pairs of lovers to congratulate, while she and Nick sat like outsiders shut out from the circle of promise and commitment. Morwenna gave a silent sigh deep within herself. She could bear it. She would have to for Nick's sake, but could he? He could not disguise the look of brooding sadness that had been in his eyes over the past weeks. His work, his hopes for the *Lady Morwenna* had helped, but they had not been a complete compensation. He and Barbie were apart now and there was a rift between them that might never be bridged—unless. . . .

Morwenna caught her breath at the possibility that had just occurred to her. They would stay apart, caught in the trap they had made for themselves, unless they were thrown together in spite of themselves. What was to stop her going to Barbie Inglis and telling her that she had nothing to hide —that Nick knew what she had done all those years before? Her spirit quailed slightly. It was not a course of action that she would ever have contemplated in the past, and she was far from convinced about its wisdom now. If it went wrong—would Nick ever forgive her? she wondered. And almost in the same moment—— But if she did not try at least to bridge the gap between them would she ever be able to forgive herself?

She sat in silence for the remainder of the journey while Mark talked exuberantly about his hopes and plans and pondered likely dates for the wedding. His remarks were largely rhetorical, demanding no more than a sympathetic ear in response, and Morwenna was able to sit smiling faintly and nodding her head at intervals while her thoughts pursued each other. She would be taking a terrible risk. Barbie Inglis might simply refuse to see her and that would make matters even worse than they were at present. But at the same time she knew that if there was nothing ventured, there was nothing gained. She did not even contemplate the prospect of Dominic's anger if he ever found out about her interference. That was best left out of the reckoning or she might lose her courage entirely.

'The yard's closing down early this afternoon,' Mark commented suddenly after a few minutes' silence. 'We always do that at Christmas, and we always all have a drink together before the closing. If you're in the vicinity, I'm sure you'd be welcome to join us.'

'Who else will be there?' she asked cautiously.

'Well—everyone. Dominic, of course—and Nick when he was well enough. There's always a little present each for the men's children which Dom hands out. Aunt Barbie used to go, but I suppose she'll hold aloof this time.'

'And Karen?'

'Naturally,' he said rather drily. 'Can you imagine her permitting herself to be left out of anything—even a works party?'

She tried to smile, but it was a dismal failure. 'I suppose she feels she has the right now.'

'Right doesn't enter into it. She'd come anyway. Well, shall I tell Dom to expect you?'

'No.' Her denial was too swift and positive. She could sense his surprise. 'I—I mean I don't think so. I'll just do my shopping and catch the bus back to Trevennon. Please don't worry about me. Parties aren't much in my line.'

'Saving yourself for tomorrow evening, eh?' He smiled, but his eyes were still slightly puzzled. 'Please yourself. Now, where do you want me to drop you?'

She answered him at random and slid out of the car with a feeling of thankfulness. She wandered up the main street, oblivious of the Christmas bustle going on around her, stepping off the pavement to avoid the laughing, chattering groups of children and adults scurrying to complete their preparations. The shops were brightly lit and decorated with tinsel and glitter, but Morwenna hardly noticed. Her heart was beating loudly and painfully and not merely because of the steep climb as she neared the top of the hill. She knew, because Mark had pointed it out to her, where the Inglis house was, standing foursquare in its own grounds just where the little town gave way to the countryside again. It was a Georgian building, of three storeys, commanding a view right over Port Vennor, and it looked neat and freshly painted, with the gardens carefully tended. Everything, Morwenna thought as she pushed open the gate, that Trevennon was not. This was the house where money had never been a problem or maintenance any particular anxiety.

Life, it seemed, had always been good to the Inglis family. Generations of them must have lived here, expecting the best and usually obtaining it, secure in the assurance of their own worth. It could never have occurred to Barbie Inglis that Robert Kerslake, the man she had set her heart on, could possibly prefer another woman. The shock of the elopement must have been punishing for her—worse even than it had been for Nick—and it must have made everything she valued seem suddenly meaningless.

So she had lashed back at Laura and at the family who had sheltered and cherished her for so long. Both of them must suffer because of the wrong that had been done her. And, in the end, because malice always turns back on itself, the one to suffer most had been herself.

Morwenna put her hand on the gate. It swung inwards on well-oiled hinges and she walked steadily up the path and rang the bell. It was a dark, grey day and there were lights on inside the house. As she heard approaching feet on the other side of the door, Morwenna found herself praying it would not be Karen.

Instead she was confronted by a tall woman in a neat green nylon overall who gave her an enquiring glance.

'I'd like to see Miss Inglis, please.'

The curiosity in the woman's eyes deepened. 'Madam isn't feeling well today. She's resting in her room. I think Miss Karen is at home if....'

'No, I'd rather speak to Miss Inglis herself,' Morwenna said firmly. 'I'm sure she'll see me. I—I have a message from Trevennon for her—a personal message.'

The woman hesitated. 'Well, miss, I don't know, I'm sure. Madam did say ... but there, if you've a message for her, I suppose it will be all right. I'll tell her you're here.'

'No, that's all right,' Morwenna halted her. She swallowed. 'If you'll just show me where her room is, I'll pop in and give her the message and be off. It is rather urgent and I'm in a bit of a hurry.'

There was a pause then the other woman said rather stiffly, 'Very well, miss, though what Madam will say, I don't know. However, if you're certain....'

She led the way up thickly carpeted stairs to a broad gracious landing running the full length of the house. She led the way briskly to the door at the end and tapped on it.

'There you are, miss.' She turned away. 'I presume you'll see yourself out when you've passed on the message.'

There was silence from the room beyond and Morwenna had to steel herself to open the door and walk in.

The curtains were half drawn across the tall windows, excluding what little light there was, and for a moment she thought the housekeeper was mistaken and that the room was empty, and then she saw Barbie Inglis lying on a chaise-longue close to the window.

'You!' Morwenna thought she had never heard such bitterness conveyed by one brief monosyllable. 'Who allowed you in here?'

'Your housekeeper, Miss Inglis. But you mustn't be angry with her. She acted in good faith—I said I had a message for you.' Morwenna forced herself to walk across the room. She stood looking down at Barbie Inglis. For a moment she wondered whether she had been doing her an injustice. She looked genuinely ill, her skin stretched tightly over her cheekbones and her eyes sunken.

'How dare you force your way in?' There was a handbell on a small table close at hand and she propped herself up on one elbow to reach for it. Morwenna quite gently put it out of her reach.

'For Nick's sake,' she said.

'You've brought me a message from Nick?' Barbie Inglis's eyes flashed. 'He couldn't be so cruel as to use you as a messenger.'

'No.' Morwenna looked steadily at her. 'He has no idea I'm here. He'll probably be very angry with me—almost as angry as you are, Miss Inglis, but I have to take that risk. I can't bear this terrible misunderstanding to go on any longer.'

'There is no misunderstanding,' Barbie Inglis said with a terrible coldness. 'I simply do not wish to visit a house where the daughter of a woman who wronged me very deeply is treated as an honoured guest—given privileges that—friends of many years' standing are denied.' There was almost a choke in her voice. 'Now go, Miss Kerslake. Leave my house. Nick has made his choice and you will not busy yourself any further.'

Morwenna bit her lip. 'I know you hated my mother, and I can understand it.'

'Thank you.' Barbie Inglis's voice vibrated with sarcasm.

There was a chair nearby, a delicate thing with gilt legs upholstered in the same striped material as the chaise-longue. Morwenna pulled it forward and sat down without being invited.

'I've asked you to go!' Miss Inglis's voice was almost hysterical.

'No, not yet.' Morwenna nerved herself. 'You talk of wrongs, Miss Inglis. But what of the wrong you did? Wasn't that a greater one? To sell the designs for the *Lady Laura* to a cheap firm like Lackingtons. How much did they pay you?' She looked round the affluent surroundings of the bedroom. 'I wouldn't have thought you were in real need of thirty pieces of silver.'

If she had any lingering doubts about the veracity of Barbie's guilt, they were banished for ever. Under her incredulous eyes, Miss Inglis seemed to shrink, her eyes widening and glazing in real horror.

Ridiculously, Morwenna found words singing inside her

head—'*The curse is come upon me,*' cried the Lady of Shalott.

When Barbie spoke, her voice was whispering like an old woman's. 'How did you know? Did—did Laura guess? I've been afraid of this always. From the moment you came back, I knew why. I've been waiting for you to come here. What do you want—money? My niece tells me you have none of your own. She said something about art lessons—trip abroad. Is that what you want?'

'No, no.' Any anger Morwenna might have felt evaporated under an onrush of pity. 'You really don't understand, do you? I knew nothing about any of this until I came to Trevennon. And my mother never told me what had happened to the *Lady Laura* because she never knew.'

'Then—who did tell you?' There was a dawning realisation in Miss Inglis's eyes, and a kind of sick dread.

Morwenna hesitated compassionately, but there was no easy way, now she had embarked on this course. 'Nick told me,' she said at last.

For a moment she thought Barbie Inglis had fainted. The older woman sank back on her cushions, her eyes closed. Her face was very white and her mouth looked pinched.

'He knows,' she muttered at last.

'He's always known.' Morwenna leaned forward and took one of the cold hands between hers, chafing it gently. 'He just wanted you to tell him, that's all. All these years he's been waiting. Don't you see there's no point in pretending any longer?' she ended on a note of appeal.

Barbie Inglis struggled upright into a sitting position. 'There's a glass in the bathroom,' she said. 'Will you get me some water, please?'

She indicated a door on the other side of the room. Morwenna went across and found herself in a small but luxurious bathroom, probably converted from the original dressing room. She poured some water into the glass and took it back to Miss Inglis, who was sitting staring expressionlessly out of the window.

'Thank you.' She accepted the glass from Morwenna and drank deeply. She was still very pale, but she appeared to have herself under control once again.

'What are you going to do?' Morwenna asked as the

silence seemed to stretch out between them.

Barbie Inglis smiled without mirth. 'What can I do? I've been considering closing the house and going away from here. A cruise perhaps—or a long holiday in the sun. That seems the obvious choice. I shall think of something, no doubt.'

'But what about Nick?' Morwenna took the empty glass from her and put it down.

'Nick?' There was pain in the way Barbie Inglis pronounced his name. 'How can I face him now, knowing that he's always—known? I could never stand the shame of it.'

Morwenna stared at her, her heart sinking. 'But you can't mean that. You've both been so unhappy for so long—and now when you have the chance to be totally honest with each other....'

Barbie Inglis gave a twisted smile. 'It's too late for that. No, I shall go away somewhere—after Christmas. That's all that's left to me now.'

'No, it isn't.' Morwenna stared appealingly into her eyes. 'It's just this—infernal pride of yours and you know it. Nick wants you. He's wanted you for years, but not with this—thing always between you. Isn't the sacrifice of a little pride worth all the happiness that might result?'

Barbie Inglis gave a faint smile. 'You're very young, Miss Kerslake. To the young, everything is always black and white. Let us accept that you meant well by coming here; however, I would be grateful if you would go now.' She leaned back against her cushions and closed her eyes again.

Morwenna got to her feet, slowly and reluctantly. 'Miss Inglis, I feel I've failed. Please believe me—all you would need to do would be arrive for dinner at Trevennon tomorrow evening. Everything would work out after that—I know it.'

Barbie Inglis seemed to withdraw in upon herself. 'I asked you to go, Miss Kerslake,' she said in a quiet monotonous voice.

Morwenna hesitated, took one last despairing look at the unyielding face before her, then walked to the door.

She was halfway down the stairs when a door at the side of the hall opened and Karen came out. Morwenna froze, hoping that the other girl would not look up and see her standing there, but it was a vain hope. Karen glanced round almost casually, but as her gaze focussed upon Morwenna, her features sharpened inimically.

'What are you doing here?' Her voice sounded shrill with shock. She swung back towards the room she had just left. 'Dominic!'

Morwenna groaned silently, her fingers gripping the banister rail until her knuckles showed white.

He came out into the hall and stood looking up at her as if he could not believe his eyes. Then he said very quietly, 'What in hell's name do you think you're playing at?'

Morwenna sighed. 'I came to ask Miss Inglis to dine at Trevennon tomorrow evening.'

Temper barely controlled brought Karen's lovely face to the brink of ugliness. '*You* came to invite her? My God, if that isn't adding insult to injury....'

'Oh, you don't have to worry.' Morwenna was very pale. She came down the remaining stairs. 'She refused—naturally, and I'm leaving.'

'I should damn well think you are!' Karen walked to the front door and flung it open.

Morwenna went blindly towards it.

'Wait, Morwenna.' Dominic's voice came after her, cool and authoritative.

'No.' She paused, but did not turn and look back at the two of them standing there united in condemnation of her. 'Forgive me, but I don't think I can take any more at the moment. I know what you must be thinking, but I can only say I meant it for the best. I'm sorry.'

She went out into the raw December air, walking quickly. As she reached the gate, she heard the front door slam shut behind her, closing them in together. As she walked away from the house, a few flakes of snow began to drift down out of the leaden sky, but she paid them no heed, and the dampness on her face had no connection with the weather at all.

'You mean,' Biddy said incredulously, 'that you've run away?'

Morwenna avoided her gaze. 'Not really. I was going to

leave anyway. I've just done it a little earlier than I intended, that's all.'

'Balderdash,' Biddy said roundly. 'No one takes off for anywhere through choice on Christmas Eve. I mean, where are you going to go? What are you going to do?' She saw Morwenna's suddenly stricken look, and her face softened. 'Oh, love, I mean ultimately. Of course you can stay here with us as long as you want, you know that. Where do they all think you are?'

'I wrote Nick a note, saying I'd decided to go back to the Priory.' Morwenna bit her lip. It had been a difficult letter to write, knowing the hurt she was going to deal the recipient. 'They'll think I've gone to Penzance to catch a train. At least that's what I hope they'll think.' She took a sip at the scalding mug of coffee Biddy had just put into her hand.

'Well, Mark won't think it for one,' Biddy pointed out reasonably. 'We can hardly hide you in a cupboard each time he knocks at the door.'

'I hadn't thought of that,' Morwenna admitted. She sighed. 'Oh, Biddy, I'm sorry to give you all this trouble. I just couldn't think where else to go.'

Biddy gave a rueful chuckle. 'Love, the only person you're making trouble for is yourself, as far as I can see. Wouldn't it have been better in the long run to have stayed behind and faced this row—whatever it was?'

'I suppose so.' Morwenna bent her head over the steaming mug. 'But I just couldn't stand any more, Biddy. I knew how angry he was going to be—and I couldn't bear it.'

'Nick?' Biddy raised her eyebrows.

'Oh, no. Dominic,' Morwenna said quickly, and flushed hotly as Biddy's expression changed from enquiry to an all too comprehensive understanding.

'Oh,' she said, after a pause. 'So that's the way of it.'

'Yes,' Morwenna pushed her hair back rather defensively. 'Biddy—please don't say anything to Mark.'

Biddy shook her head. 'I think the boot's on the other foot,' she said drily. 'Mark has already mentioned something of the sort to me.'

'Oh, no!' Morwenna was aghast. 'I thought no one knew.'

'Well, let's say he's had his suspicions.' Biddy smiled at

her. 'It's not easy to hide things from people who are living in the same house. When Mark and I were having our difficulties, I tried to pretend to Greg that I wasn't in the least concerned, but he wasn't fooled for a second.' She hesitated. 'Do you want to tell me what happened, or is it too painful to talk about?'

'No,' Morwenna gave a little sigh. 'It's a long and complicated story, but as you'll be joining the family, you'd have heard about it eventually anyway.'

Biddy listened without interruption as Morwenna recounted the facts from her mother's departure from Trevennon years before to her abortive visit to Barbie Inglis the previous day. The only thing she did not mention was Dominic's lovemaking, but she guessed Biddy would be able to see the points at which omissions were made from her sometimes stumbling narrative and draw her own conclusions.

When she had finished, Biddy whistled thoughtfully. 'It's incredible,' she said. 'I've always had Miss Inglis marked down as the stereotype English gentlewoman, very correct and rather colourless. I never dreamed she'd be capable of such passion, or such spite.' She stared frowningly into the fire for a few minutes. 'It was bad luck that Dominic happened to be at the house at the same time as you, but shouldn't you have stood your ground and explained exactly what your motives were for being there?'

'I couldn't. I'd promised Nick that I wouldn't say anything to anyone else. He wanted to protect her, I suppose.' She gave a little shiver. 'But Dominic was so angry. It was only the previous night that he'd tried to get me to promise to forget the whole thing. It must have seemed to him that I'd deliberately set out to do quite the opposite, out of malice.'

'And you didn't tell Nick what had happened either?'

'No, I went straight to my room. I stayed there all evening, pretending I had a headache.' She smiled rather wanly. 'I didn't have to pretend too hard. I—I did my packing and wrote to Nick. Then I went to bed, but I didn't sleep very well.'

'I can imagine,' Biddy muttered. 'And what was Dominic doing all this time?'

Morwenna bit her lip. 'He came back very late,' she said. 'Long after dinner was over. I'd just got into bed and switched the light out, when I heard him come upstairs. He came along to my room and tried the door, but I'd locked it, so he had to knock. I—I didn't answer. I hoped he would think I was asleep, but of course he didn't. He must have knocked for about five minutes. Then he called to me and said he knew I was awake and that I couldn't expect to stay in my room for ever, and he would see me in the morning.'

Biddy grimaced. 'It was just as well you'd already done your packing. I think after a message like that I'd probably have left half of my things behind.'

'I did leave one thing behind,' Morwenna said sadly. 'A little pearl ring that belonged to my mother. I had it on my dressing table, but I couldn't find it and I didn't have time to make another search this morning. I wanted to get out of the house before anyone saw me.'

Biddy patted her hand. 'Well, you're here now, and all's well. We've got a camp bed and we'll make it up in my room presently.' She hesitated. 'You can stay there out of the way when Mark calls for us this evening, if that's what you want. But you'll have to face him sooner or later.'

Morwenna nodded. 'I'll worry about that when it happens,' she said.

The afternoon seemed very long. She watched Biddy tie up her presents for Mark and Greg, and thought rather wistfully of her own gifts which she had placed neatly under the Christmas tree before she had left. They had an early tea and listened to a carol service on the radio, then Biddy disappeared mysteriously to make herself beautiful for the 'forthcoming ordeal', as she put it.

Morwenna sat by the fire and sketched—the spikes of hyacinths in the bowl Greg had made—the large important marmalade cat fast asleep in the opposite chair after a dinner of giblets. She supposed there would come a time when the thought of Dominic would no longer be paramount in her mind, but that time would be far distant. He filled her mind, and his dark face swam before her vision so that the image she was trying to create on the page became distorted. She groaned impatiently as she crumpled up yet another spoiled sheet and sent it spinning into the fire.

'I don't want to disturb you, but Mark will be here in five minutes.' Biddy came into the room, a little self-conscious in a full-length wool jersey dress in a charming sherry colour. She grinned, blushing a little, as Morwenna complimented her sincerely on her appearance.

'Well, I had to make an effort. Your Dominic was charm itself when he called here yesterday, but he's still a formidable character. He probably expects me to arrive in a patchwork caftan and bare feet, with a flower in my hair. Greg too,' she added, and Morwenna laughed at the image this conjured up.

She got to her feet hurriedly at the sound of a car approaching, snatching up her sketchbook and making for the short flight of stairs to the upper storey. She whisked into Biddy's bedroom and half-closed the door. She heard the cottage door open downstairs and the murmur of voices. She frowned. It did not sound like Mark, but who else could it be? She pulled the door a little further open and stood with her head bent, listening intently.

Biddy's voice floated clearly and sweetly to her ears. 'You say you've been in touch with her family at the Priory, Mr Trevennon, and they have no idea where she is? I hope your uncle isn't too worried.'

'Of course he's worried,' Dominic said. 'She's got her luggage, and a half-return ticket to London, and no money from what we can gather. Mark has been to the station to try and find someone who may have seen her, but there were quite a few people travelling because of Christmas and no one remembers her.' He paused and then said slowly, 'I suppose you have no idea where she might be?'

Morwenna stood half paralysed, her nails digging deep into the palms of her hands. Oh, Biddy, she thought desperately, don't give me away. The silence seemed endless until Biddy said smoothly, 'None at all, I'm afraid. But I shouldn't worry too much. A lovely girl like that is bound to have a lot of friends she can turn to.'

Morwenna did not wait to hear Dominic's response to this. She crept across to her bed and sat down, burying her face in her hands. Her imagination must be playing her tricks, she thought dully as she heard the door below slam and the car drive off. What other explanation was there for that note of almost desperate appeal in Dominic's voice? She had to make herself realise that he would be only too glad to be rid of her. If he was concerned, it was for Nick.

She sighed and resolutely swallowed a chokingly painful lump in her throat. Now that she was alone, she had to consider her future plans. She couldn't really do very much at all until after Boxing Day, and then she would go to London and find some sort of hostel accommodation. Dominic had been right about the pitiful state of her finances, but she couldn't allow herself to worry too much about that. She would find work somehow. Maybe she would even find some kind of living-in job like a companion or mother's help where she could paint in her spare time. There were all kinds of possibilities, she told herself, trying to shut out of her ears the memories of Dominic's voice with its unusual hesitancy.

The evening dragged by. She made some coffee and listened to the radio again, although if anyone had asked questions on the programmes afterwards, she would have been hard put to it to answer.

She found herself wondering restlessly what stage the dinner party at Trevennon had reached. Had they reached the toasts yet? Were Dominic and Karen standing hand in hand receiving everyone's congratulations and best wishes? She wondered whether they would open their presents to each other that evening, or keep them for the following day. And on the heels of that thought came the passionate wish that she had, after all, left a present for Dominic. She'd left him nothing—not a note, nor even a card, and she found herself regretting this with all her heart. Nothing could change the way things were between them, but it was suddenly very painful to know that he would always imagine she had gone away hating him. She was never going to see him again, but it was strangely important that he should know that she had not been lying when she had confessed her love for him. Even if he was sardonically amused by the knowledge, at least she would no longer be around to be hurt by his mockery.

She got up and walked restlessly round the room. But it was too late, much too late to do anything about it now. There was no chance of getting a gift for him. All the shops had been shut for hours—and besides, that wasn't the sort of thing she meant.

As she returned to her chair, her hand caught the sketch pad which was balanced on the arm and sent it flying to the floor. She knelt down to retrieve it and saw that it had opened at the page where she had made the drawing of Morwenna Trevennon on the beach in Spanish Cove. She looked down at it, her lip caught between her teeth. At the time, the brooding self-revelation of the drawing had frightened her. Now, she felt its impact anew. Her face, her eyes, all her helpless, hopeless longing for the man she loved who did not return her love. Not Morwenna Trevennon, who had loved triumphantly and died for her love without regret.

She tore the page out of her book very carefully, then went over to the big roll-topped desk in the corner of the room which Greg and Biddy regarded as their office, and found a large square envelope. She would send him this, she thought. Post it from London after Christmas.

She wrote his name on the envelope, then paused. But that wasn't what she wanted. She wanted his present to be with the others under the tree, not some kind of afterthought. She got up and went to the window, pulling back the curtain and staring out into the darkness. It had been snowing again and most of the evening too if the light covering on the ground was anything to go by.

She turned away, telling herself that what she was contemplating was complete and utter madness. It was at least two miles to Trevennon from here, if not more, along unlit lanes. And if she managed to get there, what then? If she simply posted the letter through the box, it would tell everyone that she was still in the neighbourhood and could embarrass Biddy and Greg. The only alternative was to get into the house without being seen and put the envelope under the tree with the other presents. She looked at her watch. The meal, she knew, was one of Inez's most festive spreads and would probably still be going on. If only she could get there before they moved into the sitting room for coffee.

She felt almost light-headed as she reached for the phone and dialled the number of the local taxi service in Port

Vennor. The owner was not eager to turn out, but when Morwenna persisted, he grudgingly agreed, and told her at her request what the fare would be. She had enough in her purse to cover it, but hardly anything left over once it was paid, and again she told herself that this whole idea was madness.

Yet she had to do it. It was as simple as that. She put on her boots and wound her long scarf round her head and neck. She couldn't afford to have the taxi bring her back as well. She would have to walk, and as an afterthought she armed herself with Greg's powerful flashlight from the kitchen mantelpiece.

She made the taxi-driver drop her well out of earshot of the house in case anyone with sharp ears wondered who was driving up at that time of night. She approached the front door cautiously. It had occurred to her that it might be locked and that her whole errand could be fruitless, but it swung open when she tried it and she tiptoed noiselessly into the dimly lit hall. The dining room door was closed, she saw with relief, and she could hear the murmur of voices and the clatter of cutlery coming from behind it. One of the lamps had been left on in the empty sitting room, and this and the firelight provided all the illumination that was necessary as she crept across the room and slipped the envelope in among the other gifts.

As she crossed the hall, back towards the front door, she heard movements from the dining room—the sound of chairs being moved back—and realised she was only just in time. She had left the door slightly open to facilitate her retreat, and she was through it in a second and back in the cold white world beyond.

All that was left now was the long trudge back to St Enna. She looked up at the house whose strange gaunt shape had become so dear and familiar and thought how she would miss it. There were other things too. She would miss the cry of the gulls early in the morning and the touch of spray on her face as she walked along the cliffs. And she would never see Spanish Cove when the seals came in the spring, or later in the year when the brightness of the summer sun would dance on the rocks and the restless sea.

Almost without knowing it, she began to walk away from

the house and the lane which led back to the road, towards the cliffs. One last time, she thought, to sniff the salt in the air and see the sea breaking on the shore at her feet. Then she could carry its sound in her ears like a shell to alleviate the long city days ahead.

As she came out on to the cliffs, she moved carefully, shining the flashlight ahead of her at every step. It was very calm, and very cold, and the snow which had been coming down fast had now dwindled to a few desultory flakes. Below her in the cove, the sea murmured like a siren.

She transferred the flashlight into her other hand, and gripping the handrail tightly began to pick her way down the steps. It had been bad enough the previous time when the steps had been frosty. Now, the thin covering of snow had made them treacherous in the extreme. Halfway down she paused, wondering whether it would be more sensible to retrace her steps, but that seemed a defeatist attitude so she pressed on.

She was about three steps from the beach when the handrail snapped. She cried out, losing her balance, and the flashlight flew out of her hand and landed on the sand below with Morwenna after it. She landed awkwardly, her left foot catching on a stone and turning under her so painfully that for a moment she felt sick and faint and the world swung dizzily about her. She bent her head and gritted her teeth until the spasm passed. She did not think she had broken her ankle, but she had almost certainly sprained it. Slowly and gingerly she tried to stand up, but her foot would not take her weight and with a little groan she collapsed back on the sand. She had only the dimmest notion of first aid, but it seemed a sensible idea to get her boot off before her ankle swelled too badly. It might be sensible, but it was also difficult and extremely unpleasant, and she was almost in tears by the time it was concluded. She got slowly and painfully on to her knees and felt all around her in the sand for the flashlight. She found it almost at once, but it was broken, and at the same time Morwenna became aware of several things. One of them was that no one knew where she was, and the second was that the area of beach on which she was crouching was small, and becoming ever smaller by the minute. The tide, she thought desperately, all Nick's warnings about its perilously swift advance returning to chill her. Oh, God, the tide. Why hadn't it occurred to her that it might be high tide tonight?

She pushed the broken flashlight into her pocket and crawled on her hands and knees back towards the steps. She dragged herself up on to the first one, then paused. There was no handrail to assist her now, and as well as being steep and slippery the steps sloped a little, so that she found she was sliding backwards towards the beach again. This isn't happening, she thought. It can't be happening. She was beginning to panic and she knew it, and she forced herself to calm down. Her fingers scrabbled round the stone steps, seeking some kind of hold, but her hands were numb with cold and wouldn't obey her. Besides, the steps were worn smooth with age. There were no convenient ledges or other projections to grasp.

She glanced back over her shoulder and saw that the incoming waves seemed to have made further advances even in the past few minutes. She wondered what time the tide would reach its height. The lower steps were covered in seaweed, which indicated the final limits of the rising water, but this was not her main concern. Her chief enemy was the intense cold, and she knew it.

Teeth gritted, she tried again to stand and collapsed down on the steps with a cry of pain, grazing her elbows as she fell. On a flat co-operative surface she might have been able to hobble a few feet, but the steps defeated her.

Coming down to the cove, she thought with a kind of icy finality, would be the last and most disastrous of her impulses. She looked back to see where the water had reached and saw her discarded boot, bobbing away on the ebb. Before long, she knew, the freezing water would be lapping round her feet.

She was shivering violently, light-headed with cold and fear, her mind a whirling jumble of confused thoughts and images. The sea was coming to take her, she thought, as it had taken the other Morwenna centuries before, and it would be much easier not to struggle any more but simply close her eyes and let herself go on the high tide at midnight. There were coloured lights flashing behind her closed eyelids and the sea was murmuring to her with the voice of a lover. She found herself wondering how long it had been before the sea had carried Morwenna and Esteban away from each other, or had her arms clung fast to him even in death? Nothing would seem so bad, she thought remotely, with your lover's arms around you.

The voice of the sea was louder now and more insistent, calling her name over and over again, and she gave a little soft groan in response. And the arms which held her were strong, just as she had imagined, but they could not overcome the fear that gripped her and she began to struggle weakly.

Dominic's voice said urgently, 'My darling, I've got you. You're safe, but you mustn't fight me. Try and relax and put your arms round my neck.'

And she thought, 'So it's a dream, all a dream,' and allowed an overwhelming darkness to swallow her up.

There were other dreams as well. Strange dreams of the hall at Trevennon and Nick, white-faced, standing hand in hand with Barbie Inglis. There was warmth and unimaginable softness and comfort and a liquid which trickled fire down the back of her throat. And oddly there was Dr Warner's genial figure. 'A fine Christmas present this is for us all, young lady.' His touch on her ankle was magically comforting and she tried to tell him so, but his face kept receding and it was much easier instead just to take the two small white tablets that he was offering her. Somewhere close at hand, he was telling someone, 'Yes, a bad sprain, but she's young and resilient, so we'll have to hope there are no ill effects. Rest and quiet and plenty of warmth is what she needs, but call me at once if....' His voice faded and the darkness returned, but it was a friendly darkness now.

When she opened her eyes again, a cold grey light was filling the room, and she knew that she wasn't dreaming. She turned her head slightly and looked up at the slightly ironic gaze of Morwenna Trevennon, until a more homely countenance interposed itself.

'Merry Christmas,' Inez said somewhat tartly. 'And a nice fright you give us all, I must say!'

Morwenna gave her a wan smile. 'I'm sorry.'

'Tidn't me you have to apologise to, my lover. Here's some soup I've been keeping hot for when you woke up. Sit up a little bit and I'll arrange your pillows.'

Morwenna complied, wincing a little as she moved her injured foot.

'What happened?' she asked. 'I was on the beach and I fell—I can remember that. I couldn't get back up the steps.'

Inez looked austere. 'And what were you doin' down there, I'd like to know, when you'd gone off from your home without a word to anyone?'

'It would take too long to explain,' Morwenna said wearily, beginning to eat her soup, and Inez's face softened.

'And I shouldn't be going on at you when you need rest,' she said. 'You eat the soup, my pretty, and then I'll brush your hair because Mr Dom's downstairs waiting to have a word with you.'

Morwenna laid the spoon back in the bowl. Her eyes sought Inez's apprehensively. 'I—I don't want to see anyone.'

'That's no way to talk.' Inez put the spoon imperiously back into her hand. 'Spent half the night in that chair, he did, making sure you slept easy. Besides, 'twas him that found you, and you'll want to thank him for that at least. Carried you into the house as if you were a dead thing.'

Morwenna made herself go on with her soup. She said slowly, 'Other things are coming back to me now. I thought I'd dreamt them. Did—did I see Miss Inglis here?'

'She's still here. I made up the bed for her in your old room.' Inez gave a nod of satisfaction. 'Looks as if she and Mr Nick are going to make a match of it after all these years.' She chuckled. ' 'Twas proper romantic to see them, and I'd always thought Miss Inglis a cold sort of woman. And Mr Mark's young lady seems a nice little thing, though not a lot to say for herself yet. Finished? There's a good maid.'

She took the tray from Morwenna briskly, and fetched her hairbrush from the dressing table. Morwenna protested feebly, but Inez overrode her objections. 'You don't want him seeing you like this with your hair in a snarl,' she declared positively. 'And that old nightie of your mother's isn't much cop, either. Lucky I've got something that'll cover it up proper.'

She produced a parcel wrapped in Christmas paper and handed it to Morwenna. When she opened it, Morwenna found a pretty white wool shawl, hand-crocheted with a long fringe.

'Little present for you,' Inez commented offhandedly. 'Did it when I had a moment. 'Tisn't difficult to do—in fact I could teach you how to do it, later on.'

Morwenna slipped the shawl's fleecy softness round her shoulders, sudden tears pricking her eyes. 'Oh, Inez! It—it's beautiful.'

'Well, there's no call to cry about it.' Inez sounded shocked. 'Don't let Mr Dom find you with red eyes on Christmas morning.'

Before Morwenna could speak, she gave her a ferocious wink and vanished with the tray, and the discarded wrapping paper.

Morwenna watched the door, aware that her heart was thumping uncomfortably under her ribs. When at last he came, she was shocked at the sight of him. He was very pale and there were deep shadows of sleeplessness under his eyes. He came across to the bed and stood looking down at her.

'We don't have to talk,' he said quietly. 'We've all the time in the world for talking when you're stronger. Just don't send me away, Morwenna. Let me sit in that chair and look at you, and know that you're safe.'

'No,' she halted him as he began to move away. 'There are things that must be said. You—you saved my life. I don't know how, and I can't begin to thank you....'

'Thank me?' he cut in almost incredulously. 'My God, have you any conception of what I went through yesterday when you disappeared like that?'

'Yes.' She began to pleat a fold of sheet in her fingers. 'I'm sorry I worried you all like that.'

'Never mind the others.' He sat down on the edge of the bed and put his hand over hers. She was amazed to find that it was shaking slightly. 'Later in the day they'll all be coming to see you and you'll hear all about their varying reactions *ad nauseam*. But now I've got you to myself for a while, so I'd be grateful if you'd concentrate on me and my feelings. Why did you run away?'

'Because I knew I'd made you angry again—and I couldn't bear it.' She stared wearily down at the coverlet. There was no point in dissimulation now.

'Because I found you at Barbie's?' He gave a slight groan. 'I was angry, but not for the reason you think. You see, I wasn't alone there. Nick was with me.'

'Nick?'

'Yes. He decided yesterday morning that as devious methods hadn't achieved what he wanted, then he'd better try a more direct approach. So he told me the whole story and got me to drive him over to see Barbie. Karen—insisted on knowing why we had come, and Nick was blunt with her, perhaps too blunt. She took it badly, and you suffered the brunt of it. If I seemed angry, it was more for you than with you, although I was afraid that you might have queered Nick's pitch by your intervention.'

'But I didn't know,' she began. He passed a silencing finger caressingly over her lips.

'You didn't wait to find out, my sweet. You came back here and barricaded yourself in and none of us could reach you. Then we had to spend a frantic day yesterday trying to find you. The Christmas Eve dinner was nearly cancelled for the first time in living memory. It was Nick's decision to go ahead with it. He was convinced that you'd be back in the house before midnight.' He gave a slight, rueful smile. 'But it's as well he couldn't visualise the circumstance of your return, or it might have caused him another stroke.'

Morwenna was shaking now, a little with reaction, but more, far more with his proximity and this new inexplicable tenderness.

She moistened her lips. 'So—so everything's all right with Nick and Barbie. I'm so pleased—pleased above all that Nick finally decided to go to her himself.'

'He found her more than ready to meet him halfway,' Dominic said rather drily. 'I don't know what you can have said to her, but it seemed to have touched some inner chord. He was with her for over an hour and when they came down to the drawing room she was clinging to him as if he was her rock.'

Morwenna was silent for a moment, then she said, 'But how do you feel about it, Dominic? After all, what she did affected your family so deeply. Can you forgive her and accept her as Nick's wife?'

'Nick's his own man,' he said shortly. 'As for Barbie, she's been punished enough, I think. She and Nick plan to be married early in the New Year. When they announced it last night, she looked like a woman who had been let out of prison.'

She forced a smile. 'It must have been quite a celebration. I hope Karen will also be able to accept the situation.'

He shrugged. 'I doubt if she'll be around very much longer to accept it or otherwise. I gather from Barbie she's planning another prolonged visit to California. Apparently there's a man involved.'

Morwenna was very white and her eyes were enormous. She whispered, 'But it was you—you and Karen. You were going to announce your engagement to her last night. That's the other reason I ran away—I couldn't face the idea of seeing you together.'

'I—engaged to Karen?' He stared at her, brows raised. 'Whatever gave you that idea?' His face became sardonic. 'Or maybe I should ask whoever gave it to you?'

'But she made it clear to me that you were going to be married. She talked about the changes she would make when she was mistress here. And Mark said you'd taken your mother's ring to be cleaned and altered.'

His mouth twisted drily. 'I'm aware that local gossip has had Karen and myself paired off for some time, and I'd be a liar if I pretended to you that I wasn't attracted to her, or that any relationship between us had been purely casual. She was decorative and could be amusing and she had other—attributes which I won't enlarge upon, but there was never any question of marriage, on my side at least. In fact things had cooled between us quite some time ago—long before you quite literally flung yourself across my path.'

She said, her face burning, 'But you were with her that night. The night Nick unlocked my mother's room. I saw you come home the next morning.'

'Yes, I'd been out all night.' He looked steadily at her.

'But I hadn't been with Karen. I'd just been—driving around, trying and failing to come to terms with myself and the way I was feeling about you. I was trying to argue you out of my head and my heart and failing badly. Hence my somewhat violent reaction when I saw you.'

She released her hand gently from his. She did not look at him as she said, 'Dominic—I'm not another Karen. You see, I lied to you the other night. There's never been—anyone. But I know you want me, and if that's all you want of me, then I'll make it what I want too.'

He swore softly under his breath. His hand gripped her chin and turned her head so that she was facing him.

'And where does love come into it—or were you lying about that too?'

'Oh, no.' Her eyes met his. 'I did—I do love you. But you said....'

'I know what I said.' He put up a hand and warily raked his dishevelled hair back from his forehead. 'Let's just say it was my last line of defence against you—and not a very good one at that.' He bent forward and kissed her eyes very softly. 'I love you, Morwenna,' he whispered. 'And I need you as I need to draw my next breath. I sensed it that first night when I hauled you out of the ditch. That's why I was so angry when I found out who you were. Your mother had always been represented to me as an unprincipled adventuress. Knowing you were her daughter, I was bound to misjudge your motives. I've been torn in half ever since you set foot in this house. And to cap it all, it was so obvious that everyone else in the household adored you. Especially Mark.' He shook his head. 'God, was I jealous of Mark! I saw him kissing you that night—remember? I'm afraid you suffered the backlash from that later.'

In a low voice, she said, 'Dominic—that card from Vanessa.'

'Ah, yes.' His lip curled slightly. 'I had the privilege of a conversation with your cousin Vanessa when I phoned the Priory to enquire about your whereabouts. She took a quite malicious delight in hearing you might be in trouble of some kind. And she asked if you'd received the card.'

Morwenna sighed. 'She's never liked me very much, but....'

'Don't give her another thought,' he said. 'You need never see her or hear from her again.'

He drew her to him and his mouth closed over hers with an ardent possessiveness which sent her senses reeling. When she could speak, she said, 'But you were always so hostile to me....'

'I thought I behaved with amazing restraint under the circumstances,' he said. He bent and pressed his lips to the throbbing pulse in her throat. 'I wanted so badly to believe in you—to accept all that loveliness and innocence as genuine, but all the evidence seemed to be against you, making you either a mischief-maker or a fanatic—possibly both.' He shook his head. 'When Nick told me how he'd been using you, we had a blazing row.'

'You mustn't blame him.' Shyly she put up a hand and stroked his cheek. 'He only did what he thought was right.' She paused. 'Dominic—how did you know where to find me? On the beach, I mean.'

He lay on the bed beside her, holding her in the curve of his arm. 'When I realised you'd gone, I looked everywhere for a note—some kind of message. In spite of everything, I couldn't believe you'd simply vanished without a word to me. And I had this feeling that you were still in the area.' He grinned reminiscently. 'A feeling that was confirmed when I called at St Enna to collect my future sister-in-law. She may be a loyal friend, but she's not a good liar. I guessed you were somewhere about—possibly within earshot, and that my best bet would be to return later that night or early this morning when you weren't expecting me. That's what I intended. Then I found the envelope with your drawing under the tree last night and I knew that you'd visited the house without anyone realising it during the evening. It seemed a forlorn hope, but I went to the front door and there were these footprints leading away from the house in the snow. It had to be you, so I got a torch and followed.' He shuddered. 'Thank God I did!'

His lips found hers again and she clung to him without reserve, returning his kisses with passionate ardour. They were both far too absorbed to hear the door opening.

'Rest and quiet,' Inez said severely. 'That's what that maid should be 'aving, and how's she to do that, I'd like to know, with you sprawled all over her bed, Mr Dom?' She stood, hands on hips, regarding them both like a benign fairy. 'Come away and have your breakfast, and leave 'er be.'

Morwenna began to shake with laughter and felt Dominic's arm tighten round her.

He said with a dangerous glint in his eye, 'Inez, I'll leave when I've said what I came here to say, and not before.'

'Well, get on with it, then,' Inez returned without rancour. 'You've been here long enough to make a speech in Parliament, never mind ask the maid to marry you. And if your bacon's cold, don't blame me.' On which valedictory note, she departed.

Morwenna said on a catch of her breath, 'Dominic—you —I....'

He reached into his pocket and took out a small jewellers' box. He said rather ruefully, 'Inez stole my thunder, but I had the ring cleaned and altered for you. I borrowed the little pearl ring of your mother's to make sure the size was right—the one you were crying over that day.' He sighed. 'I wanted so badly to pick you up in my arms and comfort you, but all you wanted was to sing a paean of praise to Nick for getting those damned pictures framed.'

'Well, it was kind of him.'

'Kind be damned. He had nothing to do with it.'

'It was you!' She looked wonderingly up into his face. 'But you never said anything ... and when I thanked Nick, he didn't deny....'

'I told him not to. I was afraid if you'd realised that I'd had them framed you might have flung them back at me.' He took the ring, a large square emerald flanked by two exquisite diamonds, out of the box and slid it on to her finger. 'If you cry now,' he whispered, 'I can pick you up in my arms and hold you for the rest of our lives.'

'The rest of our lives!' Morwenna gave a shaky laugh. 'And yesterday I was so miserable. I can hardly believe it!'

'You'd better believe it.' He kissed the hand that wore his ring, and his kiss was a pledge. 'Morwenna Trevennon—the bride the sea gave back to me. No more tragedies, my love, no more bitterness or looking back into the past.'

'No.' She slid her arms up round his neck, and smiled into his eyes. 'Only the future—and each other.'

His mouth was warm and demanding on hers, and as they clung together, the first Morwenna Trevennon gazed down on them serenely from her frame on the wall, and, for a second, the ghost of an understanding smile seemed to play about her painted lips.

Poignant tales of love, conflict, romance and adventure

Harlequin Presents...

Elegant and sophisticated novels of
great romantic fiction . . .
12 all-time best-sellers.

Join the millions of avid Harlequin readers all over the world who delight in the magic of a really exciting novel.

From the library of Harlequin Presents all-time best-sellers—we are proud and pleased to make available the 12 selections listed here.

Combining all the essential elements you expect of great storytelling, and bringing together your very favorite authors—you'll thrill to these exciting tales of love, conflict, romance, sophistication and adventure. You become involved with characters who are interesting, vibrant, and alive. Their individual conflicts, struggles, needs, and desires grip you, the reader, until the final page.

Have you missed any of these *Harlequin Presents*...

Offered to you in the sequence in which they were originally printed—this is an opportunity for you to add to your Harlequin Presents . . . library.

- **127 Man in a Million**
  Roberta Leigh
- **128 Cove of Promises**
  Margaret Rome
- **129 The Man at La Valaise**
  Mary Wibberley
- **130 Dearest Demon**
  Violet Winspear
- **131 Boss Man From Ogallala**
  Janet Dailey
- **132 Enchanted Dawn**
  Anne Hampson
- **133 Come the Vintage**
  Anne Mather
- **134 Storm Flower**
  Margaret Way
- **135 Dark Castle**
  Anne Mather
- **136 The Sun of Summer**
  Lilian Peake
- **137 The Silver Sty**
  Sara Seale
- **138 Satan Took a Bride**
  Violet Winspear

This elegant and sophisticated series was first introduced in 1973, and has been a huge success ever since. The world's top romantic fiction authors combine glamour, exotic locales and dramatic and poignant love themes woven into gripping and absorbing plots to create a unique reading experience in each novel.

You'd expect to pay $1.75 or more for this calibre of best-selling novel. At only **$1.25 each**, Harlequin Presents are truly top value, top quality entertainment.

Don't delay—order yours today

Complete and mail this coupon today!

ORDER FORM

Harlequin Reader Service

In U.S.A.
MPO Box 707,
Niagara Falls, N.Y. 14302

In Canada
649 Ontario St., Stratford,
Ontario N5A 6W2

Please send me the following Harlequin Presents...I am enclosing my check or money order for $1.25 for each novel ordered, plus 49¢ to cover postage and handling.

- ☐ 127 Man in a Million
- ☐ 128 Cove of Promises
- ☐ 129 The Man at La Valaise
- ☐ 130 Dearest Demon
- ☐ 131 Boss Man From Ogallala
- ☐ 132 Enchanted Dawn
- ☐ 133 Come the Vintage
- ☐ 134 Storm Flower
- ☐ 135 Dark Castle
- ☐ 136 The Sun of Summer
- ☐ 137 The Silver Sty
- ☐ 138 Satan Took a Bride

From time to time we find ourselves temporarily out of stock of certain titles. Rather than delay your order we have provided an alternate selection area on this form. By indicating your alternate choices, we will still be able to provide you with same day service.

Number of novels checked _____ @ $1.25 each = $ _____

N.Y. and N.J. residents add appropriate sales tax $ _____

Postage and handling $ .49

                                        TOTAL $ _____

ALTERNATE SELECTIONS ☐ ☐ ☐

NAME _____
(Please Print)

ADDRESS _____

CITY _____

STATE PROV _____ ZIP POSTAL CODE _____

Offer expires June 30, 1979

Put more love into your life. Experience the wonderful world of...

Harlequin Romances

Six brand-new romantic novels every month, each one a thrilling adventure into romance...an exciting glimpse of exotic lands.

Written by world-famous authors, these novels put at your fingertips a fascinating journey into the magic of love, the glamour of faraway places.

Don't wait any longer. Buy them now.

What readers say about Harlequin Romances

"Your books are the best I have ever found."
P.B.*, Bellevue, Washington

"I enjoy them more and more
with each passing year."
J.L., Spurlockville, West Virginia

"No matter how full and happy life might be,
it is an enchantment to sit
and read your novels."
D.K. Willowdale, Ontario

"I firmly believe that Harlequin Romances
are perfect for anyone who wants to read
a good romance."
C.R. Akron, Ohio

*Names available on request